Keepsakes

THE GATES MANOR SERIES
BOOK THREE

JAN HEMBY

BLUE INK PRESS

Keepsakes

ISBN: 978-1-948449-18-2

Library of Congress Control Number: 2023942647

Published in the United States by Blue Ink Press, LLC

This book is dedicated to my sister, Carol, who is a better writer than I am…and has always had my back. I love you, Cookie.

Chapter One

Julia peered over the top of the evening newspaper as Holly and Olivia made their way into her kitchen. Holly arrived with Olivia's overnight bag slung over her shoulder.

Olivia arrived with an attitude.

"I don't understand why I can't go to the concert. All my friends will be there. Besides, it's my birthday! Why can't I do what I want on my birthday?"

Setting the overnight bag down on the floor, Holly sighed. "Olivia, you just saw those friends less than twenty minutes ago at your party."

Olivia put her hands on her hips, "I just saw Grandma, too. *But here I am!*"

"From what the other moms have told me, college guys tend to hang out at that concert venue. Your dad and I don't feel comfortable about you going. Plus, Grandma Julia could use your help unpacking the rest of those boxes in her garage."

Julia folded the newspaper and set it aside. "Don't put me in the middle of this," she said as she removed her reading glasses and placed them on the kitchen table beside her teacup. "I wouldn't want moving-and-storage detail on my fifteenth birthday either! Those boxes have been sitting in my garage for several weeks. Obviously, they don't contain anything I can't live without. Besides, I'm perfectly capable of moving them by myself."

Holly and Olivia responded in unison, "No!"

Julia smiled. "I guess that settles it." She stepped over to the sink to rinse out her teacup. After drying her hands on a dishtowel, she kissed Olivia on her head. "If your grandpa was still around, he'd tell you that whatever they're playing at that concert isn't real music anyway."

Olivia's scowl softened into a smile. "That's exactly what Grandpa Bill would have said!"

Holly put her hand on Olivia's shoulder. "Did you remember to pack your cellphone charger?"

Olivia rolled her eyes. "Yes, Mom."

"Okay, give me a hug."

Olivia didn't move.

"Okay, don't hug me. I'll pick you up in the morning."

Julia cleared her throat and cast Olivia a stern look. Olivia dramatically exhaled and quickly embraced Holly as if her mother carried a deadly disease Olivia could catch.

At the sound of Holly closing the front door, Olivia's mood seemed to improve. She hopped onto the counter and smiled in Julia's direction—a smile that still turned heads despite the recent addition of braces. Her blonde hair hung in soft waves like it had when she was a little girl, but her eyes had recently turned to a deeper, more exotic shade of green. Julia understood how Olivia's stunning facial features, coupled with the fact that she'd inherited Holly's curvy figure, could cause her parents to be a little overprotective.

"Grandma, you know I love spending time with you. It's just that—"

Julia interrupted, "You don't have to explain. Let's unpack those boxes so we can order a pizza and watch a movie. How does that sound?"

Olivia grinned and jumped off the counter. "That sounds like a plan!"

Julia led the way into the garage, where a small collection of boxes remained unpacked. One in particular caught her attention. She gingerly touched it and separated it from the pile.

"Grandma, let me get that for you."

Julia ignored Olivia's offer, carried the box inside, and set it down on the kitchen table.

"Hand me that letter opener over there on the counter."

Olivia complied and Julia carefully cut through the packing tape and opened the box. She brushed aside a layer of Styrofoam to reveal an outdated telephone.

Olivia stood beside Julia. She looked down at the telephone and then back up at Julia. "Is this *the* telephone?"

"Yep," Julia answered as she lifted it out of the box. "This is *the* telephone."

"What's that for?" Olivia pointed to the compartment that contained the answering machine tape.

Julia chuckled. "That's a little magnetic recording device that stored the messages callers would leave. Of course, now wireless phones record those messages digitally."

"Wow," Olivia said. "That's really old."

Julia cut her eyes over to Olivia. "Be careful what you call *really old.*" She wistfully stared back down at the telephone. "I can remember when this was cutting-edge technology."

"Does it still work?" Olivia asked as she turned it from side to side.

"Only one way to find out! Let's see if we can find the plug."

Julia removed another layer of packing and found the adapter and telephone cord underneath. She held both in her hand as she scanned the lower part of the wall near the table.

"I'm still learning where the receptacles are and which light switch goes to what in this house," she mumbled.

"I think that's a phone jack beside that receptacle right over there," Oliva pointed. After Julia connected the telephone cord and plugged in the adapter, the machine beeped to life.

Olivia's eyes grew wide. Julia found it amusing how the old phone fascinated her. Decades ago, it represented one of the thousands that looked and functioned just like it. Now it could be a collector's item.

"Pick up the receiver," Julia instructed. "Do you hear a dial tone?"

"What's a dial tone?"

"It's a steady sound that lets you know the phone is working properly. Only a handful of older landlines still support phones that feature a dial tone. Nowadays, most home phones function just like a cellphone, but that hasn't always been the case."

Olivia nodded. "I hear it!"

"Okay, now dial…uh…your cellphone number."

Oliva pressed the small, square numbers on the phone.

Her phone began ringing from her overnight bag.

"It worked!" she exclaimed.

Julia smiled. "Of course it worked."

Oliva put the receiver back down and pointed to a piece of paper taped to the front near the tape compartment. "What's that?"

Julia picked up her glasses from the kitchen table and leaned in closer to the phone. "Oh, that was our telephone number back when I was growing up. The telephone company assigned it to my mom and dad in the 1950s. I'm certain it's obsolete now."

"This is *so* cool," Olivia said. "It's like going back in time!"

Julia raised an eyebrow. "As cool as going to the concert?"

Olivia darted over to the corner of the kitchen where Holly had left her overnight bag. She glanced over her shoulder at Julia. "Even cooler!" She unzipped a compartment and took out her cellphone. "I'm going to call Kelly and let her know that I'm not going tonight. Then we'll get those other boxes unpacked."

"Sounds like a plan." Julia winked. Oliva laughed and bounded upstairs.

As the sound of Olivia's footsteps faded, Julia directed her attention back to the phone. Box-shaped and the color of wood putty, it wasn't much to look at. Yet God had used it years ago to do something miraculous. She smiled as she thought about how He always shows up in plain clothes—even when working through inanimate objects.

Julia recognized the handwriting on the faded piece of paper as her dad's. He'd probably jotted down their number and taped it to the phone when Julia's mom began having memory issues. She assumed that the number had been out of circulation for years. Then again, what if the phone company had assigned it to someone else? Her curiosity got the best of her.

"What the heck, why not?" she asked herself. She carefully dialed all ten digits and then she waited. To her astonishment, the number started ringing. She held her breath. What if someone answered? Should she apologize for the call or simply hang up?

Then she heard a voice on the other end—a familiar voice. Her breath caught in her throat.

"Hello?"

Julia wanted to respond, but she couldn't form the words.

"Is anybody there?"

Julia stuttered, "Mom? Is that...is that...you?"

Then the line went silent.

Chapter Two

Across town at an old, abandoned apartment complex, Detective Norman Lasko stepped out of his car. He kicked aside rocks and debris to clear a path across the parking lot. He was met by a construction supervisor wearing a yellow hardhat.

The man stuffed the clipboard he was holding under his arm and extended his hand.

"Officer?"

"*Detective* Lasko," Norman corrected, and shook his hand. "And you are?"

"Tom Johnson. I'm the foreman of the demolition project. Are you familiar with this neighborhood?"

"Unfortunately, yes. This place has produced more crime reports than cockroaches over the years. I'm glad they're finally tearing it down."

"Don't be too quick to check it off your list just yet. You need to take a look at what we found behind a cabinet in one of the units."

Even though Norman had served on the police force for nearly twenty years, crime scenes still made him nervous. Finding the remains of a missing person or watching a gunshot victim take their last breath never got any easier.

Putting on a pair of latex gloves, he followed Tom up what was left of a second-story wooden staircase. As they entered the apartment, two workers stood across from where Norman assumed the kitchen cabinets had once hung. One of the workers pointed to an exposed stud in the wall.

Norman turned on his flashlight, directing the beam towards an opening behind the sink. He placed the flashlight on the counter and unfolded an evidence bag he had retrieved from his jacket pocket. Reaching into the space, he carefully removed a plastic bag from a long, rusty nail.

"It doesn't make any sense to me," Tom remarked. "I don't know much about drugs, but that looks like cocaine to me. If it is, then I'd guess someone in this part of town could have made a lot of money selling it on the streets back in the day."

Norman set the evidence bag on the counter. "*Could have* is right. If it is cocaine and it's been here since the building was built, it's probably worthless now. I'll send a sample of the contents to forensics and have them dust the outside of the bag for prints."

After slipping the plastic bag into an evidence sack, Norman glanced around the room. "Whose apartment was this? I realize no one has lived here for a long time, but do you know the name of the last tenant?"

"Actually, I do. The property manager provided us with a roster in case we came across anything suspicious. You'd be surprised what people leave behind, especially if they're on the run." Tom began flipping through the pages of paper on his clipboard. "Here it is. The last tenant was a woman…a Margaret Gates."

Julia stood speechless as she hung up the receiver. What just happened? How could she have heard her mother's voice? The possibility that she could have experienced another phone call from the past made her dizzy. She eased herself into a chair at the kitchen table. There had to be a logical explanation for this.

Before she could collect her thoughts, Olivia came back downstairs engrossed in a lively conversation on her phone.

"I can't believe he did that! She should break up with him."

Olivia opened the refrigerator door and rummaged through a shelf containing water bottles and juice cans. She mouthed at Julia across the room, *Do you have any Diet Coke?*

Julia shook her head. "I don't think so."

Olivia's brow furrowed. "Hey Kelly, can I call you back?"

She cautiously approached Julia. "Grandma, are you okay? You look a little pale."

Julia didn't know what to say, or if she should say anything. She needed time to regroup. "I'm fine, sweetie. I just think I may have overdone it."

Olivia put her hand on Julia's shoulder. "You should have let me bring in that box from the garage."

Julia patted her hand. "There's some cash in my purse. Why don't you order a pizza and some Diet Coke and get that movie started? I'm going to lie down for a few minutes. I'll join you a little later."

Oliva smiled. "You know you don't have to entertain me. I'm fifteen now. I'll be fine. And I'm sorry for how I acted earlier. I was mostly just mad at my mom. You of anyone should know how annoying she can be."

Julia suppressed a laugh. Despite the occasional mood swing, Olivia was a normal, healthy fifteen-year-old. Julia's mind went back to when she herself was fifteen. It was then that her best friend Margaret—also fifteen at the time—began being abused by her father's business partner, Horace Bennington. At that age, Margaret should have been like Olivia: carefree and only concerned about teenage drama and which movie to watch on a Friday night. Margaret was a productive, well-adjusted adult now. But the pain she'd endured as a young girl still tugged at

Julia's heartstrings, especially now that Julia had a grand-daughter that age.

Julia focused back on the present. "It's okay. I understand. Believe it or not, I used to be a teenager myself. It's funny how annoying your mom can be when you're fifteen." Julia looked around and lowered her voice as if she was telling Olivia a secret. "But don't worry—she'll grow out of it."

Olivia laughed and Julia excused herself to her room.

She sat down on the side of her bed and reached for her Bible on her nightstand. "I think a few 'fear not' scriptures are in order," she said out loud. "Wait, where is that concordance Bill always used?" She set her Bible on her bed and began searching through the bottom drawer of her nightstand.

"Gee, there's a lot of junk in here," Julia said as she pulled out expired coupons, a pair of spare reading glasses, a bag of cough drops, and a few stray Christmas cards.

"There it is!" she said as she picked up the worn, paperback topical concordance. She was about to squeak the drawer shut again when she spotted the corner of another book. She slid aside a stack of bills bound together by a rubber band to reveal *her* book, the one she had penned several years ago. She picked it up and thumbed through the pages. She could still picture herself sitting in front of her laptop for hours, writing and rewriting each chapter. When it first was published, she'd proudly displayed a copy on the den coffee table. It made her a little sad to think that it now resided at the bottom of her nightstand drawer.

She sat down on the side of her bed. After reading through the first several pages, she chuckled. "Well, Julia, the geriatric apple doesn't fall far from the tree. Here you are on page sixteen complaining about how many items your parents had stored in their guest room closet." She glanced back over at the open drawer and quoted from the book, "'*A small space that contains a lot of junk.*' Hmm. I definitely inherited that trait from Dad."

Julia closed the book and thought for a moment. *But it wasn't all junk, was it? The tape recording I found in that closet led me to the Morgans and eventually to Margaret. What if—*

Her eyes fell on the book once more. Even though she'd penned every word, she felt a strong urge to go back and read through it again. It was, after all, the account of what had taken place when she'd encountered another mysterious phone call from the past; a call that had changed her life and the lives of so many others. If nothing else, maybe it would serve to revive her desire to write again, something she'd allowed to go dormant since Bill's passing.

Julia slipped off her shoes, adjusted the pillows behind her, and stretched out on the bed.

"Let's start back at the beginning," she said. "Chapter one."

Chapter Three

Norman set his keys down on his desk and flipped the switch on his computer. As he poured himself a cup of coffee, he began issuing voice commands. "Identify the owner of Durledge Apartments. Locate information on Margaret Gates."

As he sat down at his desk, his computer screen populated with numerous links to public records and newspaper articles. He clicked on one that caught his attention.

"Well, would you look at that?" he muttered.

Julia had only planned to read a chapter or two and then close her eyes for a few minutes. Before she knew it, she was already on the twelfth chapter, and an hour had passed. Olivia had assured her she'd be fine on her own, but Julia still wanted to watch at least part of the movie with her.

As she entered the den, she spotted Oliva curled up on the sofa. Olivia had begged Holly to let her attend a concert that would have kept her up past eleven. Yet she had already fallen asleep, and it was only nine-thirty. Julia found the remote underneath a plate of pizza crusts and clicked off the television. She grabbed a throw blanket from the rocking chair across the room and tucked it around Oliva, brushed her hair back, and kissed her on the forehead.

Julia paused for a moment to marvel at how much Olivia resembled Holly. Julia had just read the section of her book where Holly arrived for a visit after Julia's mother had passed away. Seeing Holly walk up the sidewalk that evening had been like a breath of fresh air for Julia. The two of them had planned to stay up and chat, but Holly had fallen asleep on the sofa before they'd gotten the chance. Julia smiled. Once again, the apple didn't fall far from the tree. Like Holly, Olivia wasn't one for late nights.

Julia made her way through the kitchen. She was reaching for the light switch when, out of the corner of her eye, she spotted the telephone. What if she dialed her parents' phone number just once more? Perhaps what happened earlier had been a fluke, like an old recording playing from the answering machine tape. She remembered how that could happen if someone answered the phone after the machine had already started recording.

She chuckled and shook her head. Why hadn't she thought of that before? The explanation made perfect sense. She carefully opened the compartment and removed the old tape, confident that nothing would happen when she tried calling the number this time.

She took a deep breath and punched in the digits.

The line began ringing.

"Hello?"

Once again, it was her mother's voice. Julia couldn't believe it. *This can't be happening!*

Julia spoke loudly into the phone. "Mom? Can you hear me?"

To her amazement, her mom answered, *"Julia, honey, is that you? I'm sorry for getting you out of class. I hope your teacher isn't upset."*

Julia stood up straight. Her heart raced. Her voice shook as she replied, "Yes, Mom, it's me!"

"Frances just called. She can't drive you and Margaret home from school today. She didn't sound well. I hope everything is okay. I just wanted to let you know that I'll be picking you up."

Julia was frantic. "Mom, it's me! But I'm not young Julia anymore."

"Hello, Julia? Are you still there?"

Julia heard what sounded like a thunderclap on the other end, and the line went silent once again. She hung up the receiver and waited a few seconds before redialing the number. This time nothing happened. She tried it once again—still nothing.

She sat down and rested her elbows on the table. *Dear Lord, what is going on?*

Then she smelled something burning. A spark flew from the receptacle where she'd plugged in the phone. A popping noise followed, which made her jump. The light over the kitchen table flickered off.

"That can't be good," she said under her breath.

She stepped over to the electrical panel by the garage entrance and flipped the breaker. The light came back on over the table. But when she sat back down and tried to get the answering machine to turn on, it wouldn't work.

She jumped again when she saw Olivia standing over her.

Olivia cocked her head to one side. "Grandma, who were you talking to?"

Julia panicked. She knew with certainty that she had heard her mother's voice. What if no one believed her? She didn't need anyone questioning her state of mind, especially at her age, and with her mother having passed away from Alzheimer's.

She looked up. "I'm sorry. Did I wake you?"

Olivia yawned and tucked a strand of hair behind her ear. "Were you talking to someone on the old phone? You were kinda loud."

Julia picked up the receiver, handing it to Olivia. "Actually, it stopped working. No dial tone anymore."

Olivia listened and then handed the receiver back to Julia, "Yeah, I don't hear anything."

Julia continued, "It blew a fuse which startled me. That's probably what you heard." She paused and then put her hand on Olivia's shoulder. "Did you get extra banana peppers on that pizza?"

Olivia grinned. "You're right. It was probably just a banana pepper pizza dream. Can I crash in the guest room?"

"Of course. There's an extra blanket in the closet if you need it."

Olivia kissed Julia on the cheek and then lumbered upstairs.

Julia felt relieved. At least *that* was over. She had successfully sidetracked Olivia's question, but in reality, she *had* heard her mother's voice. And what was she saying about Frances, Margaret's mother?

Julia looked down at the phone. It was dead now, so it certainly couldn't provide her with any answers. Then again, the last time something like this happened, the pieces fell into place when Julia reconnected with her middle school band director, Caleb Morgan, and his wife, Minnie. What she wouldn't give to have them to talk to right now!

Yet, she knew what they'd tell her to do.

She stepped out onto the front porch and walked past the rocking chair to the right of the door. It often remained unoccupied as Julia preferred sitting on the steps where she had an unobstructed view of the sky. Tonight, the cloudless firmament boasted the glow of half-moon and a host of twinkling stars. Her mind traveled back fifteen years to her perching on her parents' front porch steps when the first mysterious phone call had occurred.

She sat down on the top step and looked heavenward. "Lord, I feel alone. I don't have Mr. Morgan, Minnie, or Bill to talk to this time. Worse, I'm older now. Sometimes I feel like my family is on standby, just waiting for me to start showing signs of Alzheimer's like my mother. If I tell them what happened tonight, will it only serve to reinforce their fears? Will they think my mind is slipping?"

An evening breeze stirred the fragrance of the gardenia bush next to Julia's porch. While it now bloomed in her yard, it hadn't started out there. It had been one of several that had grown next to the Morgan's front steps. Julia had asked their son, Kenneth, if she could dig up a bush to plant in her yard before he'd sold his parents' homeplace. This was the one she had selected.

She reached over and snapped off a bloom. It amazed her how such a tiny little flower could produce such a powerful fragrance. She fought a lump in her throat as the aroma took her back to the numerous times she'd visited the Morgans in their home.

Gazing heavenward once more, she continued her prayer. "Heavenly Father, what is it with me and telephones?" She raised her eyebrows. "Or with me and *that* telephone?"

She shook her head. "I thought you had finished using that old machine, but maybe you haven't." She paused and thought for a moment. "In some ways, it's like me. I'm not a new model anymore. Some of my parts are wearing out, and, hey, I even blow a fuse now and then!" She looked down at the ground. "But that doesn't mean you're finished with me."

Julia felt a sudden rush of emotion and her eyes filled with tears. "When I moved into this townhouse, I boxed up my memories from the past. Did I do the same for any hopes or dreams for my future?" She set the gardenia bloom on the porch and laughed dryly. "I guess that old telephone wasn't the only thing that needed to come out of storage."

She took a deep breath and checked the time on her watch. The evening certainly hadn't gone as she had planned. Then again, in her experience, life rarely did. Standing to go back inside, she cast a parting glance up to the sky.

"Even though this is scary, I have a feeling you're getting ready to write an amazing story." She smiled. "Again."

Chapter Four

An attractive woman in her late-thirties with dark brown skin and shoulder-length brown hair stepped into Norman's office. Norman looked up briefly.

"Good morning, Monica. Grab a cup of coffee."

"Don't mind if I do," Monica replied. She poured a cup, took a sip, and then scowled over at Norman. "What is *this*? Didn't I stock your office with some decent joe?"

"Sorry," Norman snickered. "I still reach for the cheap stuff. Old habits die hard."

Monica rolled her eyes. "*Old* being the operative word here. You're not that much older than me, but your coffee tastes like something they drank on *The Tonight Show*…when Johnny Carson hosted."

Picking up the container of coffee sitting beside the pot, she shook her head. "First of all, it's in a *can*. You're a smart guy; you should know that decent coffee doesn't come in a can anymore."

She began digging through a cabinet beneath the coffee pot. Pulling out a bag of unopened coffee, she turned towards Norman and pointed to it. "If you're going to utilize my expert detective skills, you need to be fueling my brain with something other than knock-off coffee."

"Fair enough," Norman retorted.

Norman couldn't help but smile as he watched Monica pour the old coffee into the sink and proceed to brew another pot. Even though it had been years now, he could still remember when she'd first joined the force fresh out of the Academy. Having graduated top of her class, she'd moved up through the ranks quickly. Her attention to detail balanced Norman's knack for seeing the big picture. Together, they made an effective team.

So effective, in fact, that their work associates often accused them of behaving more like a married couple than colleagues. Each knew—and understood—the other's nuances. Even the completing-each-other's-sentences cliché applied to them. Moreover, neither held back when communicating an opposing point of view. But the closeness never went any further, and Norman often wondered why. Then again, he valued his and Monica's professional relationship and would never want to jeopardize it by attempting to make it anything more. It felt safe and familiar, and he was content with that.

She looked over her shoulder. "So, what's so important that you took me off the Guthrie case?"

Norman leaned back in his office chair. "Have you heard of the Durledge Apartments they're tearing down, over by that old car dealership?"

"Heard of them? How about that's where I spent most of my time as a rookie. I lost count of the number of domestic disturbance complaints I responded to over there. That place was a breeding ground for crime. They should have demolished it years ago."

"The construction crew made an interesting discovery while gutting one of the units: a large bag of cocaine hidden behind a wall."

Monica poured two cups of coffee and brought them over to Norman's desk. She took a sip of hers and said, "So, why would anybody hide coke behind a wall and leave it there? Who was the last tenant?"

"That's just it. The last tenant was Margaret Gates, who now—"

Monica interrupted, "Runs that place that helps teens with addictions."

Norman clicked a few keys on his computer. "Right. But what you may *not* know—because it was before your time—is that Margaret Gates hasn't always been a saint."

He turned his computer screen towards her. "Check out this rap sheet."

"Whoa. Do you think the coke could have been hers?"

Norman grinned. "Not so fast, Sherlock. There's even more that you don't know. One of the reasons the Gates Manor got started was because Margaret had been sexually abused for years."

Monica shook her head. "A plausible explanation for the drug abuse?"

"That's her story. But look at who the abuser was."

He clicked a few more keys on his laptop.

Monica's eyes grew wide. "*Horace Bennington*? *The* Horace Bennington?"

"Yes, James Gates' business partner."

Monica all but choked on her coffee. She cleared her throat. "James Gates as in Margaret Gates' father?"

"Legend has it that James knew about the abuse. Not only knew about it but allowed it."

Monica's eyes flashed with anger. "Not exactly father of the year, this James Gates."

"It gets better—or worse, depending on how you look at it. It turns out Horace was the biological father of Margaret's brother, Preston. Horace's son Joseph donated part of his inheritance money to start the Gates Manor after Horace died. A way to make up for his father's sins, I guess. Then he ended up marrying Margaret Gates."

Monica's eyes narrowed. "Wasn't there another brother?"

"Oh, yes. Wyatt. He was a big shot who got his clock cleaned when he tried to kill Margaret. Dalton Larkins was his attorney and got the charges reduced. He only served six months. He apparently had a change of heart behind bars. Now he leads a prison ministry."

Monica raised an eyebrow. "Was that a history lesson or a recap of yesterday's episode of *The Young and the Restless*?"

Norman smiled wryly. "You know what they say. Truth is stranger than fiction."

"But what does all of that have to do with a bag of coke found in an apartment once rented to Margaret Gates?"

"I'm glad you asked. Look at whose name is on the deed of the Durledge property."

Monica looked at the computer screen and then at Norman.

"I don't understand. Why on earth would James Gates and Horace Bennington buy a worthless piece of property like that?"

"That's where it gets interesting. I did a title search and found out they weren't the original owners."

"So, who was?"

Norman clasped his hands behind his head and leaned back in his chair once more. "Their wives."

Feeling guilty for having been distracted the night before, Julia got up early and prepared Olivia's favorite breakfast: chocolate chip pancakes complete with all the syrup she could drown them in. Afterward, the two of them moved the rest of the boxes out of the garage and put the items away. Julia mentioned the old phone only in the context that she was glad Olivia got to see it and hear a dial tone before it had stopped working.

By the time Holly returned to pick up Olivia later that morning, Julia felt satisfied that she had successfully executed her duties as a grandmother. Olivia left full of pizza, chocolate chip pancakes, and a few good memories.

Julia waved goodbye from her front porch and watched until

Holly's car was out of sight. Then she stepped back inside and located her cellphone. Dialing a number, she waited impatiently. After several rings, a voice answered on the other end.

"Julia? I was just thinking about you!"

"Margaret, we need to talk. Can I come over?"

"Uh, sure. When?"

"Now, if that's okay."

"Joseph is getting ready to take J.J. to soccer practice, so now actually works. Are you okay?"

"I've been better. Something really strange happened last night. I need to sit down and discuss it with you in person."

"I'll put on some coffee. See you soon."

Margaret sat quietly for a moment, looking down at her phone.

"I don't think it was a coincidence that Julia called you," Joseph said.

Margaret looked up at Joseph. She found it hard to believe they had already been married thirteen years. The two of them began working together when the Gates Manor first opened. Margaret taught music and provided counseling for the students. Joseph served as the hospital liaison for the students' medical needs. What had started out as a professional relationship turned into love. They'd opted for a Christmas wedding; a fairytale-like event held at the Manor. Only days later, they adopted a baby boy. The family that Margaret had always dreamed of—but had lost hope of ever having—came to pass within a short period of time. Some days it still felt like a dream.

"You know you can talk to her about this."

"You're right," Margaret said. Her chair squeaked against the kitchen floor as she got up and retrieved a container of coffee from the freezer. She separated a filter from a stack on the counter and looked over to Joseph. "I just don't understand why it's happening, especially after all this time."

The newspaper rustled as Joseph set it aside. He stepped over to where Margaret was standing and embraced her from behind. "Your journey of faith has been defined by trusting God for what you don't understand. You still don't know how Julia received that phone call years ago, but it was God's way of rescuing you. He may not give you *all* the answers, but He'll give you the ones you need. Even counselors—*especially* counselors—need a sounding board from time to time. If anybody would understand what you've been going through, it's Julia. Talk to her."

He smiled as he pointed to the coffee pot. "You might want to get that going. Julia's a fast driver, and her blood type is Dark Roast."

Margaret laughed and turned to face him. She took his hands into hers. "Thank you for always being there for our son and me."

Joseph pulled away and looked at his watch. "Speaking of which, I do need to get J.J. to soccer practice. What do you think Julia wants to talk to *you* about?"

Margaret shook her head as she picked up the coffee carafe and filled it with water from the sink. "I don't know. She sounded upset. It's interesting that we both need to talk to each other at the same time."

Joseph's car keys jingled as he slipped them off a hook on the wall. He craned his head up towards the staircase and called out, "Let's go, son. Make sure you've got all your gear."

J.J., short for Joseph Jr., clunked down the stairs in his soccer cleats and uniform. He was on the smaller end of the spectrum for boys his age. He had soft brown curls that framed his deep-set, brown eyes. He flashed a handsome smile to Margaret, a smile that always melted her heart. From what she had heard, it had also begun melting the hearts of his female classmates.

"See ya, Mom!" he called as he headed out the back door.

Joseph stepped back into the kitchen and gave Margaret a quick kiss on the cheek. "Maybe Julia is just overdue for some BFF time with you. I'll see you in a couple of hours."

Margaret forced a smile, clicked the coffee pot on, and then leaned back against the counter.

"I've got a feeling it's more than that," she muttered. "Much more."

Chapter Five

1975

It was a crisp fall morning in mid-October 1975. The cool air provided a welcome relief from the intense North Carolina summer heat that had stubbornly refused to abate. Frances Gates wearily sat down in the park swing. She could feel the extra weight in her mid-section shifting her center of gravity. She lifted her feet off the ground to gently set the swing in motion. The fallen leaves that blanketed the grass crunched as a woman in her late thirties walked across the park to join her.

Frances had always thought that Ellen Bennington possessed true beauty, both inside and out. Her brown, shoulder-length hair was always perfectly coiffed, and her pixie nose powdered. Frances suspected that she would look just as lovely with dripping wet hair and no makeup. Her most stunning feature was her eyes—a rare, robin-egg blue. While attractive, Frances took note that they rarely displayed happiness.

Ellen held a reputation in the local community for being strong, confident and, at times, outspoken. Frances had witnessed those traits in Ellen, but she'd also seen her demonstrate generosity and compassion as she opened her arms—and her home—to those less fortunate. It was this tender side to Ellen that Frances would appeal to this morning.

Frances and Ellen maintained a cordial acquaintance, but they weren't what Frances would define as close friends. They had been thrown together through James and Horace's business relationship. What friendship did exist between them could be destroyed by what Frances was about to tell her.

"Good morning, Ellen."

"Good morning! How are you feeling these days?"

Frances' attempt at a smile fell short. "A little tired, but not too bad. Nausea comes and goes. You?"

"Oh, you know," she said as she opened her purse and shook out a cigarette from a gold case. After lighting it, she took a draw. "I'm constantly running one of the boys to this practice or that. Horace had another meeting last night that went past bedtime." She briefly made eye contact. "I have a manicure scheduled for noon today." She crossed her arms and looked off into the distance. "Business as usual, I guess."

Frances could feel her heart pounding. Her grip on the swing tightened. Could she go through with this? Her stomach felt sick, and not from the pregnancy. Her breath quickened. She had to will herself to remain calm.

"Thank you for coming here this morning. I realize that we may not be as close as I'd like for us to be, but I do consider you to be a friend."

Ellen's eyes darted at Frances and then immediately looked away. Frances could tell she wasn't prepared for the conversation to divert from the superficial so abruptly. She appeared to regroup, and her reply sounded rehearsed as if she was merely playing the role of a proper, southern wife with a noon manicure appointment.

"That's very kind of you. Everyone needs a good friend."

"I've been sitting on something for a long time, Ellen. I thought I could keep it a secret indefinitely. Not because I wanted to, but because I didn't think I had a choice. I'm at the end of my rope. I can't do it anymore."

Ellen took a seat in the swing next to Frances. Frances reached over and took her hand.

"You're the only friend I can talk to about this."

"Why me?" Ellen's eyes narrowed.

Frances hesitated. "Because it has to do with your husband."

Ellen jerked her hand away and stood up. "What about my husband? Look, I know Horace isn't the most honest businessman in the world, but neither is James. There's nothing you can tell me he's done that James isn't equally guilty—"

"I'm carrying his child," Frances interrupted, unable to believe that she had actually spoken the words out loud.

Ellen's mouth dropped. "No, it can't be…"

Frances regretted the pain that this would cause Ellen. It was as if she was spreading her own heartache like a deadly disease. Having to voice it out loud was also forcing her to relive it in her mind. She forced herself to continue, hearing her voice thicken with tears, "He raped me. And do you know why he raped me?"

Ellen took another draw from her cigarette. And then another. She started pacing. "This can't be happening! Oh, dear God. This can't be happening."

Frances had come too far to stop now. She raised her voice and repeated, "Do you know why he raped me?"

Ellen became silent. She extinguished the cigarette with her foot and brushed away the tears escaping from her eyes. "Why?" she asked, looking down at the ground.

As tears streamed down her own face, Frances responded barely above a whisper. "Because I told James to order Horace to leave Margaret alone."

Ellen's eyes flashed with anger. "What did you say?"

"Horace has been abusing Margaret. It was a twisted way of James repaying Horace for a business deal that James allowed to go sour." She shook her head. "I'm not privy to the details. All I know is that it's been going on for weeks. When I found out, of course, I was furious. But you know as well as I do that I can't go to the police. Horace and James are too powerful."

Ellen didn't say anything for a moment. Frances held her breath. Either Ellen would side with her, or she would destroy her. If the latter happened, it wouldn't matter; the situation had already destroyed her. She had nothing to lose at this point.

Looking off into the distance, Ellen quietly asked, "Does James know it's Horace's child?"

Frances hung her head. "No."

Ellen sat back down in the swing. Frances saw compassion in her eyes.

Her bottom lip quivered. "I'm so sorry, Frances. I know it doesn't change anything, and it's completely inadequate, but I am truly sorry. And you're right. You can't go to the police."

Neither of them said anything for a moment. Frances felt like they both needed a pause to let everything to sink in…if that were even possible.

Ellen looked at the swing where Frances was sitting. "You can't be comfortable. Why don't you come out to the estate and we'll have tea?" She smiled weakly. "I can get that manicure anytime."

Chapter Six

After ringing Margaret's doorbell, Julia snapped off a couple of dead geranium stems from a pot on her front porch.

As Margaret opened the door, Julia handed them to her bouquet-style. "You really should break these off when they start to die."

"Aren't you getting bossy in your old age?" Margaret teased. She took the flowers in one hand and embraced Julia with the other. "Come on in!" As she walked ahead of her, she looked over her shoulder. "The garage needs cleaning out, too, if you want a *real* project."

Julia laughed. She needed a dose of Margaret's humor. Even though the two of them had remained best friends, they each had their own lives and hadn't spent as much time together recently. Julia had been preoccupied with getting settled in her new townhome. Margaret still worked a few days a week at the Manor and otherwise stayed busy raising a teenage boy.

"You still take two sugars in your coffee?" Margaret asked.

Julia set her purse down on the counter and pulled out a chair at the kitchen table. "Still do."

Julia watched as Margaret poured two cups and then set

them on the table. Margaret had long since cut her shoulder-length blonde hair and now sported a short bob. She did continue to color it, though. Raising a thirteen-year-old son, she wasn't quite ready to go completely gray yet. She was still tall and lovely with bright blue eyes that served as windows to a happy soul.

"How is J.J.?" Julia started and then stopped. "Actually, can we skip the small talk?"

Margaret folded her hands on the table. "J.J. is fine, and yes, we can. You sounded upset on the phone. What's going on?"

"It happened again."

"What happened again?"

"A phone call."

Margaret's eyes looked expectant as if she was waiting for Julia to get to the point. *Why can't you figure it out without me having to say it?* Julia thought. Of course, it was ridiculous to think that Margaret would automatically assume it was another phone call from the past. Why would she?

"Last night, Olivia came over to help me move the boxes out of my garage. I found the one that contained my parents' old phone."

Margaret raised an eyebrow. "*The* phone?"

"*The* phone. I was showing Olivia how it worked. When she left the room, I dialed my parents' old number. I assumed it would be out of service, but I was curious to see what would happen."

Margaret took a sip of her coffee. "And?"

Julia took a deep breath. "My mom answered the phone."

Margaret didn't even blink as she set the coffee cup down on the table. "What do you mean your mom answered the phone?"

Julia's tone was matter of fact. "Exactly what I said. I heard my mom answer the phone."

Margaret's expression didn't change.

"Later that same night, I redialed the number, thinking it had been a fluke with the answering machine. But, lo and behold, my mom answered again. This time I could talk to her. She was telling me that your mom couldn't pick us up from school and that she would be picking us up instead. When I tried to explain that I wasn't young Julia, she couldn't hear me anymore. I heard a loud noise, and then the line went dead."

The silence was palpable. Margaret looked so distracted that Julia snapped her fingers in front of her face.

"Did you hear anything I said?"

"Oh, yes. I heard it."

"Then why aren't you saying anything? Do you think I'm crazy?"

"No, Julia, I don't. I'm just stunned. First, that this is happening...*again.*"

"Tell me about it! What else?"

Margaret shook her head. "That it can't be a coincidence. When you called me today, I couldn't believe the timing because I've needed to talk to you, too. I didn't want you to think *I* was crazy, so I've been putting it off. Julia, I've been having dreams again. I used to have dreams about the abuse all the time. The memories were bad enough, but the dreams made it feel like it was happening all over again."

"Are you having those dreams again?"

"No. Now I'm having dreams about my mom. I'm overhearing conversations I suppose I overheard as a teenager. I can't remember the details of each one; you know how dreams are. One felt so real that when I woke up, I wrote it down so I wouldn't forget."

Julia watched as Margaret picked up a notepad with some scribblings on it. She reached for a pair of reading glasses on the table and put them on. She cleared her throat. "*I'm around fifteen years old in the dream. Julia's mom had just brought me home from school. I'm walking through our house looking for my mom. I walk up to her bedroom door, which is closed. I'm just about to knock when I hear her talking to someone on the phone.*"

"What did she say?" Julia pressed.

Margaret turned the page in the notebook. "'*Are you sure this is going to work? What if this blows up in our faces? I can't afford to take that kind of risk.' Before I wake up, I hear a noise that sounds like a crack of thunder, and then —*"

Julia sat back in her chair. Her heart was pounding. "Read that last part again."

Margaret looked up briefly, then back down at the notepad. "'*I can't afford to take that kind of risk.*'"

"No, not that part. The very last sentence."

"'*Before I wake up, I hear a noise that sounds like a crack of thunder, and then —*'"

Julia cupped her hands over her face. "I can't believe it!" she exclaimed. "At the very end of the call with my mother, I heard the same thing. It sounded like a thunderclap. I didn't think it was important; I was focusing more on what she had said. I just assumed the noise happened when the phone line went dead."

Margaret's eyebrows snapped together. "What do you think it means? Or does it mean anything?"

Julia took a sip of her coffee. "I don't know. Right now, my head is still spinning from the fact that this is happening in the first place. What are the chances?"

"The last time you thought you were losing your mind from a phone call, God was scheming a plan to rescue me," Margaret said as her eyes twinkled.

Julia chuckled. "Ah—if you remember correctly, it wasn't just the phone call. It was the visit to high school after I found that old band concert tape. Going back in time thirty years does have a way of making a girl question her sanity."

"Of course, I remember. After all, I was one of the lead characters in your book."

Julia looked down. *Her book!* She had stopped reading at the twelfth chapter. What if there were clues in the book? What if that was one of the reasons Mr. Morgan had wanted her to write it in the first place? Maybe it wasn't meant only to provide hope and answers for others. Could answers be hidden in it for her?

Julia looked back up at Margaret, her eyes thoughtful. "It's interesting that you mentioned my book. When the phone call happened the other night, I started rereading it. Prior to that, I hadn't looked at it in years."

"You did write it, you know." Margaret winked and took a sip of her coffee.

"It was as if I needed to be reminded of how God worked everything out the first time this sort of thing happened. Now…I wonder."

"I can see your wheels are turning. What are you thinking, Julia Burch?"

"Do you remember how emphatic Mr. Morgan was about my writing that book?"

"Well, yeah, it was an amazing story! You'd always wanted to write a novel. I think he saw that you had potential. The book contained a powerful message of redemption."

"What if there was another reason? Something even Mr. Morgan couldn't have known back then?"

"Okay, you lost me."

"Your dreams have to be connected to the phone call with my mom. What if there are clues in the book that could help us sort this out?"

Margaret's expression softened. She hesitated but then said, "I know we both want to figure this out." She paused. "Hey, God's done it before, right?" She gave a quick, nervous laugh. "All of that aside, how did it feel to hear your mom's voice again?"

Julia sighed. "She's been gone a long time, Margaret. With Alzheimer's, her mind was gone years before we actually lost her. To answer your question?" She looked at Margaret as her eyes welled with tears. "It was wonderful. I didn't realize how much I missed hearing her voice. In my head, I knew it couldn't be real. In my heart? I desperately wanted it to be her on the other end of that phone call."

"I understand," Margaret said as she reached for Julia's hand and gave it a quick squeeze.

Julia picked up her coffee cup and walked over to the carafe to refill it. She tore off a paper towel from the roll on the counter and blew her nose.

"I don't know what I'd do if you didn't understand. I thought my heart would never heal after Mom died. Then Bill —" Once again, she began to cry.

Margaret got up from the table and walked over to where Julia was standing. She put her arm around her.

"I'm not sure which kind of loss is worse," Julia said as she wiped her eyes. "The kind where you feel helpless against a disease or the kind where—"

"We've talked about this before," Margaret said softly. "What happened to Bill wasn't your fault."

"I could have taken the car that day. But he wanted me to be safe, so he left me with the heavier vehicle. If I'd had my wits about me, I would've insisted that he drive the SUV. He had much farther to travel than I did."

"That transfer truck was driving way too fast for those icy road conditions. It wouldn't have mattered what Bill was driving."

"What if it *would* have mattered?"

"Julia, you can't—"

"I know, I know." She sighed and took a moment to regroup her thoughts. "I guess what I'm trying to say is that each situation leaves you with a different kind of pain."

"I'd say they both suck," Margaret said as she pulled Julia into a hug.

Julia laughed and cried at the same time. "Yes, they do."

Margaret turned to face Julia and put her hands on her shoulders. "Joseph reminded me this morning that we have to trust God for all the things we don't understand, and that includes the sucky stuff. One day it *will* make sense. Maybe not in this life, but one day. Until then, we *have* to give it to Him."

"I know. You're right." Julia blew her nose once more and then located the trashcan in the corner by the refrigerator and tossed in her paper towel. Gaining her composure, she picked up her coffee cup. "So, what do you suggest we do next?"

Margaret rubbed her chin. "Two heads are better than one. How about we *both* read through your book?"

Chapter Seven

Norman ducked under the crime scene tape and then held it up for Monica. He had ascended halfway up the rotting, wooden staircase when he stopped and turned around. There was a sound that he should be hearing but wasn't.

"Monica? Are you coming or not?"

Monica put her hand on her hip. "Not at the same time as you! Those rickety stairs can't hold both of us."

"Where's your sense of adventure?" Norman called out as he walked up the rest of the steps.

"Where's your *common* sense?" Monica mumbled.

"I heard that," Norman yelled from inside the building.

Once he and Monica were both inside the apartment, they each slipped on latex gloves and turned on their flashlights. Norman walked over to where smoke-stained blinds covered the one window in the living room. He pulled at the cord, and the blinds squeaked up the glass. The morning sun filtered through several years' worth of dust that had been released.

Monica waved her hand in front of her face. "I think I'd just as soon use my flashlight!"

Norman shook his head as he walked through the room. "This place really is a dump. I know it looks even worse now because it's been abandoned for years, but I can't exactly imagine it was featured in *Southern Living* before that."

Monica made her way into the bedroom as Norman directed his flashlight around a worn-out sofa and a chair that looked like a rat had gnawed through the cushion.

"Norm, come look at this. It's a box of some sort."

Norman stepped into the bedroom, where Monica had squatted down and aimed her flashlight under the bed.

He squatted beside her and stretched his hand under the bed as far as it would reach. He retrieved what appeared to be a container that was a little smaller than a shoebox. It was heavier than he thought it would be. He handed it to Monica, who sat down on the side of the bed.

"What is a nice box like this doing in this cesspool?"

"Nice?" Norman scoffed as he waved dismissively. "It's all tarnished and covered in cobwebs!"

"You'd be tarnished and covered in cobwebs, too, if you'd been stashed underneath a bed for God knows how long."

Monica turned the box from side to side. "For your information, it's silver-plated and, most likely, a family heirloom. Focus your flashlight on the center."

Norman brushed off a few remaining cobwebs and aimed his flashlight where Monica had instructed.

"It's monogrammed, see?"

"Okay, so what's in this box?"

"Let's find out," Monica replied as she opened the lid.

"Okay, what do we have here?" Monica said as she began taking the items out one by one. "Evidently, this was a keepsake box. We have a silver-plated baby rattle, a small silver picture frame, a picture of a mom with a baby, and a diary." She tugged at the lock. She looked in the box once more and then turned it upside down and shook it. "We have a diary but no diary key. I wonder where the key is?"

Norman pulled an evidence bag from his coat pocket. "Let's put it in here for safekeeping until we get back to the office." He suppressed the urge to laugh. "And Monica, it's a diary. I think we can manage to get it open."

"Don't be a smartass," Monica quickly retorted as she began rummaging through other items in the room. "I just know that where there's a diary, there's a key somewhere. If we can find it, we might find other things Margaret didn't want anyone to know about."

Norman shook his head in frustration. "The chances are slim to none that we would ever find a key in all this mess."

"Okay, Margaret," Monica said as she rummaged through an old nightstand. "Where did you hide things?"

This was one of those times where Monica's attention to detail annoyed Norman.

Suddenly Monica lifted her head. "Where's that hole in the wall where you found the cocaine?"

They retraced their steps back through the living room and entered the kitchen.

Norman pointed to where the cabinets used to be. "There's a hook in there. That's where we found it."

After checking to see if it could support her, Monica eased herself onto the counter. Norman stood behind her as she shone her flashlight into the wall.

"Do you see anything?"

Monica handed him her flashlight as she reached her hand down and pulled out a thin silver necklace chain with a key at the end of it.

Grinning, she handed it to Norman. "I've got fifty bucks that say this little key goes to that diary. But that's not all. Hang on."

Norman reached over Monica to shine his flashlight into the wall again as she carefully pulled out a small box.

"Where was that?"

"It was sitting on a cross board in the wall." She opened it and pulled out a key that appeared to be a little larger than the key on the necklace chain. "I hate to say I told you so—"

"I thought you rather enjoyed it," Norman said as he smiled

and placed the box in a separate evidence bag. "Good job. Your attention to detail saves the day once again. Let's get these items to the lab and see if they start talking."

"You know we may have a problem now," Monica said as she lowered herself from the counter.

"Yep," Norman agreed. "If that's Margaret Gate's keepsake box and Margaret's diary key—"

Monica sighed. "It could be Margaret's cocaine."

Chapter Eight

1975

Frances Gates watched as Gina Merino, a young Hispanic girl, poured her a cup of steaming hot tea. Frances couldn't help but stare. Gina was strikingly beautiful, with her long dark hair and hourglass figure. Her warm and friendly smile struck Frances as an attempt to portray her life as a happy one. Her sad, almond-shaped brown eyes, though, suggested a different narrative.

Frances wondered what her story was. She'd read in the newspaper about the scholarship fund Horace had started for foreign exchange students. If Gina had been one of those recipients, why wasn't she studying at a university instead of serving tea? Granted, working for the Bennington's was no small honor. Yet somehow this young lady looked out of place.

Frances' thoughts were interrupted as Ellen stepped back out onto the terrace. She took a seat in one of the remaining white, wrought iron chairs encircling a matching table. She lit a cigarette. Blowing the smoke away from Frances, she quipped, "They say these things are going to kill me one day."

Not wanting to agree or disagree, Frances smiled and took a sip of her tea. Her porcelain cup rattled on the saucer as she carefully set it back down.

"Thank you for having me here, Ellen. I can't remember the last time I was invited to tea, much less treated like a princess."

Frances caught the slightest hint of a smile from Gina as she filled Ellen's cup. It was almost as if Frances' words had encouraged her. Ellen must have picked up on it, too, as she used her hand to shade her eyes from the morning sun and looked up at Gina.

"Gina knows I speak the truth when I say that nobody could take her place. I don't know what we'd do without her."

Only Gina's lips smiled; her brown, almond-shaped eyes remained sad. "Thank you, Mrs. Bennington," she responded politely. "Is there anything else you need?"

"I think we're good for now. I'll ring if I need you."

Gina nodded and quietly went back inside the house.

Frances couldn't shake the feeling that there was more to Gina's situation than met the eye. But that's all it was: a feeling. She forced herself to focus on why Ellen had invited her to tea in the first place. As if on cue, Ellen tapped her cigarette into an ashtray on the table and leaned back in her chair. Her tone was a mixture of anger and pain. Frances sensed that neither was new or unfamiliar to Ellen when it came to Horace.

"Do you want to start from the beginning?"

Frances nodded weakly and then looked down. "First of all, I want you to know that there was absolutely nothing between Horace and me. I only wanted him to leave Margaret alone. If he had agreed to do that, I would have been willing to let the whole thing go. But James told him that I knew. I was home one afternoon—"

Ellen interrupted. "Does Margaret know that you know?"

That was the one question Frances had dreaded the most. Her posture sagged. "Ellen, I've betrayed my own daughter. I've wanted to talk to her, hold her, and tell her that everything will be okay. If I could, I'd take her for counseling and arrange for the best medical care. But James—"

Once again, Ellen interrupted. "Let me guess. James threatened to twist the whole situation around to make it look like Margaret instigated it if you dared to do that. Let's face it; you'd have to leave the state to find a doctor or a counselor who doesn't owe James some kind of favor. And let's not forget how he has law enforcement and even congressmen under his thumb." Ellen took a draw from her cigarette. "If I didn't know better, I'd say we were married to the same person."

Tears raced down Frances' cheeks. "He also threatened to cut Margaret and me off financially. He's done it before when I've challenged him. I'd go to the bank to make a withdrawal and the account would be frozen. Once I couldn't even buy groceries."

Ellen angrily put her cigarette out in the ashtray. Lighting another one, she took a draw. Smoke escaped through her nose as she talked. "It's so unfair. Even though it's the 1970s, women still don't have equal rights. How is it that our husbands can do this to us?"

"Because they're powerful and corrupt, that's why." Frances glanced around the terrace. "We both know that they didn't achieve all of this by being smarter than the next guy—just more cut-throat."

They both became quiet for a moment. Ellen was the first to break the silence.

"I apologize for interrupting you. I think you were going to tell me how it happened."

"Don't apologize. All of that needed to be said." Her mouth was dry, so she took a sip of her tea before continuing. "It happened one afternoon last spring. I was in my bedroom, and I heard someone enter the house. Margaret had already come home from school, and James was out of town. I knew it couldn't be either of them. Then I heard Horace call my name."

"Did you confront him about barging into your house uninvited?"

"No. I knew I had to pick my battles. So, I simply asked him what he wanted. He informed me that Margaret was part of a business arrangement and that nothing would change. Then he…" Frances' voice began to shake.

Ellen slid her chair closer to the table. She put her hand on Frances'.

"It's okay. Go ahead."

Frances' eyes narrowed as she forced out the words. "He told me that if I interfered, he would kill Margaret. I pleaded with him. He slapped me so hard that it knocked me down. Then he got on top of me—"

Her chin lowered to her chest as her words trailed off. Once again, she couldn't believe she'd said them out loud, and to Ellen Bennington of all people. Could she trust her? What if this had been a mistake? In her peripheral vision, she could see Ellen leaning back in her chair. When Frances lifted her head, Ellen's robin-egg blue eyes were wet with tears.

"Sick bastard," Ellen whispered.

Frances was relieved that, once again, Ellen appeared to be on her side. She leaned over and found a package of tissues in her purse and wiped her eyes. "James has done some despicable things before. But allowing Horace to sexually abuse Margaret, which then led to Horace raping me? No, I can't let this go."

"Nor should you." She looked thoughtful and then said dryly, "Nor should I."

"What can we do? And I'm so sorry. I know this is devastating for you, too. I didn't want to hurt you. I can't imagine what you're going through."

Ellen scoffed. "I've been through worse. At this point, I'm more angry than hurt. However, I do think I can help."

"I'm listening."

"First, I need to ask you a critical question. How fed up are you? Are you ready to follow through with a plan that will give James and Horace a taste of their own medicine?"

Frances thought for a moment. "Yes, of course. But I can't afford it to blow up in our faces. It has to be calculated and, well, safe."

"In other words," Ellen said with a half-grin, "it has to be legal, which is how I can be of assistance. I'm meeting with that new lawyer in town, Dalton Larkins. He's supposed to be brilliant, good-looking, and—the best part? No ties whatsoever to Horace and James. My parents left me a sum of money in their will earmarked for Wyatt and Joseph. I've scheduled an appointment with Mr. Larkins to establish a trust fund for their college education. Maybe while I'm there, I could ask him about our...options?"

Frances squinted her eyes. "I don't understand."

"What do Horace and James value more than anything? Think about it for a moment."

"I don't have to think about it. The answer is money and power."

"You left out one," she said, leaning back in her chair once more and folding her arms. "Their reputations."

"Okay, but short of going to the press, how do we do expose them for the crooks they are? Without it hurting us or, more importantly, our children?"

Frances watched as Ellen looked off into the distance as if she was deep in thought. She took several draws from her cigarette before putting it out in the ashtray.

"How would you rather die?" Ellen asked.

"I beg your pardon?"

"Would you rather someone shoot you and get it over with, or kill you by torturing you...slowly...over time? Which is worse?"

"What on earth? The latter is worse, of course!"

Ellen chucked, followed by a wheezy cough that sounded like she needed to cut back on the cigarettes. "We may need to exchange instant gratification for more of a long-term solution. Something that will hit them where it hurts—over time."

The pieces were beginning to fall into place in Frances' mind. "So, we're talking about putting a tiny puncture wound in the tire as opposed to slashing it?"

Ellen smiled and raised her eyebrows. "The tire still goes flat; you just don't know it's happening."

Frances took the last sip of her tea, which was now lukewarm. She carefully set the cup down and looked at her watch. "I should be going. I'll be glad to split whatever fee Mr. Larkins charges you."

Ellen shook her head. "This one's on me. It's the least I can do."

Frances picked up her purse and paused. "Please tell Gina thank you for the tea."

Ellen stood and put her arm around Frances as they walked to the terrace stairs. Then she looked into her eyes.

"I'm sorry my husband is such a monster. I chose to marry him, so I have to deal with it. But other people shouldn't have to suffer."

Ellen's choice of words made Frances wonder. She took a chance. "Other people? I'm not the only one, am I?"

Once again, Ellen's robin-egg blue eyes filled with tears.

Now Frances understood why they always looked so sad.

Chapter Nine

Julia had complained about moving at first but was now beginning to feel settled in her new townhouse. It was more compact than the sprawling home where she and Bill had raised their two children, Holly and Claire. In fact, it was Holly and Claire who had encouraged Julia to downsize, reasoning that a smaller, newer house would require less upkeep and would be easier for her to manage. Leaving behind forty years of memories had been difficult. Moving on without Bill had been next to impossible.

She picked up their wedding picture which she kept on her nightstand. They would have celebrated their forty-fifth-anniversary last month. She felt a lump in her throat. Even though it had been decades since they'd exchanged vows, it felt like yesterday. She examined the old photo; how young they both looked! She set it back on her nightstand and leaned back on her pillow. When she closed her eyes, she could still see the snow falling on that December evening and feel the sting of the cold air as she had approached the front door.

"Claire? I think I heard the doorbell. Will you see who it is? I've got my hands in dishwater."

"Sure, Mom. Hey, have you looked outside? It's snowing again!"

"Yes, I've been watching for your dad. I still can't get him to answer his cell. Our first white Christmas in ages, and he's going to be late for the celebration."

Julia could hear Claire opening the front door. A muffled conversation followed.

Claire's voice sounded different this time when she said her name. "Mom?"

"Hang on, I'm drying my hands."

As she approached the door, Julia's heart raced as she saw two uniformed highway patrolmen standing on the front porch. Out of the corner of her eye, she could see that Claire's face had gone pale. The two men removed their hats.

"Mrs. Burch, we're so sorry to inform you..."

Julia grabbed a tissue from her nightstand and wiped her eyes. She had always pictured her and Bill watching their grandchildren grow up and perhaps even traveling abroad after Bill retired. Instead, she was left to navigate this season of life alone.

"Okay, Julia," she said out loud. "You've felt sorry for yourself long enough. It's time to get back to business."

She picked up her book. She had earmarked where she'd left off earlier.

Margaret was one for protecting the things that were special to her. In the corner of her dining room stood the curio cabinet which displayed her porcelain doll collection. It was one of only a few items she'd kept from her childhood—and the only one that provided her with positive memories of her dad. She had stored it at the Manor house for years, but she recently had it moved home for safekeeping.

Margaret had chosen a top shelf on the den bookcase as the location for Mr. Morgan's Bible. His wife, Minnie, had presented it to her shortly after his death. Margaret had referenced it so many times that the pages had begun to tear. Wanting to preserve it for as long as possible, she no longer carried it to the Manor to conduct Bible studies with the students. She only referenced it when she needed the extra comfort that reading Mr. Morgan's notes in the margins provided.

Julia's book represented another keepsake. It was Julia's story, but it contained Margaret's as well. She owned several copies and kept them in the same bookcase as Mr. Morgan's Bible. One in particular held intrinsic value, as Julia had both signed it and written a note for Margaret on the inside cover. Unlike the other things she considered precious, Margaret regularly picked up this book. Reading—and re-reading it— reminded her that if God could deliver her from drug addiction and the brink of suicide, He could certainly help her with any day-to-day challenges and trials she might encounter.

Not wanting to be disturbed, Margaret had waited until both Joseph and J.J. had fallen asleep before she settled in with Julia's book. Draping a blanket over her feet, she reached for the cup of tea she'd steeped a few minutes earlier. She closed her eyes and took in the aroma of cinnamon and orange oils released in the steam. She set the teacup down and picked up the book. This time, she'd be reading it to see if it contained any clues from the first time Julia experienced a phone call from the past.

She was so familiar with the story that she had to be intentional about reading it word for word. The first few chapters went quickly. Then she arrived at the section where Julia visited their old high school. Expecting to find Mr. Morgan tutoring there, she had encountered something unexpected: her classmates as they were thirty years earlier. No one could see or hear her, which made the experience even more frustrating and frightening.

Wait a second, Margaret thought as she licked her thumb and turned back a few pages. Her eyes narrowed as she re-read one of the sections. Flipping forward a couple of pages, she read another paragraph or two. Reaching for her cellphone, she looked at the time. It was late, but not that late. She dialed Julia's cell number. After a few rings, Julia answered.

"Hello?"

"Hey, I'm sorry to be calling at this hour."

"It's okay. I was having a hard time falling asleep, and I thought I'd read a little more in the book."

"What chapter are you on?"

"I just started chapter thirteen."

"Then you missed an important detail. I don't understand how it all fits together, but it has to mean something. Go back to chapter seven, your visit to the school. Now, turn to page thirty-one and read the entire page."

Margaret could faintly hear the rustle of pages as Julia followed her instructions.

"Do you see it?" Margaret asked impatiently.

At first, there was silence on the other end. Then Margaret heard Julia gasp.

"The storm!" she exclaimed.

"When you went to the school that day, you had to run through a downpour to get back to your car. Last night, you heard a thunderclap at the end of the phone call with your mom. I heard one in my dream. Could it be connected?"

"I don't know how, but my gut tells me that it is."

Margaret smiled and put her glasses down on the table. "I think we may have found our first clue."

"But what does it mean?" Julia asked.

"Let's think about it. It was the middle of May when you visited the high school. Our class was there attending sopho-more orientation. Maybe something in that section of the book can help us. It doesn't make sense, but neither does you hearing your mom's voice on a phone call…twice. We didn't think some-thing like this would ever happen again. That ship sailed two days ago."

"You're right. Having been through this before—"

"We should be able to put on our big girl pants and trust God."

"With that in mind, let's start from the beginning. I walked into the building. I could smell fresh paint from the new panther mascot emblem displayed on the lobby wall. I studied the names on the awards in the trophy case, saw Bobby Tyler and my other classmates, and then later spotted Greg what's-his-name standing in the student smoking area. Other than that, nothing stands out except that no one could see or hear me. Oh, and that teacher was trying to get the students in line. She was upset with two girls who—"

Margaret finished Julia's sentence, "Who didn't get permission to go to the bathroom."

"She seemed a little tense. Then again, teachers could be strict back then."

Margaret sat up in her chair. "Julia, it's not you who can fill in the blanks from that day. It's me."

"What are you talking about?"

"I'm sorry. I'm going to have to call you back."

Margaret's hands were shaking as she attempted to put the phone on the lamp table. It slipped off and landed on the floor as she hurried into the kitchen. Turning on the kitchen sink faucet, she splashed some cold water on her face. After blotting it dry with a paper towel, she stood there for a moment, trying to slow down her breathing.

"So much for putting on your big girl pants, Margaret," she said. Her lip quivered as she looked heavenward. "Lord, will this ever get any easier?" Leaning her elbows on the counter, she put her face in her hands and wept.

Chapter Ten

Julia glanced at the time on her phone. If Margaret didn't call back in a few minutes, she would call her. She picked up the book again but couldn't focus on reading it.

What did Margaret remember?

Evidently, the trigger was when she mentioned the students who got into trouble for going to the bathroom without permission. What was in that statement that could have caused Margaret to get so upset?

Her phone began to vibrate. "That could be my answer," she said.

"Hey! Are you okay?"

She could hear Margaret sniff.

"I'm sorry for hanging up like that, but I was completely caught off guard. I've read that section of your book more times than I can count. I don't know why I didn't see it before."

Even though Julia was eager to hear what Margaret had remembered, she didn't want to gloss over the fact that whatever it was had surfaced some strong emotions. She thought for a moment before responding.

"Maybe seeing it wasn't *important* until now, like the dreams you've been having. Do you recall years ago when you first started this journey? One of the things you learned was that healing comes in stages, especially healing from something as devastating as sexual abuse."

"So, you're suggesting that there's something hidden in my heart that still needs healing?"

"I'm saying that healing takes a lifetime. Whether we've been abused or not, as Christians, we're in the process of being conformed into Christ's image until we leave this earth. You may not understand why this memory has stayed in the shadows, but you can trust God's timing in exposing it."

"I know what you're saying is true. It's just that, right now, remembering hurts."

Julia paused. "Are you ready to tell me what it was?"

"I was supposed to be a part of that sophomore orientation. I was in line talking with my friends when I saw Horace enter the lobby doors with Wyatt and Joseph in tow. For some reason they were late and he was bringing them to school. I'm sure it was one of the few times he lowered himself to such a task. Of course, being the philanthropist that he was—particularly with scholarship donations—every teacher and administrator who caught a glimpse of him was treating him like royalty."

Julia could hear Margaret sniff again. "Then what happened?"

"We made eye contact. He smiled at me, but it was a sardonic smile. Pure evil."

"That had to have been so upsetting for you."

"It would have been upsetting to run into him *anywhere*. But school, and especially band class, was my outlet. It was where I could be a normal teenage girl—or at least pretend to be. Seeing Horace that day made me feel like the one place where I felt safe wasn't safe anymore. I asked the teacher if I could go to the bathroom. I told her I was sick to my stomach. I'm sure my face was as pale as a ghost, and I must've looked like I was about to throw up. So, she believed me. Besides the fact that those girls should have asked for permission anyway, I think she would have instructed them to go to a different bathroom in case I was contagious."

"But in the bathroom, you were—"

"Crying my eyes out. But not so that anyone could hear me. I'd become quite proficient at doing whatever I had to do to keep my secret. The only people I ever told were the Morgans."

Julia thought for a moment. Even though she didn't understand everything yet, one thing was no longer a mystery: God was using this situation to bring Margaret more freedom and healing.

Julia could hear what sounded like Margaret turning her head and blowing her nose. "But enough about me," Margaret said. "What does this have to do with my mom calling your mom about picking us up from school?"

"Not so fast!" Julia said. "What God does along the way of us trying to figure this out is just as important as us figuring it out. What you shared is something that's been hidden for years. At that point in time, you no longer felt safe. Anywhere. Am I right?"

Margaret didn't say anything.

"Are you okay?"

"Yes, and you're right. That was the point in time when I began turning to drugs and alcohol. Not overnight, of course. But it's when I started looking elsewhere for that feeling of safety and comfort. I never made the connection until now."

Julia felt a lump in her throat. "What you were looking for was someone who could make you feel loved again. Then, the One who is love found *you*."

"He'd been pursuing me all along, but my pain had blinded me. You know, while there are still unanswered questions about this whole thing, some of it is beginning to make sense. We're pretty good for over-the-hill sleuths, wouldn't you say?"

Julia chuckled. "Speak for yourself with that over-the-hill talk. Although, we *are* investigating one of the greatest mysteries of all time: God's amazing love."

They both were quiet for a moment, which seemed appropriate. Then something occurred to Julia. "You alluded to the fact that Horace bringing the boys to school seemed unusual."

"Only because I knew that, like my dad, Horace only showed up for big events like award ceremonies or graduations where he could smile for the camera. Taking us to band practice and helping us with our homework—you know, the day-to-day parenting? Our moms did all of that."

"When my mom said your mom couldn't pick us up from school, she indicated that your mom had sounded upset. What if all of this happened on the same day? What if my time jump wasn't merely to see my classmates and learn a lesson about how our choices would determine our futures? What if there was more going on behind the scenes? Something that we wouldn't need to see—"

"Until now," Margaret interjected.

"Exactly," Julia responded, and then she paused. "But there's something that still puzzles me. *Why now?*"

Chapter Eleven

M onica threw her keys on the counter and started thumbing through a pile of mail: electric bill, sales paper, credit card offers, car registration notice, and a letter from her brother. She set aside the electric bill and the car registration notice. The rest she tossed into a wastebasket.

The Durledge Apartment case baffled her. However, she smiled as she thought about how the key on the necklace chain did, in fact, go with the diary. She always found it satisfying when she could "one-up" her senior partner. It wasn't that Norman wasn't great to work with; he was. The two got along well and had solved numerous cases together. Still, being right felt good.

She hadn't had a chance to read through Margaret's diary entries yet; just walking through the apartment had made Monica feel depressed and hopeless. She couldn't imagine how Margaret must have felt living there for as long as she did. All that Margaret had accomplished since then was nothing short of miraculous.

The second key Monica found in the kitchen wall had a number inscribed on one side. She and Norman had no clue yet as to what it unlocked.

Monica opened the refrigerator door and pulled out a plate of leftovers. She placed them in the microwave, gave a voice command, and the machine hummed to life.

The wine rack on the kitchen wall contained several bottles. Monica had planned her dinner menus for this week and had paired a bottle with each meal. She popped the cork from a Cabernet and poured herself a glass. Sitting down at her kitchen table, she glanced down at the wastebasket and sighed. She pulled out the letter from her brother.

"You're not going to give up, are you?" she mumbled.

She set the letter on the table. Before the microwave's digital voice announced that her food was ready, the aroma of Italian seasonings filled the kitchen. As she opened the door and picked up the steaming plate, a piece of melted cheese slid onto her hand.

"Son of a—"

She jerked her hand back and all but dropped the plate onto the counter. Turning on the cold water at the sink, she put her hand under the faucet. She dried it off with a dish towel and examined it under the sink light.

"Well, that scar will just blend in with all the rest."

Carefully placing the plate on the kitchen table, she took a seat and a sip of her wine. She extended her hand to pick up the letter but hesitated.

"Oh, what the hell," she said as she slid it over to her and ripped it open. Typical of her brother, it was meticulously hand-written and annoyingly polite.

> *Dear Monica,*
>
> *Since you won't answer my phone calls, text messages, or emails, I'm writing you this letter. I understand why you're avoiding me, but you can't avoid the situation forever.*

"That's where you're wrong," Monica said as she took another sip of wine to wash down a forkful of lasagna.

Pop has asked to see you. He doesn't have long. The doctor said he's down to weeks, maybe days. He's changed, Monica. He's not the man you grew up with. And he's still your father. Please make the trip and pay your respects. Or come and tell him how much he hurt you. Just come. I'm praying that you will.

Love always,

Calvin

Monica threw the letter on the floor. Calvin could never understand, and she didn't expect him to. He was a toddler when their mother passed away. There was so much he didn't remember. And she didn't have the heart—or the stomach—to fill in the gaps for him.

She'd made three promises to herself over the years in the wake of her father's mistreatment of her. The first was that she would never pursue a relationship with anyone like him. She broke that promise her senior year of high school when she dated the captain of the football team. She chalked it up to being young, inexperienced, and smitten by biceps and a letter sweater.

The second was that she'd never judge anyone who had experienced a difficult childhood. Working as a police officer had caused her to break that one—occupational hazard, she'd told herself. But when she left Louisville, Mississippi, and headed east, she vowed never to return. That was one promise she intended to keep.

She jumped when she heard her cellphone chiming. It was Norman. She gave herself a second to regroup before answering.

"Hey, Norm. What's up?"

"The box you found in the wall? We dusted it for prints."

"And?"

"Nothing."

"'Nothing' as in it was wiped clean, or 'nothing' as in it wasn't somebody in the database?"

"The latter. So, it's a dead end."

"What about the cocaine bag?"

"It looks as though someone attempted to wipe it but left a partial print behind. We traced it to one Dominic Martin."

"Should I know who that is?"

"Not necessarily. He was way before your time."

"What was he in for?"

"What he *wasn't* in for is a better question. He was charged with possession with intent to sell, possession of a stolen weapon, and that's the shortlist."

"Sounds like every mother's dream for her little girl," Monica said as she cradled the phone between her neck and shoulder, sunk her fork into a corner of the lasagna, and took a quick bite.

Norman laughed. "Yeah, a real model citizen. Unfortunately, someone offed him in prison back in the late 1970s, so, he won't be much help. But speaking of help, I've got someone working on that key. We should know something in the morning."

Monica swallowed another bite. "Sounds like a plan. Thanks for giving me an update."

"Hey, can I ask you something?"

"Sure. What is it?"

"When are you going to have me over for some of your home cooking? I'm eating frozen pizza...again. You know, the kind where you can't pronounce the ingredients?"

"Hey, I only cook for me," Monica said emphatically. "But the next time I have leftovers, I'll bring you a plate to work. How's that?"

"That's not the same. How can you be so hardhearted? How long have we worked together?"

"Too long," Monica retorted. "Now, let me finish my dinner while you eat...whatever it is you're eating."

Norman chuckled. "I'll see you tomorrow."

Monica ended the call and put the phone down. The fresh burn on her hand had turned to a bright shade of pink. Her eyes filled with tears.

"Norman, you're a great guy, and I like you more than I let

on. I wish it could be as simple as me having you over for a meal. But nothing in my life has been simple. I'm sorry, but I only cook for me now."

She glanced down at her brother's letter on the floor. She leaned over, picked it up, and then tossed it over into the sink. She wiped her eyes with her sleeve and rummaged through a kitchen drawer. Finding a box of matches, she stood at the sink and stared down at the letter. Her eyes displayed no emotion as she struck a matchhead against the box. She picked up the letter and held the match against a corner of the paper. She watched it burn until the flames nearly licked her hand, then she dropped it back into the sink and turned on the faucet before the smoke alarm could sound.

"That's what I think about your letter...and our father. He can burn in hell for all I care."

She picked up her glass of wine, turned off the kitchen light, and went to bed.

Chapter Twelve

"You look rough," Norman commented as Monica hurried into his office, tucking a strand of hair into her ponytail. "And you're late. You're never late."

Monica didn't turn around as she busied herself making a pot of coffee.

Okay, Norman. Don't ask too many questions.

As the coffee pot gurgled to life, she turned to face him. "I'm sorry. I had a family issue to deal with last night. Can we drop it?"

Norman's eyes looked pensive, as if he knew there was more to it than that. She hoped he wouldn't push the issue.

Evidently, he chose not to. He simply shrugged his shoulders and said, "Okay. I'm here if you need to talk about it."

Monica pressed her lips together and nodded. "Any luck with the key?" she asked as she poured a cup of coffee.

Norman took a sip from a red and white Styrofoam takeout cup on his desk. "The guys in the lab researched it online but couldn't find anything helpful. So, I contacted Tom Kimball. He's an old family friend who used to work as a locksmith in Enoburg. He's retired now and has been for years. Since we could be dealing with a key that someone forged when he was in business, I thought he could be of assistance. I sent him a photocopy, and he called to say he wanted to meet with us. He'll be here any minute. Oh, and one detail about him: he's very religious. I just wanted to give you a heads up."

"I should have slept in later," Monica quipped as she rolled her eyes.

At the sound of someone quietly knocking, Norman stood and stepped over to open his office door. He glanced back at Monica and pointed his finger. "Be nice!" he whispered emphatically.

"Mr. Kimball, please come in," Norman said as he shook hands with a tall, lanky man who appeared to be in his late seventies. He wore a long-sleeved, blue and white plaid shirt neatly tucked into a pair of khakis that sported a crisp crease down the front. His hair was white and his beard closely trimmed. He carried an old-fashioned briefcase. What stood out to Monica were his piercing, blue eyes.

"This is my partner, Monica Berry. Please, have a seat."

Norman slid a chair across the floor and placed it beside Monica's.

Monica remembered Norman's instructions to be nice. "May I get you a cup of coffee?" she asked.

"Monica, if I hadn't already had a cup before I left the house, I'd take you up on it. I don't know what's in the pot over there, but it smells really good!"

Monica seized this opportunity, albeit a small one, to take credit where credit was due. "You have me to thank for that. Norman would rather drink that fossil fuel he picks up from a convenience store down the street."

Tom leaned his head back and laughed. "She's got your number, Norman!"

"That's one way of putting it," Norman said as he cast a sideways glance at Monica before settling into his office chair.

"I appreciate your help with this, Mr. Kimball."

"Call me Tom. Nobody calls me Mr. Kimball anymore.

Nobody, that is, except for the nurses at the doctor's office. And those telemarketers. They're annoying, but you've got to admire their tenacity!"

Monica noticed that as Tom talked, he alternately looked both of them in the eye. And there was something about how he'd said her name when she'd offered him a cup of coffee. In her experience, few people made an effort to be personable like that anymore.

Norman folded his hands on his desk. "So, you said you may have found something that can help us."

"Yes, in fact, I think I have."

Tom picked up his briefcase by the handle and set it up on Norman's desk. Clicking it open, he pulled out a board filled with keys.

"I worked as a locksmith for over forty years. I started my apprenticeship when I was just a teenager, so I know a little bit about keys. Without boring you with details about keyways, biting numbers, and manufacturers, I can pretty much tell what this one goes to."

"Does it have anything to do with the biting numbers and all of that other stuff?" Monica asked inquisitively.

"That's part of it," Tom nodded. "Norman, where is that key? I examined the photo you emailed me, but I wanted to see the key in person to make sure I've got the exact copy."

Picking up an evidence bag from his desk, Norman handed it to Tom.

Tom examined it and then looked through several rows of keys.

"In addition to that, Monica, I've kept a copy of every key I ever made. That way, if a customer lost one, I could give them a spare. It was easier than having to travel to the location for a fitting." He looked over at Monica and winked. "And there was no charge for the spare."

She couldn't help but smile. What Norman said about Tom couldn't be true. He didn't act like other religious people she'd known in the past who either looked down their noses at her or who came across as downright strange. Tom seemed so happy and full of life.

"These keys went to lockboxes, bank boxes, and safes. Ah, here it is." Still keeping the key in the plastic bag, he paired it with a key in his briefcase.

"Do you see the number at the top? That's a post office box number."

Norman leaned forward in his chair. "So, this is a post office box key?"

"Yep, which you won't be able to use because—"

"Nobody uses post office box keys anymore," Monica completed his sentence. "A key card opens everything." Her eyebrows snapped together. "Damn! We can't catch a break with this case!"

She remembered Norman saying that Tom was religious. Her stomach clenched. *Did I just swear in front of this man?*

"I'm sorry, Mr. Kimball. I didn't mean to use profanity. It's just that every time we think we're making progress on this case, we start spinning our wheels again."

"No need to apologize, Monica. I know you and Norman care about your work."

Monica shook her head. "Still, I need to watch my language."

Tom turned to her and smiled. "The only thing you need to watch is calling me Mr. Kimball!"

Something about this man was different. She couldn't put her finger on it, but the atmosphere in the room had changed since he arrived. Plus, his experience as a locksmith could prove valuable. She was glad Norman had asked for his assistance with the case.

"Is there anything else you can remember—anything at all— about this particular key?" Norman asked. Monica sensed he was as frustrated as she was at how this case had stalled.

"There is indeed," Tom responded. "When the most prominent family in the community hires you to make a key, you don't forget."

Monica swallowed hard as she and Norman exchanged glances. "You're telling us that this key goes to a post office box owned by Horace Bennington?"

Tom shook his head. "Not Horace Bennington. His wife, Ellen."

Monica and Norman's eyes locked once more. Monica knew what Norman was thinking because she was thinking the same thing: Maybe Tom could provide more help than any of them had realized. Monica quickly jumped to her feet to top off her coffee and offered to pour Tom a cup.

This time, he accepted.

"Just one sugar," he said, holding up his right index finger. Looking at Norman, he cupped his hand over one side of his mouth and stage whispered, "Doc says I need to curb my sweet tooth!"

Norman smiled before clearing his throat and changing the topic. "We'd like to ask you a few questions about the day Ellen Bennington hired you to make that key," he said as he powered up his laptop. "I'll be taking notes while we talk. Some of the questions we'll be asking you may be hard to remember, given how long ago this happened, and they also might sound trivial, such as—"

Monica interrupted, "What Ellen was wearing, what the weather was like outside; those sorts of things."

"Exactly," Norman said. "Sometimes, the tiniest detail can be the very thing that breaks a case."

Tom took a sip of his coffee. "I'll be glad to help in any way that I can."

"For starters," Monica said, as she set her own cup down on Norman's desk, "did Ellen make an appointment with you?"

"I was a small-town locksmith. My customers didn't need to make an appointment. I loved my work. It was the perfect occupation for me."

"Why was that?" Monica asked, momentarily thrown off from her original line of questioning as genuine curiosity tugged at her.

"I could make a good living from an honest trade, provide for my family, and share the love of Christ."

If Monica hadn't liked Tom, she would have recoiled at his last statement. Instead, she felt comfortable enough to probe further.

"What do you mean *as a way to share Christ*?"

Tom set his cup down beside his chair and smiled. "You left out a critical word in that question, Monica. It was the *love* of Christ that I wanted to share with people."

"How did being a locksmith help you do that?"

Norman's eyes widened as if he was beginning to feel nervous with Monica's questions as they seemed wholly unrelated to the case now.

"Monica—" he began.

Tom smiled and put his hand up. "It's okay, Norman. That's an excellent question. I wish more people would ask it!" He turned in his chair to face Monica. "You see, as a locksmith, I helped people unlock things. All sorts of things: house doors, car doors, safes—you name it. Do you know what's the most difficult thing to unlock?"

Monica wanted to look away, but his eyes displayed a gentleness that made it almost impossible to do so.

"The human heart...especially one that's been hurt. It's similar to a lock. A lock chamber that's been damaged or that's full of buildup won't open. It takes someone who understands locks to apply the proper tools and cleaning agents to fix it. It's the same with our hearts. The one thing I've found—the only thing—that can unlock a heart is love. God's love."

Monica's heart began to beat faster. *I've just met this man. Why do I feel like he knows my story?*

Determined to keep her emotions in check, she forced herself to focus back on the case.

She cleared her throat. "Did you sense that Ellen Bennington was experiencing some sort of emotional pain?"

Tom nodded. "Most people are. Some are just better at hiding it than others. Ellen dropped by my shop around twelve-thirty. I remember the time because it was when I took my lunch break each day."

Norman typed as he asked, "So, she came in and asked you to make a key? Do you remember anything unusual about how she acted or how she was dressed?"

"Let me think about that." He paused, appearing thoughtful. "She acted normal enough. She wasn't very talkative, but it wasn't like we were close friends. I barely knew her; I just knew the name. She was wearing a khaki raincoat that looked a little short on her…like it didn't fit quite right, I think. And she had on a scarf that tied underneath her chin. Ladies used to wear those back then. This one matched her raincoat."

Norman looked up from typing. "So, it was some sort of rain hat?"

Tom stared off into the distance for a moment. "Yes, come to think of it, it *was* raining that day. A downpour, in fact. I guess she was trying to keep her short, teased blonde hairdo from getting wet."

"Did anything else seem out of the ordinary?"

Again, Tom paused. "She was wearing these big sunglasses. I remember that because I wondered why she would be wearing them when it was raining outside. I assumed it was because she was Ellen Bennington and she wanted to keep her identity private."

Monica had been fidgeting with a paper clip she'd picked up off the floor. Several things simply weren't adding up.

"Did Mrs. Bennington ever take off her sunglasses?" she asked.

Tom shook his head. "She only lifted them for a brief moment when I asked for her signature on the bill of sale."

Monica leaned in closer to Tom's chair. "I need for you to

think, Tom. Think back. Did you see her eyes at all? What color were they? Did she look like she'd been crying? Did she have any facial bruising?"

Tom closed his eyes as if trying to concentrate. After a moment, he opened them and shook his head. "I'm sorry. I can't remember. As I said, it was only for a second so that she could sign the bill of sale."

"Would you still have a copy of that bill of sale?" Norman asked.

"I shredded all of my old paperwork a few years ago."

Monica wanted to swear again but bit her tongue.

"But," he smiled as he said, "I held onto *that* receipt. Back then, Ellen Bennington's autograph was like a souvenir."

He produced a business-sized envelope from the side pocket of his briefcase and handed it to Norman. "I hope I've been at least a *little* help to you today."

"You've been a big help," Norman said as he set his laptop aside and stood to his feet. "But I'm ready to take a lunch break. I thought I'd grab a bite at that new restaurant down the street. It's getting good reviews. Would you like to join me?"

Tom's face lit up. "I never turn down an opportunity for good food and even better company."

"One out of two isn't bad," Monica teased, cutting her eyes over at Norman.

"Wait a second," Tom said. "Speaking of lunch, I just remembered something. It probably doesn't mean anything, but, as you said, you never know. Evidently, Ellen wasn't a fan of tuna fish. She smelled my sandwich as soon as she walked up to the counter. I thought she was going to throw up right then and there. Too bad I didn't bring something else to eat that day!"

Monica's mind raced. "Yeah, too bad," she said, her eyes narrowing.

"Will you be joining Norman and me for lunch?"

"I've got some, uh, paperwork to catch up on. I'll have to take a raincheck."

She hoped her excuse sounded convincing enough. She had way too much on her mind to even think about socializing right now.

Tom reached around and pulled a wallet out of his back pocket.

"Here," he said, handing Monica and Norman each a business card. "This has all of my contact information on it. Don't hesitate to call me if there's anything else I can do."

"Well, shall we adjourn?" Norman asked, giving Tom a friendly slap on the back.

"It was so nice to meet you," Tom said, extending his hand to shake Monica's. "You've got your work cut out for you here. And I'm not talking just about keeping criminals off the street, I'm talking about keeping ol' Norman in line. At least try to teach him to have a little class about the coffee he drinks!"

Monica chuckled. "I'll do my best!"

As she watched him walk out with Norman through the lobby, she took a deep breath.

I've got news for you. That wasn't Ellen Bennington in your shop that day.

Chapter Thirteen

Margaret awoke with a start. It was daylight outside. She couldn't believe she'd fallen asleep in the recliner. The table lamp was still on, and Julia's book was open and resting sideways on her chest. She adjusted her reading glasses which had slid down her nose during the night.

"I must have been exhausted," she said to herself as she set the book aside. She checked the time on her cellphone. It was two minutes past eight o'clock. She'd missed a call one minute earlier from a number she didn't recognize. The sound must've been what had awoken her.

I don't know who you are but thank you for calling and waking me up!

She yawned and made her way into the kitchen where a murky, morning sky diffused a calm shade of grey through the windows. This would normally make Margaret want to crawl back under the covers, or as was the case today, back into the recliner. However, it was the middle of May, and spring was in full bloom. She opened the kitchen door, stepped out onto the back porch, and breathed in a cocktail of gardenia and honeysuckle. The bouquet made her feel invigorated, despite the dense cloud cover.

She thought she heard a bee buzzing nearby, so she quickly closed the door. Once inside, she realized her phone was vibrating on the kitchen counter. Again, she didn't recognize the number, but she saw that it was the same one from earlier.

This is the second time they've called. Maybe it's not a telemarketer or a wrong number.

"Hello?" she answered as she retrieved a box of waffles from the freezer.

"Is this Margaret Gates…I mean, Bennington?"

Margaret's stomach turned. Whoever this person was, they knew her maiden name. She hadn't been addressed by her maiden name in years and felt thrown off. "Yes, this is Margaret," she said cautiously.

"I'm sorry to be calling so persistently and so early, but I was wondering if I could stop by and speak with you and your husband sometime today."

Margaret set the box of waffles on the counter. "May I ask who's calling?"

"This is Detective Monica Berry with the police department. I'm working on a case that I think you and your husband may be able to help me with. I just have a few questions to ask you. It won't take long."

Margaret's heart raced. "What does this case have to do with my husband or me?"

"I'd rather not say too much over the phone. Would this afternoon, say, around three o'clock, work for you?"

Margaret heard Joseph coming down the stairs. He set his Bible on the counter and adjusted his necktie. Margaret furrowed her brow as she made eye contact with him. She pointed to her phone.

"Of course. We're happy to help. See you then."

"Thank you, Mrs. Bennington."

"What was that all about?" Joseph asked. "Please don't tell me I have to get to church early today to usher."

"That was the police," Margaret said as she set her phone down on the counter.

Joseph looked surprised. "The police? Hey, I paid that parking ticket months ago!"

"I'm serious, Joseph. It was a detective. She wants to ask us some questions about a case she's working on. She thinks we could be of help."

"Maybe we can. I'm always willing to support our law enforcement."

"Me, too, of course. But this detective knew my maiden name."

"Margaret, *everybody* knows your maiden name. You were a Gates, for heaven's sake."

"But nobody *calls* me by that name anymore. It felt strange, especially coming from a police officer. What if this case has something to do with my past?"

"Then we'll deal with it together. But I highly doubt that's it. The only person you ever hurt was you."

"And Preston," she said as she cut her eyes over towards him.

"True, you did cause your brother a lot of heartache and stress. But I don't think he's going to press charges after all this time."

Conversations like this one reminded Margaret of how perfect Joseph was for her. His positive outlook and sense of humor kept her from taking situations like this one—and life overall—too seriously.

She chuckled. "Okay, you win. I won't worry that it's my past coming back to haunt me. But don't make any plans for this afternoon. She'll be here at three."

"Darn, I'll have to postpone that bank heist J.J. and I had planned!"

"Speaking of our son," Margaret said as she stepped over to drop two waffles into the toaster. "Will you make sure he's awake?"

Joseph called over his shoulder as he walked into the den. "Already did. He's in the shower."

"Well, aren't you a keeper?" she said as she grinned and started the coffee.

"Don't you forget it!" Joseph called from the other room.

"Not a chance," Margaret said to herself.

Julia pulled her car into the gas station. She had just enough time to fill up and make it to church before the service began. The cloud cover had begun to produce tiny droplets of rain that felt cool against her face. After starting the gas pump, she caught her reflection in the car window.

Yep, my hair is going to be one frizzy mess today.

Her attention was diverted to an expensive-looking vintage car entering the parking lot. *Probably owned by a collector,* she thought as she leaned over to get a better look.

She returned the gas hose to the tank as the machine announced how many gallons she'd purchased, and the amount deducted from her bank card. She ignored it as she watched the car's driver step inside the gas station convenience store.

Why does this car look familiar?

She walked over to see the pale, yellow Cadillac. It appeared to have been perfectly restored except for one small—but deep—scratch. It looked as if someone had attempted to repair it but had been unsuccessful.

Without thinking, she carefully touched it.

"That was the only blemish he couldn't fix."

Julia jerked her hand back as a large man carrying a plastic grocery bag approached.

"I'm sorry," she said sheepishly. "It's just that it's such an elegant car. What year?"

The man smiled as he tossed his purchase into the back seat.

"No need to apologize. This car gets a lot of attention. It's kind of like having a pretty lady on your arm. Everyone wants to stare!"

She felt relieved that he didn't seem to be upset with her.

"It's a 1975 Cadillac," he continued. "My dad bought it from an estate sale, oh, some fifteen years ago. It was in great shape except for that one scratch there. He would've had to replace the whole back quarter panel. He couldn't find the parts on a car this old. So, he had it touched up the best he could. She's a beauty, isn't she? My son just got his license and is begging me to let him drive it to school."

Julia smiled and nodded. "I can see why. For some reason, it looks familiar to me, like I've seen it before. You said your dad found it at an estate sale?"

The man's eyes narrowed as he opened the driver's side door. "He bought it from some rich guy that used to live around here. Bennington? Yeah, I think that was his name."

Julia's heart skipped a beat.

"You have a good day, ma'am," the man smiled before closing the door and starting the car.

Julia forced a smile as she watched the car leave the parking lot.

The rain began to pick up, as did the wind. Julia quickly got back into her car and closed the door. What were the chances that this particular car would have belonged to the Benningtons? Even more puzzling was the fact that she remembered it. She rarely had any contact with the Benningtons growing up.

She checked the time. That short conversation had cost her precious minutes. She'd have to hurry to make it to church on time. As she pulled back onto the highway, she couldn't help but wonder. *Was that just a random thing? Or was there a purpose in me seeing that car?*

She shook her head as she prayed. "Heavenly Father, what was that all about?"

A few hours away in the small mining town of Wynlow's Mill, Virginia, an older woman winced as her nurse helped pull her arms through the sleeves of a sweater.

"I'm sorry, Miss Hannah," the nurse said, gently stroking the woman's hair back in place.

"It's okay, Flora. It's better than getting cold sitting in an air-conditioned room."

Flora squatted down in front of Hannah's wheelchair. She gently put her hand on her knee. "Are you sure you want to go today? The weather is supposed to be messy. And you barely touched your breakfast."

Hannah nodded. "Yes. There's something I need to do. I may not get another opportunity."

Flora stood to her feet. "It's going to be a long drive to Raleigh. If we're going to make it to the eleven o'clock service, we should leave soon. Are you sure you don't want anything to eat?"

"No, just coffee this morning."

"You know you're not supposed to travel too far."

"I'm not worried. Not anymore."

Flora sighed. "Okay, if you say so. I'll get your oxygen set up and let the driver know you're ready."

After the nurse left the room, Hannah slowly maneuvered the wheelchair over to her vanity. Her hands, gnarled from arthritis, shook as she touched her face. It had long lost its youthful glow, now resembling a roadmap of lines and creases. Everything had changed over the years, the most significant being her name. At least she still had one feature that stood out, even at ninety.

It was the one that, according to her now deceased husband, had swept him off his feet when they first met. She smiled as she remembered how he doted over her in those early days.

In the 1970's, Joan Baez released a song that referenced this somewhat rare physical attribute. Her husband used to hum it nonstop. As Hannah's mind went back to happier times, she began to softly sing about eyes that were bluer than robins' eggs.

Chapter Fourteen

1975

Frances caught her reflection in the window outside of Dalton Larkins' office. She had circles under her eyes that her makeup had failed to conceal. Her hair was sticking out on one side. She discreetly licked her finger and smoothed it back down.

A bell on the inside of the door jingled as she pushed it open. Dalton was renting an office in an older building that had been recently renovated. The reception room smelled of leather books and new carpet. Behind a walnut desk—that must have set him back several hundred dollars—stood a tall, thin lady who looked to be in her early forties. Despite skin that appeared to have spent too much time in the sun, she was quite attractive. Her blonde hair was styled in a page-boy haircut that was slightly teased on the top. She wore a black and white tweed jacket with a matching pencil skirt. Her make-up was heavily applied, but it worked for her.

"You must be Frances," she said in a loud, hoarse voice that, for some reason, made her sound sophisticated, wealthy, or both. "My name's Barbara. Let me show you to Mr. Larkins' office. Ellen only beat you here by less than a minute, so don't let her give you a hard time, okay?"

Barbara stretched out the word "okay" for more than two syllables. Before Frances could respond, Barbara looked over at her stomach and exclaimed, "Looks like we've got a baby on the way! Isn't that just wonderful? Well, here's his office. You let me know if you need anything."

Barbara had already made her way back down the hall to her desk before Frances could get a word in edgewise.

"Thank you," she said quietly, looking in Barbara's direction.

The first thing she noticed when she walked into Dalton's office was that Ellen had been right about one thing: he certainly was handsome. It was the kind of handsome that takes your breath away. He had thick, dark brown hair neatly parted and combed to one side. Long, black eyelashes framed his deep-set brown eyes. He displayed a dashing smile complete with the whitest teeth she'd ever seen.

He stood and shook her hand. "It's nice to meet you," he said.

Even your voice is handsome, Frances thought.

She and Ellen greeted each other, and she took a seat in a chair next to Ellen and across from Dalton's desk. As Dalton sat back down, he reached for two sets of documents that were the only papers on his desk. He picked them up by the corners where they were stapled together and set them down in front of Ellen and Frances, respectively.

"I've already said this to Ellen, but I'll repeat it for your benefit, Frances. I hold everything you tell me in confidence. As your attorney, I'm bound by law not to disclose any information you share with me. I know this is especially important with husbands as prominent as yours."

Frances wanted to believe that she finally had legal recourse. But this young man obviously wasn't experienced enough to understand just how intimidating Horace and James—and others like him—could be. He hadn't witnessed the bloody battlefields strewn with decaying integrity and fallen belief systems. She, on the other hand, was all too familiar with the stench.

"Mr. Larkins," Frances began and then stopped.

How do I say this? she thought.

She cleared her throat. "I believe you're sincere in what you're saying. I don't mean to offend you, but I've seen men cow-tow to our husbands who had much more to lose than just their license to practice law. If I may be so blunt, what makes you different?"

Dalton smiled. "That's a fair question. Two things: first, I'm a Christian. This holds me to a higher standard beyond my allegiance to the law. Also, I fear God more than bullies. Whenever I'm tempted to let someone intimidate me, I just think of them compared to God. That usually takes care of it!"

Frances watched as Ellen leaned forward in her chair. As usual, there was a lit cigarette in her hand.

"What's the second?" she asked.

Dalton smiled sheepishly. "Have you heard of William H. Stockton?"

Ellen wheezed as she laughed. "Heard of him? Supreme Court Justice William H. Stockton?"

Dalton folded his hands on his desk. "He's my maternal grandfather."

Frances couldn't believe her ears. She glanced over at Ellen, who looked incredulous with eyes bugged and jaw dropped. The ashes at the end of her cigarette were dangerously close to falling. Just as Frances was about to warn her, she tapped them into an ashtray on Dalton's desk.

"That's your grandfather?" Ellen asked with a raised eyebrow.

Dalton nodded. "My mother is his only child. So, you'll understand, ladies, when I say that I have pull and power that far outweighs and supersedes anything your husbands can throw our way. That, coupled with the fact that I graduated top of my class at Yale, is why I'm confident I can assist you."

"Wait." Ellen put up her hand. "If you're that smart and have such powerful connections, why are you in Enoburg of all places? Why aren't you in Washington or New York?"

"While I'm proud of my heritage, I didn't want to build a career based on it. I wanted any success to result from my own hard work and accomplishments. My grandfather started out in a modest law firm in a small rural town, so I thought I'd follow in his footsteps. Plus, I don't like big cities. Enoburg is a better fit for me. When I have clients with situations like yours, it makes me think that maybe God sent me here for a time such as this."

Frances smiled. This young man could be the answer to her prayers. She felt something stir in her heart that she hadn't felt in years: hope.

She put her hand on Ellen's. They looked at each other and nodded.

"Okay, Mr. Larkins, you're hired," Ellen said.

Dalton smiled. "First things first. Call me Dalton."

"Okay, Dalton," Frances said as she picked up her copy of the paperwork. "What's this?"

"The corporate world has begun to change due to the Women's Equal Rights movement. Opportunities exist for women that would have been unheard of, say, ten years ago."

"Such as?" Frances asked.

"Low interest—or interest-free—business loans that don't require a man to cosign. With the right financing, which I can arrange for you, you can start a business venture."

"I don't understand," Frances said. "We don't want to start a business venture. Horace and James would never allow it."

"There are legal ways to work around all that, such as what you call the venture. The best part is you can put it into a trust and name a recipient who, at a certain date, will then become the beneficiary of all profits or, in your case, all liabilities and debts."

Ellen rustled through a few more pages of the document. "You want us to purchase *this* property? Are you out of your mind? It's in the worst part of town!"

Dalton appeared to be unfazed. "Yes, it is."

Frances' eyes lit up. "You're going to arrange for us to start a business which will end up in our husband's names. Except, over time, this business is going to fail?"

Dalton nodded. "Terribly."

Frances looked over at Ellen and smiled. "Puncture wound in the tire."

Chapter Fifteen

The conversation at the gas station had put Julia behind schedule. She preferred arriving at Margaret's presentations early to secure a seat up front. Today, however, she found herself rushing into the building as the congregation finished singing the first hymn. She could only locate a few available chairs, and those were scattered along the back row.

Today, as in prior years, Margaret would update the local community on how the Gates Manor was continuing to help troubled teens. Not only did the staff there teach these students music and provide counseling and health care, but they also imparted something even more life-changing: the love of God. Margaret would remind everyone of the ongoing financial needs required to successfully operate such a ministry.

As Julia took her seat, she wondered how long Margaret would continue to speak at fundraisers, not to mention work at the Manor. Margaret—like Julia—was approaching her late sixties. She had recently mentioned retiring, but she'd first need to find a successor—a task easier said than done. Her shoes would be big ones to fill.

Seeing Margaret stand behind the microphone never got old for Julia, even after all these years. Every day that Margaret was alive and fulfilling her God-given destiny was nothing short of a miracle; a miracle Julia felt grateful to have been a part of.

"Good morning, everyone!" Margaret said with a friendly smile.

The congregation replied, "Good morning!"

Margaret's update marked an annual event that traditionally packed a full house with people from all over the community attending. Today was no exception. She was a few minutes into her presentation when the back doors of the church creaked open. Julia and several others looked over to see a uniformed nurse pushing an older woman in a wheelchair. The nurse maneuvered the chair over to the aisle seat next to Julia's.

At one point during Margaret's speech, Julia heard a sniff coming from the older woman's direction. She had a thin, clear oxygen tube in her nose. Her hand trembled as she attempted to catch a tear that was slipping down her face. Julia reached over and patted her hand. When she did, she noticed an exquisite ruby and diamond ring sparkling on the woman's right ring finger.

The woman made eye contact with Julia and smiled faintly. She whispered the words, "Thank you."

Margaret finished her talk, which proved moving and challenging as always. As soon as she gave the microphone back to the pastor, members of the congregation began reaching for their wallets.

The pastor stood back up at the pulpit. "Well, that's a hard act to follow!"

A chuckle rippled through the crowd. Through the maze of heads and shoulders in the pews ahead, Julia had a crescent view of Joseph putting his arm around Margaret and giving her a quick kiss on the cheek. Julia looked at the empty seat next to her where Bill would have sat. Suddenly, she felt a rush of emotion. She'd learned over the years that, in the grieving process, certain triggers can come out of nowhere.

This was one of them.

Julia, this is not the time or the place, she scolded herself silently.

Having Bill sitting with her in a church service was a small thing, but it was something she missed. She could still feel him slipping his hand into hers, as he often did, when someone sang a particularly inspiring song. Julia's vivid memories of Bill made her feel like she could reach out and touch him. Instead, she reached for a tissue in her purse and dabbed her eyes.

The pastor's message was brief this morning and, after two more songs, the service ended. Julia had hoped to speak with the older woman, but her nurse wheeled her out during the benediction. Julia stood and began excusing her way past people chatting with one another until she reached the front of the church, where she spotted Margaret and Joseph. As she got closer, she caught bits and pieces of comments as supporters took turns greeting them.

"Thank you so much for sharing today."

"We're so excited about what the Lord is doing at the Gates Manor!"

"Just wanted you to know we're praying for you."

Before Julia could get Margaret's attention, the pastor came up behind Margaret and Joseph and said something to them. Julia assumed it had to do with the offering collected. Margaret and Joseph followed him through a side door in the front of the sanctuary.

Over the noise of the crowd, Julia thought she heard someone say her name. She dismissed it and walked over towards the door from which, she assumed, Margaret and Joseph would return in a few minutes.

"Are you Julia Burch?"

This time she was sure she heard it. She spun around to see a tall man who appeared to be about her age. He was wearing a navy suit and was clean-shaven with salt and pepper hair.

His greeting had surprised her and so she stammered slightly in response, "I'm sorry, uh, what did you say?"

"Are you Julia Burch, the author?"

Julia rarely found herself at a loss for words. But, for some reason, in these few awkward seconds—which felt like hours—she couldn't find any. At all. She couldn't decide if it was because few people ever asked her about her book anymore, or because this man was incredibly handsome.

"Yes, I am," she finally managed. "And you are?"

He smiled. "A fan of your writing! Your novel was one of several I had set aside to dig into when I retired. I really enjoyed reading it—twice, in fact."

His smile was making her knees feel like jelly. *For Pete's sake, Julia, you're not fourteen years old.*

"Thank you!" she responded. "Do you go to church here? I don't remember seeing you before."

"I'm a member at First Methodist. I only beat you here today by a couple of minutes. I was sitting a few seats over from you. *Back Row Baptists*, they call us. Except that I'm Methodist."

The man rolled his eyes as if embarrassed at his awkward attempt to start a conversation. "I'm sorry," he said, extending his hand to shake hers. "My name is Perry Thomas. I'm an attorney with Larkins, Thomas, and Stewart."

"Oh, you must have worked alongside the infamous Dalton Larkins?"

Before Perry had a chance to answer, Julia felt a hand on her shoulder and heard Margaret's voice.

"Hey, you! I didn't see you come in today!"

"Margaret!" Julia said with a little more enthusiasm than she intended. "Great presentation today. We should probably leave now and beat the Sunday rush at that restaurant, right?"

Her eyes looked intently into Margaret's. It was a classic cry for help communicated with just a look when directed to your best friend. Julia wanted to escape this conversation with Perry.

She knew it didn't make sense; after all, why *wouldn't* she want to talk to this handsome, kind, and engaging man? Did she feel guilty? She hadn't even *looked* at another man since Bill's death. Did she doubt that another man could be interested in her? All of this was crazy thinking—she'd only met the guy twenty seconds ago. But there was a connection, and she didn't like how it was making her feel.

She could analyze it all later. Right now, she just needed to be rescued.

Margaret's eyebrows narrowed as if she detected the panic in Julia's expression. Then she glanced past Julia and saw Perry. When she looked at Julia once again, she was smiling. Her smile made Julia panic even more.

Julia's eyes widened, communicating the unspoken once again, loud and clear.

Margaret, don't you even think about it!

It became apparent that Margaret *had* thought about it as she immediately transitioned into match-maker mode.

Margaret stepped towards Perry and said, "I don't think we've met?"

Julia looked down at the floor. "Um, Margaret, this is Perry Thomas. He's an attorney who worked with the late Dalton Larkins."

Margaret shook her head. "Of course! You took over Mr. Larkins' law practice when he passed away. I'm sorry, I guess it's been a while."

Perry smiled and shook Margaret's hand. "It *has* been a while. I was just telling Julia that I was impressed with her work as a writer." Then, as if it was an afterthought, he quickly added, "And with your work at the Manor, of course."

Margaret grinned. "Of course. You know, we were just going to grab some lunch. Would you like to join us?"

Julia held her breath, but Perry declined. "I'd love to, but I've got a stack of folders on my desk I need to sort through. I've just taken a new case. It's my first in over a year. In fact, I came out of retirement to work on it."

Julia opened her mouth to say how nice it had been to meet

Perry when Joseph, making his way from the back hall to where they were standing, spoke loudly.

"Perry Thomas?"

The next few seconds were marked by Joseph and Perry exchanging a hearty handshake and a few friendly back slaps.

Joseph shook his head. "How long ago has it been? Ten years?"

Perry took a step back. "Has it been that long?"

Joseph chuckled. "I'm afraid so, my friend. It looks like we've both acquired a little more grey hair since then!"

Joseph turned to Margaret and Julia. He put his hand on Perry's shoulder. "When Dalton Larkins passed away several years ago, Perry took over his workload. Now Perry's retired, and I've been passed on to one of the younger partners."

"Yes, Brent Forrester," Perry responded. "He may be young, but he's sharp. You're in good hands with him."

"So, how are you enjoying retirement?"

"I *was* enjoying it a lot. I played a little golf, did a little reading." Julia could feel her cheeks get warm as Perry shot a glance her way.

"You say that in the past tense," Joseph said, raising an eyebrow and folding his arms.

"Yes, I was asked to take a case for a lady who was one of Dalton's clients many years ago. Before my time, I guess. The name didn't ring a bell."

"Oh," Joseph said thoughtfully. "Well, I've lived here my entire life. Maybe I'd recognize it."

"I've just started working on it," Perry said as he slipped his phone out of his coat pocket. "Let me make sure I'm pronouncing her last name correctly." He keyed in a few prompts. "There it is. Her name is Hannah Vinmeyer."

Joseph looked off into the distance for a moment. "Nope. Never heard of her."

"Well, that's probably because she's ninety years old—not exactly one of your peers!"

"I guess it's safe to assume she's getting her will together and making her final arrangements? It must be a complicated case for the younger partners to send it your way."

"I don't know if *complicated* is the word, but I have a feeling it's going to be interesting." Perry smiled. "However, I don't want to bore you nice folks with attorney talk and keep you from your lunch plans."

Julia couldn't help but notice how kind Perry's smile was. It put her at ease. She began to feel silly for having reservations about talking with him. She extended her hand. "It was nice to meet you. I'm glad you enjoyed my book. I don't run into many people anymore who've read it or would take the time to encourage me. It was very thoughtful. Thank you."

From the corner of her eye, Julia could see Margaret's jaw dropping ever so slightly.

Chapter Sixteen

J ulia had hoped she wouldn't need her umbrella. As usual, she'd left it by the back door—a bad habit she'd had for as long as she could remember. The rain had subsided, but more was on the way according to the weather report. Hopefully, it would hold off until she got back home. She scanned the restaurant and smiled when she saw Margaret waving to her from a booth by a row of windows.

"We're going to have to keep an eye on the time today," Margaret said as Julia took a seat across from her and Joseph. "As much as I'd love to gush about Perry Thomas, I'm afraid Joseph and I need to get back home."

"Oh, does J.J. have soccer practice today? That kid is going to go pro. He's amazing!"

Instead of beaming with pride—like Margaret usually did with any mention of J.J.—her countenance fell. "No, J.J. is at a friend's house, which may be a good thing." She sighed. "A local detective is stopping by this afternoon to speak with us."

Julia's eyes ping ponged back and forth from Margaret to Joseph. "You both look concerned. What's this about?"

Joseph reached over and took Margaret's hand. "We don't know, exactly. Margaret received a phone call this morning from detective Monica something-or-other. She didn't volunteer a lot of information. She just said that she's working on a case and wanted to ask us a few questions. She addressed Margaret by her maiden name before correcting herself and it's got Margaret a bit rattled."

Julia thanked the waitress who filled her glass of iced tea. Then she looked over at Margaret. "So, without any more specifics, you're concerned that it could be connected to your past somehow. Is that what you're worried about?"

Margaret's eyes welled with tears. "Of course that's what I'm worried about! Honestly, I'm surprised that something like this hasn't happened sooner."

Julia shook her head. "You don't know that this has anything to do with you. You paid for your crimes of drug possession—or whatever else there was—decades ago. I'm not trying to minimize that; you *did* break the law. But all of that's been dealt with."

"You don't understand." Margaret's voice was shaking. "It's not like I'm worried that there's an unpaid traffic violation out there somewhere. I just don't know what kind of a ripple effect my actions could have caused. Does that make sense?"

"It does make sense. But you've also seen the ripple effect of God's redemptive love. He took those mistakes you made and used them to help countless others."

Joseph nodded. "My first inclination was that perhaps there's been a drug-related crime in the area. With the work that we've done helping addicts over the years, the police might see us as a valuable resource. I mean, call me Mr. Logical, but I don't see a reason to panic."

Margaret had just taken a sip of her iced tea. Her eyes bugged as she set the glass down on the table. She glared at Joseph. "Are you suggesting that I, of all people, am being illogical? Me?"

Joseph looked at Julia and winked. "Of course not, dear. I would never suggest such a thing. That would be illogical."

~

Margaret rushed everyone through lunch; Julia all but felt like she had eaten her food without chewing it. She briefly hugged Joseph and Margaret in turn and offered Margaret final reassurances before watching her and Joseph hurry through the parking lot and get into their car.

The warmth outside should have been a welcome change from the chill in the air earlier in the day, but the added humidity only served to create a steam-room experience. The wind had picked up, too, and Julia's drive into her neighborhood was punctuated with the sound of pinecones and twigs tumbling onto the streets. The sky had darkened to the west, indicating a late spring thunderstorm brewing. She now felt grateful that they hadn't lingered at the restaurant. It was only minutes after she'd settled into her recliner with a cup of hot tea that she heard the first rumble of thunder.

She picked up her book, determined to get through a few more chapters. What other clues could it contain? She flipped through several pages but couldn't concentrate. In her mind, she kept replaying her conversation with Margaret and Joseph at lunch. She set the book in her lap and picked up the teacup from the lamp table beside her recliner.

Maybe Joseph is right, and the visit from the police this afternoon isn't cause for concern. But why would the detective call Margaret by her maiden name? Not that it necessarily meant anything, but it was a bit odd.

A thunderclap that seemed to shake her entire house interrupted Julia's thoughts. She immediately checked her cellphone for any severe weather alerts. She used to enjoy thunderstorms before Bill passed away. The two of them would sit out on their screened-in porch and witness the wonder of it all. Now that she lived alone, storms made her nervous. She no longer viewed them as cozy and romantic, but as the culprit of power outages, messy lawns, and roof damage.

She set her teacup on the table by her recliner and stepped over to the window in the kitchen where she could get a better look outside. A bright flash of lightning was followed by the power blinking. When it did, Julia heard a beeping sound. She couldn't believe her ears—or her eyes. From where her parents' phone sat on the kitchen table, a red light began flickering. She could hear the familiar sound of the answering machine tape rewinding as it would do when the device was first turned on.

How on earth could it still be operable? She'd assumed it had quit working when the fuse blew the other day. Perhaps it had only shut down temporarily. Or maybe the power surge from the storm had some effect. Either way, she watched as the tape finished going through the re-setting process.

Then it became quiet. It was as if the old machine was waiting for Julia to make the next move. She stood in silence for a moment trying to process what had just happened. Then she thought about the small cassette tape inside the casing. Unless her dad had erased it, it would still contain decades-old messages. She shook her head as she remembered how her dad was someone who never got rid of anything, hence the clutter in the closet at her parents' house that now resembled the clutter in her nightstand.

With that in mind, she suspected the tape would be full of messages. Plus, in the later years of her dad's life, he'd devoted his time and attention to his wife's illness. Chances were good he would have overlooked a menial task such as erasing an answering machine tape.

Julia pulled a kitchen chair out from the table. It creaked as she sat down. She slid the phone closer to her, squinting as she searched for the playback feature. When she found it, she paused.

"What secrets do you have to tell me?"

She pressed the button.

Chapter Seventeen

Margaret understood the importance of remaining calm in this situation, but evidently her hands didn't get the memo. She could feel them shaking as she poured Detective Monica Berry a cup of coffee.

She set the cup and saucer in front of Monica and then took a seat next to Joseph.

"Wow, this is a delicious dark roast!" Monica exclaimed after taking a sip.

Her comment made Margaret relax a little. "We're coffee snobs around here." Margaret chuckled as she glanced at Joseph. "Life's too short to drink sub-par coffee!"

Monica rolled her eyes. "Try telling my partner that."

Joseph spoke next. "So, Detective Berry, how can we be of assistance today?"

Monica wasted no time as she promptly produced a folder from a satchel she had placed in the chair next to hers. She began snapping photos onto the kitchen table like she was dealing cards.

"Do any of these look familiar to you?"

Margaret felt her heart racing. She immediately recognized her old apartment in the photos. She hadn't been back there since Julia and Bill had arrived that fateful night years ago. Seeing the dark, dingy rooms brought back painful memories of her old life. After a glance, she turned her head to look away.

Monica was all business. "This was your apartment, right?"

Margaret nodded nervously. The pictures rattled her to the point that she barely noticed Joseph gently slipping his hand into hers under the table.

"Now, I want you to look closely at photo number three," Monica said as she slid one of the photos closer to Margaret. "Were you aware that there was a bag of cocaine stashed behind your kitchen cabinets?"

Margaret examined the photo. She shook her head and looked up at Monica. "No, I wasn't."

Her stomach churned. She felt helpless, just like she had during police interrogations years ago. She turned in her seat to face Joseph. When she spoke, her tone sounded pleading, like someone desperate to be believed.

"Joseph, that's not mine. I've never seen it before. I had no idea it was there!"

Joseph squeezed her hand. His eyes were reassuring. "Nobody is accusing you of anything."

Monica seemed unfazed. She shuffled the photos around until she had a picture of a small key. "Have you ever seen this key?" she asked.

Margaret adjusted her glasses and picked up the photo. "No, I'm afraid it doesn't look familiar." She slid the picture back in Monica's direction.

Monica sighed and sat back in her chair. For a moment, she seemed to be studying the rain that pelleted the kitchen window. Finally, she leaned forward and folded her hands on the table.

"Can I be frank with you folks?"

"Of course," Joseph replied. "We're here to help in any way we can."

"You may or may not know this, but they're tearing down the old Durledge Apartments. The demolition crew was working in your old unit, Mrs. Bennington, when they discovered the cocaine. This led to a title search to learn who owned the property. What turned up was Bennington and Gates Enterprises. But the original purchase had two names on the deed: your mother's and your mother's," Monica said as she pointed to Margaret and Joseph in turn.

Margaret and Joseph looked at each other.

"Are you sure about that?" Joseph asked. "I don't remember my mother owning any property independent of my father."

Margaret's brow furrowed. "Wait, you just said that it was owned by both of our mothers, as in, they owned it together?"

"According to the deed, that would be correct," Monica replied. "The purchase occurred on..." she flipped through another folder she'd retrieved from her satchel. "Let's see. Oh, there it is. November 12, 1975. It looks as though attorney Dalton Larkins handled the transaction."

"Detective Berry, with my past arrest record, I can understand why you'd want to question me about the cocaine. And you *did* find it in my old apartment. But when did our mothers' less-than-lucrative property investment become police business?"

"That's a fair question," Monica replied with a slight smile. "First of all, the cocaine we found wasn't an insignificant amount that would have belonged to a small-time user. It was close to a kilo—worth about forty grand on the street today if it were fresh. That much coke is usually found on a dealer, and it could earn them some serious time behind bars. For the record, we didn't find your prints on the bag. But you're right; it was your old apartment. Nobody else rented it after you moved out. If nothing else, with the people you have helped over the years, we thought you might be a valuable resource at helping us sort this out."

Joseph mumbled under his breath, "Told you."

"Plus, where we found the cocaine, there was also a silver necklace hanging with a small key on the chain. We figured out that the key on the necklace chain went to an old diary of yours."

Margaret's head was spinning. She was about to speak when Joseph interjected. "Okay, let me get this straight. You find a bag of cocaine and a diary key stashed behind the wall of an apartment complex that, unbeknownst to us, was originally owned by our mothers. Obviously, this was a doomed venture from the get-go. They had to have known it would become low-income, subsidized housing. Why on earth would they purchase it?"

"That's another thing we had hoped you and Mrs. Bennington could help us to understand. One other item stashed behind the wall was a small cardboard box. It contained a key. Monica pointed to the photo she'd asked Margaret to look at. "This key. It turns out it was an old post office box key that was a copy of the original. The locksmith is still around and remembers making it for one Ellen Bennington. Except that…" Monica paused.

"Except that…what?"

"I don't think it was your mother, Joseph. I think someone else had that key copied."

Joseph's eyebrows narrowed. "What makes you think it wasn't my mother?"

"I never met Ellen Bennington in person, but I've seen photos. The description given by the locksmith doesn't even come close. And, rest assured, he had no problem describing her since she'd identified herself as Ellen Bennington. From what I've been told, people viewed Ellen as a celebrity in Enoburg back then. The locksmith's recollection was that she was tall and wore a raincoat that looked too short and, overall, didn't fit quite right. She wore a scarf tied around her neck that loosely covered her hair, which he described as blonde and teased. She sported large sunglasses. Oh, and there was one other detail. It may not mean anything, but he said that she got nauseous when she caught a whiff of the tuna fish sandwich he'd been eating for lunch."

Margaret's mind was racing. *December of 1975…tall…blonde teased hair…Her brother Preston was born the following March…*

Margaret gasped and cupped her hand over her mouth. "Oh my God."

"What is it?" Monica asked.

"You're absolutely right, Detective Berry. That wasn't Joseph's mother."

"How do you know?" Monica pressed.

Margaret took a deep breath. "Because it was *mine*. But something that *wasn't* mine? That key on the chain and the diary that it unlocked. I've never owned a diary."

Monica sat back in her chair. "Well, this just got really interesting."

Chapter Eighteen

1975

"Frances! Frances! Wake up!"

Frances slowly opened her eyes. Her husband, James, was squatting down by the side of the bed. She could smell his aftershave. His kiss on her cheek felt cold, as if he'd been outside.

"Good morning, darling," she replied, more out of habit than genuine affection.

"I want you to see something!" he said in childlike excitement, taking her hand and gently pulling her to a sitting position.

After pushing the covers aside, Frances instinctively rested her hand on her belly. James must have noticed.

"Our little guy is growing, isn't he?" he said tenderly.

"Little *guy*?" She shook her head. "You sound like you've been talking to our housekeeper, Esther. She thinks he is a boy, too."

She looked up at James. His eyes twinkled. For a brief moment, she felt the way she had years ago when they'd first met.

It was mid-December, her junior year of college. The campus looked deserted as she made the brisk walk from her dorm to the English

Department building. Most of the students had already finished exams and had headed elsewhere for the Christmas break.

Frances had one exam remaining. She'd been sick with a cold and hadn't felt well enough to take the test with her classmates. Even though the delay had postponed her reuniting with her family for the holiday, she was grateful for the extra time to study.

A winter storm system was approaching. Weather forecasters had predicted that it would dump several inches of snow in the area. Frances wanted to finish her exam as quickly as possible so she could begin her drive home to northern Tennessee before the road conditions became hazardous. The snowflakes had already started to fall, producing a dusting on hard surfaces.

"Thank you, Professor, for staying so I could make up this exam. I hope it didn't interfere with any travel plans you might have had."

Frances' teacher, Dr. Roberts, stood over by the windows that lined one side of the classroom and overlooked the courtyard. Frances slid her arms into the sleeves of her wool coat and fastened the buttons up around her neck. She pulled a toboggan down over her ears and slung her purse strap over her shoulder. Placing the completed exam in the center of the professor's desk at the front of the room, she made another attempt to get his attention.

"Excuse me, Dr. Roberts?"

Maintaining his gaze out the window, the short, balding gentleman in a musty-smelling sweater and wire-rimmed glasses replied, "Yes, yes, of course. You're welcome."

Again, without as much as looking in her direction, he motioned for her to come over to the window.

"What on earth is this idiot doing?" He pointed down to a young man who was twirling around by the flagpole with his mouth open towards the sky.

Frances couldn't help but giggle. "Maybe he's catching snowflakes?"

Professor Roberts wasn't as amused. He shook his head in disapproval. "Well, let's just hope that's all he catches. Look, he's not even wearing a proper coat! He'll most likely contract pneumonia."

For some reason, Frances couldn't take her eyes off this young man —whoever he was. She was intrigued by how he seemed so carefree.

As she exited the building through the double doors, she spotted the same young man attempting to make a snow angel from the inch or so of snow that had stuck to the grass.

She smiled and walked over to where he was flailing his arms and legs on the ground.

"I think you need a little more snow before you can make a snow angel. Give it another hour or two."

The young man stopped moving. He raised his head and looked up at Frances. After a brief pause, he smiled and said, "I'd say you're an angel who doesn't need any snow."

Frances wasn't one to fall for someone easily. She tended to approach relationships rationally, rarely allowing her emotions to chart her course. But she was instantly taken by this young man's quick wit and charm. The fact that he was ruggedly handsome didn't help matters.

"Well, you got half of it right. I don't know about the angel part, but I did grow up in the Tennessee hills, where I saw enough snow to last a lifetime. It doesn't excite me. But you? You must love snow. And where is your coat? I mean, your winter coat."

The young man stood to his feet and brushed off the back of his clothes.

"Where I come from, most folks don't even own a winter coat." He opened his zip-up jacket as if he were a street merchant displaying a selection of watches. "There are parts of North Carolina where this is the heaviest coat you'll ever need. It rarely gets below freezing." He leaned in towards her as if telling her a secret. He raised his eyebrows and whispered, "And it never, ever snows."

Frances suppressed a chuckle. "Well, how about a little advice? If you're going to survive three and a half more years here, you might want to ask Santa for a winter coat for Christmas."

The young man's brow furrowed, and he tilted his head to one side. "Three and a half more years? What makes you think I'm a freshman?"

"For starters, you're still wearing your high school class ring. And

Dr. Roberts had no idea who you were. He teaches English and litera-ture to all the upperclassmen. It's a small college. He would have recog-nized you."

The young man hung his head and then sheepishly made eye contact again. "Okay, you got me. I'm a mere freshman, the lowest of the low."

Frances laughed. "I wouldn't go that far!"

"How far would you go?"

"Excuse me?"

"Would you date a lowly freshman? Or am I too young for you?"

Frances wanted to say, "Yes, you're too young for me. I'm on track for graduate school. I don't need a fling with a guy who doesn't have enough sense to come in out of a snowstorm. You're having too much fun, and I don't have time for fun. It would never work."

But that's not what came out of her mouth.

"Why don't you talk to Santa about it when you ask him for that coat?"

The young man inched closer. Frances' heart began to flutter.

"Should I still believe in Santa Claus?"

Frances looked into this young man's steel-blue eyes. She willed herself to stay calm and in control. "I guess we'll find out after Christmas break, now, won't we?"

She winked and smiled as she backed away.

The young man called after her. "Hey, I don't know your name!"

Frances shouted over her shoulder as she walked in the direction of her dorm. "It's Frances."

"That a pretty name, Frances," he shouted across the courtyard. "I'm James. James Gates."

He was so full of life back then. Over the years, he'd lost that spark. Love became dry and mechanical, and life revolved around profit margins and stock market reports. It was a slow fade; one that got faster when he'd formed a business partner-ship with Horace Bennington. It hurt to know that the fun-loving, passionate young man she'd fallen head over heels in love with was just a distant memory.

Until it snowed, that is.

She looked outside the bedroom window where a fresh blanket had fallen overnight. James would not only be beside himself today, but he would be his old self. It wouldn't last but, in her experience, nothing good ever did.

She smiled as she looked up at him.

"Let's wake up Margaret and make snow angels!"

Chapter Nineteen

Holly Sparrow added a bit of water to the chicken stir-fry she was sautéing on the stove. She backed away as a burst of steam shot up from the pan.

She wiped her hands on a dishtowel she had draped over her shoulder and smiled with satisfaction. "That ought to do it!"

She heard the click of the front door unlocking and the sound of Olivia tossing her bookbag on the floor and heading upstairs.

"Something smells like a winner dinner!" her husband, Stephen, chirped as he bustled into the kitchen. Holly picked up a wooden spoon and scooped up a sampling of what she considered to be a culinary masterpiece, or, at the very least, an entrée tasty enough to receive an award at the upcoming Bake-N-Cook competition.

"Hold that spoon!" Stephen said, raising his index finger. He playfully snatched the dish towel from Holly's shoulder and tied it into a blindfold around his head. He opened his mouth and leaned in towards her.

"Be prepared to be amazed, *mon amour!*" Holly said in a dramatic French accent as she emptied the contents into his mouth.

Stephen's lips turned downward, and he winced. "*Je ne sais pas*...are you sure this wasn't a frozen concoction, *madame*, grabbed from *le* grocery store?"

Holly untied the blindfold, threw it on the floor, and then waved the spoon in front of Stephen. She furrowed her brow and shouted, "You dare to suggest that Chef Holly Sparrow would cook something from *le* frozen food section? Are you *tres stupide*?"

"You both have seriously lost your minds," Oliva said flatly as she shuffled into the kitchen in her socked feet and took a seat on a barstool at the counter.

Holly and Stephen both laughed. Then Stephen rested his hands on Holly's shoulders. "Honey, you have perfected that dish. There's no way you're not going to win."

Holly's face broadened into a big smile. "Do you really think so?"

"Of course! And with the—"

"So, what does a girl have to do to get a meal around here?" Olivia interrupted.

Stephen cast a corrective glance in Olivia's direction. Reaching into the cabinet, he pulled out three plates and three salad bowls and set them in front of Olivia.

"*A girl* can start by setting the table. Chop, chop!"

Olivia rolled her eyes and reluctantly picked up the plates and bowls.

Holly carefully poured the stir-fry over a platter of steaming rice. After Olivia had set out the plates, bowls, and silverware, the three of them sat down at the kitchen table.

"Who's going to ask the blessing?" Olivia asked as she unfolded her napkin and placed it in her lap. "I'm starving!"

Holly looked across the table at Olivia. Nothing could have prepared her for the roller coaster ride that would define Olivia's teenage years. There were days when Holly felt outdated and extraneous, like she did nothing more than clutter up Olivia's young world. But then Olivia would wake up from having a bad dream and ask Holly to snuggle with her until she went back to sleep.

On countless occasions, Holly longed to be able to dial back the clock—and the hormones. She knew the only way to forge ahead was to shape Olivia into an adult who understood that growing up meant accepting responsibilities and contributing to the greater good. She tried to snatch little opportunities to reinforce this. One involved Olivia helping her grandmother unpack boxes instead of going to a concert. Asking the blessing at supper would be another.

"Why don't you ask the blessing tonight?" Holly asked nonchalantly.

"Why me?" Olivia asked. Holly detected a twinge of defiance in her tone.

"Why not you?" Holly retorted.

Olivia scoffed. "Duh, because you or Dad always ask the blessing."

"What do Dad and I say when we ask the blessing?"

"I dunno. You never say the same thing twice."

"Exactly. We're just talking to God. You know how to talk to God. So, thank Him for the food."

Olivia's eyes darted back and forth between Stephen and Holly.

Stephen raised his eyebrows. "While we're young, Olivia."

Olivia sighed and then bowed her head. "Thank you, Lord, for this awkward blessing I'm about to offer. I don't have any experience with this, so you probably won't be all that impressed. Uh...thank you for the food my mom has prepared for us. If it tastes as good as it smells, we're in for a treat. And *please* help my parents not to be so annoying. I'm sure they get on your nerves as much as they do mine. In Jesus' name. Amen."

"Now, that wasn't so hard, was it?" Holly asked, suppressing a chuckle.

Stephen wasn't going to let that last part go unpunished. He wadded up his napkin and threw it in Olivia's direction.

"So, you think we get on God's nerves, huh?"

Oliva ducked and giggled.

Holly laughed as she took a sip of her water. "I've been meaning to ask you, how was your time at Grandma Julia's house the other night?"

"Dad, will you pass the salad? It was fun," Olivia said as she took the salad bowl from Stephen. "But I'm worried about her. I overheard her talking on that old answering machine phone contraption. She thought I was asleep, but I wasn't."

Holly put a serving of chicken stir-fry and rice on her own plate and then passed it to Stephen.

"Wait. What? Did you say she was talking on the old phone?"

"What old phone?" Stephen asked.

Olivia used her index finger to catch the dressing dripping down the side of her salad bowl. "*The* old phone, Dad. The one that belonged to her parents when she got that weird call, like, a hundred years ago." Olivia licked her finger. "It was strange. I hope it's not dementia or anything."

Holly put her fork down. "Olivia, that's a pretty serious term to toss out. We all forget names from time to time and misplace things. It doesn't necessarily mean we have dementia."

"It wasn't like that, Mom. She was talking to somebody. On the phone."

"Does that old thing still work?" Stephen asked through a mouthful of salad.

"Believe it or not, if you connect it to a receptacle and a phone jack, it does," Olivia responded.

"So, she called someone on the phone. Why does that concern you?" Holly asked.

"It's *who* she was talking to."

"Who was it?"

"Her mom."

Holly felt as if someone had just punched her in the stomach. "Are you sure?"

Olivia's expression softened. "Yes. I heard it loud and clear. She thought she was talking to her mom. Now, do you see why I'm worried?"

Chapter Twenty

J ulia reached for another tissue.

Listening to the answering machine messages was like taking another trip back in time. Several were community members calling to offer their condolences after Julia's mom had died. There were a few that she could only assume her parents had saved on purpose, like audio keepsakes. One was her calling about a young man named Bill Burch. Julia played it again—for the third time.

"Mom and Dad? It's me, Julia. I've met someone, and his name is Bill Burch. We've only been on a couple of dates, and I know it's kind of soon, but I think he might be the one. I can't wait for you to meet him! I love you, and I'll talk to you soon."

As she played other calls on the tape, she heard random messages, such as the exterminator calling to confirm a quarterly appointment. One began with a lot of static. Julia was about to skip it when she heard a woman's voice.

"Ava, it's Frances Gates. I hope you can hear me. I'm in my car trying to use one of those bag phones. Plus, it's raining cats and dogs outside. Would you mind picking up Julia and Margaret from school today? I know it's my turn, but I'm not feeling well. I guess morning sickness isn't just for mornings. Oh, and remind me never to get

around fish again, at least not while I'm expecting. Well, anyway, thank you...Bye."

Julia pressed the "stop" button and sat back in her chair.

She looked at her watch. Maybe Margaret and Joseph had finished their meeting with the detective by now. She'd risk it.

She dialed Margaret's number.

"What makes you think that was *your* mom?" Monica asked Margaret.

"She was tall. Her hair was blonde back then, and she wore it teased. This could be a coincidence, but she would have been pregnant with my brother at the time."

"That would explain why the raincoat didn't fit; if she was wearing Ellen's in order to impersonate her."

"She wore a scarf to cover her hair—" Margaret began.

"But our attention-to-detail locksmith still noticed the color and style."

"Regardless of who made that key—and why—the fact that our moms went into business together to purchase property in the worst part of town perplexes me. Bequeathing it to our fathers is even *more* perplexing. It makes me think that they had no idea what they were doing. Or—"

Monica's eyes lit up as she finished Margaret's sentence. "They knew exactly what they were doing.

"But why?" Joseph asked, leaning back in his chair. "What did they stand to gain?"

"How about revenge?" Monica said, shrugging her shoulders. "After all, it *was* the scandal of the century in Enoburg when word got out that Preston Gates was your father's biological son. In my experience, people with money and status don't usually pick up a baseball bat and beat someone to death. They attack them in other ways. They deplete their bank accounts, tarnish their reputations, and expose dirty secrets from their private lives and relationships."

"One way for sure we can settle the mystery of who made that key is to compare signatures. Joseph, if I show you the receipt from the locksmith, do you think you could identify whether or not it was your mother's handwriting?"

"Of course," Joseph replied. "That would be easy. My mother had beautiful handwriting. I have a sample I can let you see. She wrote the inscription in the Bible she gave me before I started college. My mother was private about her faith, but she told me that reading the Bible would keep me on track in college, and it did. It's upstairs in my study. I'll be just a minute."

Monica stammered when she responded. "Oh, a Bible. Okay, sure. Let's take a look at the handwriting."

Monica's tentative response did not go unnoticed by Margaret. As Joseph left the room, she studied Monica for just a moment. She was all too familiar with the expression on Monica's face. It was the classic, *I'll be polite, but I'd rather not hear any religious talk, thank you very much.*

"Wow, it's kind of warm in here. Can I get a glass of water?"

"Of course," Margaret responded cheerfully as she picked up Monica's empty coffee cup.

"It did get humid all of a sudden this afternoon," Margaret commented as she stepped into the kitchen. She peered out the window over the sink. "It looks as though the storm has calmed down a bit, though."

Monica seemed relieved to be talking about the weather. "Yes, it does. It looked pretty bad earlier when I was driving over here."

From the kitchen where Margaret was filling a glass with water from the refrigerator, she could see Monica fanning herself with a folder.

"I can turn on the air conditioning if you'd like!"

"That won't be necessary. You know how it is this time of

year in North Carolina. It can feel like January in the morning and June in the afternoon."

Margaret laughed. "That's true."

Margaret set the glass of water on the table, along with a napkin. Monica picked it up to take a sip. When she did, Margaret caught a glimpse of Monica's wrists. Even after helping troubled teens for the past fifteen years, she was still taken aback. She had witnessed it all: needle marks from drugs, scars from cutting, and everything in between. But the disfigurement on Monica's wrists was the worst she'd ever seen.

She realized she'd just met Monica, and this was a business meeting—police business, at that. She didn't want to cross any lines. Her heart hurt for Monica. What was her story? Margaret was about to gently ask her when she heard a buzzing sound coming from her purse on the counter.

"Can you excuse me for just a second?"

Margaret left the table and retrieved her phone from her purse. She saw on her caller ID that it was Julia calling.

Julia, why are you calling me right now? You know we're in the middle of a meeting.

Then it occurred to her that Julia wouldn't call at this time unless she deemed it absolutely necessary. She answered and spoke in low tones. "Hey Julia, we're still talking with Detective Berry. Can I call you back in a few minutes?"

"I'm sorry. I took a chance that you had already finished. I was listening to the tape from my parents' old answering machine. One of the messages was from your mom. I think she left it on the same day as that thunderstorm. We can talk about it later. Make sure you call me as soon as the detective leaves."

"Hang on. What did the message say?"

"Are you sure you've got the time?"

"Yes. Just make it quick."

"It was your mom calling to ask if my mom could pick us up from school. She said she wasn't feeling well due to morning sickness, which was more like all-day sickness for her. What caught my attention was the heavy downpour outside. Your mom even mentioned it. She was calling from her car using a bag phone. Do you know what that is?"

"Yes, it's a prehistoric version of a cellphone. Did my mom say anything else?"

"No. Well, nothing important, that is. She mentioned not ever wanting to get around fish again since that's what triggered this bout of nausea."

Margaret's mouth dropped open.

"Are you still there?"

"Yes. That unimportant detail is actually very important. I'll fill you in on everything later this evening."

While Margaret spoke on the phone with Julia, Joseph had returned with the Bible. He opened to the page where his mother had written his name and the date. He sat down in the chair next to Monica.

"You weren't exaggerating," Monica said as she looked on with him. "Her handwriting looks just like calligraphy."

Margaret stood behind and looked over his shoulder. "Where did your mother learn to write like that?"

"When she and my dad were preparing for their wedding, they couldn't find a calligrapher to address the wedding invitation envelopes. So, my mother came up with her own version that looked just as professional. She used that handwriting to sign her name—her married name—from then on."

Joseph ran his hand gingerly across the page as if it somehow would connect him with his mother once again.

Margaret put her hand on his shoulder before taking her seat at the table once more. She took a deep breath. "That was Julia on the phone. I think we have more evidence that it was my mom making that key."

Perry Thomas took off his glasses and rubbed his eyes. He counted the sound of four chimes coming from the mantle clock in the living room.

"And I'm only halfway through," he said, looking down at the stack of papers on his desk.

He stood and stretched his arms up over his head. When he did, a light-footed, yellow tabby cat quietly jumped up into his chair, swishing its tail along the back of Perry's pantlegs.

Perry lowered his arms and turned around. He lovingly patted the cat on the head. "Hey, George. Are you here to help me with this case?"

George purred for a moment, swished his tail a time or two more, and then jumped down from the chair. Perry watched as the cat ambled out of the room.

"I'll take that as a no," he said as he took his seat once again and put his glasses back on.

He leaned back in his chair and swiveled it around to face the window. The rain outside had subsided, but the wind hadn't. Perry watched as it tossed his late wife Becky's hummingbird feeder back and forth. He made a mental note to have the groundskeeper fill it with whatever hummingbirds eat. Becky wouldn't be happy to know that he had neglected it.

Oh, how he missed her, especially during a late spring thunderstorm. She would get excited the minute she noticed the dark clouds forming. She made the event special by pouring them each a glass of wine and insisting they watch it together from the porch.

They had also enjoyed rolling up their sleeves in the kitchen and experimenting with recipes. Perry continued to cook after Becky's passing, but more out of necessity than a hobby. He'd picked it up more seriously recently and had even entered a local cookoff. A little friendly competition might be just what he needed to get him out of the house…and back into life again.

Of the two of them, Becky was the one who'd brought adventure into their lives. In the three years since she had died, he'd become the person that she'd always kept him from becoming: boring and all-business. The image of an estate attorney that makes everyone yawn. Yes, that was him now—an old man with a cat.

He'd hoped this case that had pulled him out of retirement would also help pull him out of the rut in which he'd found himself. Wills and estate settlements can be interesting, especially if there's a significant amount of money involved. However, so far, this one was dull, just like his life without Becky.

He spun his chair back around and picked up her picture from his desk. He gave it a quick kiss before selecting a folder from the pile.

He flipped through a few pages before he stopped abruptly.

"What the—"

He adjusted his glasses and reached across the desk for another file he'd already looked through. He shuffled through the pages until he found what he was looking for.

He compared the two documents. He shook his head and leaned back in his chair.

"This family is in for a big surprise."

<h1 style="text-align:center">Chapter Twenty-One</h1>

"That was Julia on the phone. She moved recently and is still in the process of unpacking. The other day when she was sorting through the remaining boxes in her garage, she found her parents' old phone. This afternoon she played back the messages. One was from my mom. She had called to ask Julia's mom to pick up Julia and me from school that afternoon. She indicated she wasn't feeling well and mentioned that it was pregnancy nausea."

Monica's eyes narrowed. "Okay, I'm trying to connect the dots. How is this relevant?"

"It's relevant for two reasons. First, she mentioned how hard it was raining outside. My mom, or whoever that was in the locksmith's shop that day, was wearing a raincoat."

Monica nodded. "The locksmith remembered it was raining when," Monica used her fingers to make quotation marks in the air, "*Mrs. Bennington* came into his shop that day."

"There's more," Margaret continued. "Frances disclosed in the message that the bout of nausea was triggered from her—get this—smelling fish."

"Whoa," Monica said, her eyes growing wide. "What are the

chances that the message Julia heard on that old answering machine could be related to this case?"

Monica's question pierced Margaret's heart.

"Monica, there's a rich history with that phone. God used it in a miraculous way to pursue me when I didn't think I was worth *anybody* pursuing, let alone God Himself. I'll have to tell you my story sometime. Or better yet—" Margaret bounced out of her seat and stepped over to a bookcase in the den. She returned with a book in her hands.

She placed it on the table in front of Monica. "This is Julia's book. It recounts my story better than I ever could. One thing I can tell you is that God is a caring God. He cares about me, He cares about you, and He cares about this case. If it matters to us, then it matters to Him…because we matter to Him. I'm sorry if I'm coming on too strong, but I'm a living example of what God's love can do. I wouldn't be here if He hadn't rescued me. Anyway," she pointed to the book, "it's all in there. You can have this copy."

Monica didn't say anything for a moment. She picked up the book and thumbed through it. Without making eye contact, she said, "Thank you. Thank you so much."

Margaret was encouraged by Monica's response, grateful that she didn't pick up her satchel and run out the door. Today represented a success regardless of the progress they did or didn't make on the case: Margaret had planted a seed of God's love.

Monica cleared her throat and checked her watch. "Wow, it's getting late. Let's see if we can wrap this up. Even though we no longer need to compare Ellen's signature with the one on the bill of sale," Monica said as she pulled out a piece of faded yellow paper from a folder in her satchel. "Here is the receipt from the locksmith."

Joseph chuckled and shook his head. "That definitely is *not* my mother's signature."

He passed the paper to Margaret, who looked at it closely. It felt odd to be holding something that could be a clue to, well, whatever all of this was.

"I'm not a handwriting expert, but this doesn't look like my mother's handwriting either. The only thing that makes me think it could have been hers was how she put a circle instead of a dot over her i's. But a lot of people do that. We need to keep in mind that my mother wouldn't have *wanted* it to look like her own handwriting. She would have wanted it to look like Ellen's. If it was something they'd planned, she should have at least known what Ellen's signature looked like."

Joseph chewed on the arm of his glasses. "Unless they didn't think your mother would have to sign anything."

"Or," Monica said as she looked off into the distance, "they didn't have *time* to plan it or think it through. Maybe this was something they had to do quickly."

"What do you mean?" Margaret asked.

"What if that post-office box belonged to Horace, and Ellen needed to intercept a piece of mail before he saw it?"

Joseph's eyebrows drew together. "Then why didn't she have the key made herself? Why get Margaret's mom to do it?"

Monica paused and then said, "Okay, this is pure conjecture. But what if she was distracting Horace while your mom had the locksmith forge the spare key. Maybe Ellen needed to keep Horace away from their house, his office, or wherever he kept the original key."

"That sounds plausible," Joseph said.

"So, let's assume for a moment that that's what happened," Margaret said. "My mom dresses like Ellen, signs Ellen's name, and for all intents and purposes pretends to be Ellen Bennington when getting that key made. She returns the original key and the spare to Ellen. The next question would be, what was in that mailbox that Ellen didn't want Horace to see?"

Monica raised her eyebrows. "Unfortunately, we still have a bigger problem on our hands: Who owns that cocaine? Why were the post office key and the diary key hidden in the same location?"

"And since it wasn't my diary," Margaret said and she looked at them in turn. "Whose was it?"

"I guess finding the answers to these questions is why they pay me the little bucks," Monica said with a dry laugh as she stood from the table. Joseph and Margaret followed suit.

"Thank you for your time today," Monica said as they walked her to the door. She looked at Margaret. "And thank you for the book."

Margaret could feel God's love for Monica burning in her heart. "You're more than welcome." Without thinking, she stepped towards her and briefly wrapped her arms around Monica's shoulders. Monica didn't hug her back, but Margaret hadn't expected her to.

Joseph extended his hand and shook Monica's. "Don't hesitate to call or stop by if we can be of further assistance."

"Or if you get a hankering for an exceptional cup of coffee!" Margaret added with a wink.

Monica smiled and nodded. "I'll keep that in mind."

Joseph and Margaret stood at the front door as Monica got into her car. They waved to her as she backed out of their driveway and drove up the street. Joseph's tone was somber as he maintained his gaze.

"What a precious young lady. What do you think happened to her?"

Margaret's eyes narrowed. "I noticed several suspicious scars on her wrists."

"From cutting?"

"I don't think so. These looked different. If it's what I think it is," Margaret said and shook her head, "it's worse." She sighed as the two of them turned and stepped back into the house.

Margaret kept her word and called Julia to fill her in on the details of Monica's visit. The two of them decided to meet at

Julia's house the following morning for a much-needed time of prayer.

Afterward, Margaret rummaged through the refrigerator for leftovers she could heat for dinner. She pulled out last night's roast and potatoes and popped a couple of servings in the microwave.

Tomorrow was a teacher workday, so J.J. was spending the night at a friend's house. Perhaps the absence of their son—and his teenage energy—made for the unusually quiet dinner. More than likely, it was because the food wasn't the only thing she and Joseph needed to digest.

They were in the process of clearing the table when the house phone rang. They rarely received calls on their landline anymore, so the ringtone sounded almost foreign.

Joseph looked over at Margaret from where he was loading the dishwasher. He shrugged his shoulders. "Julia, maybe? She must've tried to reach you on your cell."

"I doubt it. We talked earlier, and we're getting together again in the morning at her house."

Margaret pressed the palms of her hands together and poked out her lip. "Will you answer it, please? I'm exhausted, Joseph. If it's not Julia, it's probably a telemarketer, and you'll be able to get them off the line quickly. You're the best at getting rid of tele-marketers...and you're so handsome." She giggled as he rolled his eyes.

"Fine, I'll answer the phone." He brushed past her on his way to pick up the receiver. "You can poke that lip back in now." He picked up the receiver. "Hello, this is the Benningtons!"

"Hello, is this Joseph?"

"Speaking," Joseph replied.

"Joseph, this is Perry Thomas."

"Perry, how are you?"

Margaret's eyes lit up. "Do you think he's calling about Julia?" Before Joseph could even answer, Margaret whispered, "I want to hear!"

"Perry, what a pleasant surprise! I thought you were going to be a telemarketer calling," Joseph said as he pressed the speaker button on the phone. "What can I do for you?"

"I'm sorry to bother you on a Sunday evening, but could we schedule a time to meet? There's a matter I'd like to discuss with you."

Margaret mouthed the words, *Ask him if it's about Julia!*

Joseph mouthed the word *No!* and waved Margaret away.

"Of course! I don't have my calendar in front of me, but I think I can carve out time later in the week."

There was a pause. "Joseph, this can't wait. Can you come by my office say, tomorrow morning?"

Margaret felt a twinge of anxiety.

"Is everything alright?" Joseph asked.

"Yes, it's just something I'd rather discuss in person."

"I should be able to shuffle a few meetings around. How about we shoot for, say, ten o'clock?"

"That would be great. Thank you, Joseph. I look forward to seeing you."

Joseph hung up the phone and then turned to Margaret. "Is it just me, or is it strange that we saw Perry at the church today and now he wants to meet?"

"It's not because he saw us; it's because he saw *Julia*. Didn't you notice how googly-eyed he was around her? I'm not trying to play matchmaker—"

Joseph raised an eyebrow.

"Okay, I *am* trying to play matchmaker. What else could it be?"

"I guess I'll find out tomorrow morning. Meanwhile," Joseph draped his arm around Margaret's shoulder, "we have a teenager-free Sunday evening."

"Which means?"

Joseph sighed. "Exactly what you think it means. We'll watch a movie and fall asleep by nine-thirty."

Margaret took his hands into hers. The ends of her lips curled into a mischievous smile. "What if we skip the movie and don't fall asleep, you know, right at nine-thirty?"

"I still won't let you go with me to meet with Perry Thomas."

Margaret immediately dropped his hands and sighed in frustration. "Joseph, that's not fair!"

He put his index finger to her lips. "However, I'll call you as soon as the meeting is over. Plus, you're getting together with Julia tomorrow morning, right?"

"A meeting I could easily reschedule. Just promise me you'll put in a good word for her."

"I'll see what I can do. Now, let's get back to skipping that movie!"

Chapter Twenty-Two

"You met with the Benningtons without me, or at least without checking with me first?"

Monica had prepared herself for Norman's reaction. It was a chance she'd been willing to take. Still, standing in front of his desk, she felt like a misbehaving student whose teacher had sent her to the principal's office.

"Norman, it was a Sunday."

"Even worse!" Norman slammed the folder he was holding down on his desk. "The local newspaper published a writeup last week about Margaret speaking at a fundraiser on Sunday. What if your little phone call had spooked her, and she'd canceled? Would you like to be the one responsible for that money not getting raised? The Gates Manor helps troubled teens so that they don't become *our* problem later on."

Monica sighed. "I just wanted to make some headway on this case. I felt like we were spinning our wheels."

"No," he said as he pointed at her. "You wanted to prove you were right about Ellen Bennington not being the person who made that key."

"Okay, busted. But guess what? I *was* right; it wasn't Ellen Bennington."

"Haven't you heard anything I just said? Monica, this isn't a murder case. We don't have a family out there waiting for us to bring them closure about a loved one. This case is about drugs found in a bad part of town—no big surprise there. I want this case solved as much as you do, but I'm not going to upset one of the most powerful families in the area to do it."

Monica made an extra effort to speak calmly, hoping it would subdue Norman's anger. "It wasn't like that. They were very hospitable *and* helpful. They provided me with answers, Norman. Not all the answers, but it did kick the ball a little further down the field."

Norman's expression softened as he slid a pencil behind his ear and leaned back in his chair. "The end doesn't justify the means, but grab a seat and fill me in."

Julia leaned over and tossed aside a leafy stick from her doorway. The morning sun competed with a procession of fast-moving clouds, casting shadows across her lawn. Julia shielded her eyes as she observed the collection of leaves and limbs that littered her yard from the storm the afternoon before.

"I guess I know what I'll be doing today after Margaret leaves," she mumbled under her breath as she picked up the newspaper and headed back inside. She placed the newspaper on the counter and picked up a piece of toast she'd prepared for herself moments earlier. She heard a car door shut and glanced over at the wall clock. "Margaret, if that's you, you're early."

Pulling back the curtain in her living room, she was surprised to see Steven and Olivia picking up the debris from her front yard. She opened the front door and called out, "You don't look dressed for yard work, but it's good to see you!"

Steven was in the middle of snapping a large limb in half so it would fit into the mulch bag he'd brought along. He briefly waved at Julia before stuffing the two pieces into the bag and setting it on the sidewalk. He brushed at his pants to remove a few clinging leaves and bits of pine straw.

"Good morning! I hope you don't mind a little unannounced storm cleanup."

"Oh, I'm *so* disappointed that you showed up," Julia replied with a wink. "There's nothing I look forward to more than a sore back and splinters in my hands!"

Julia watched as Olivia seemed to absentmindedly pick up a few sticks that had fallen over by the driveway. Julia found it odd that she hadn't spoken to her yet. Maybe she wasn't too happy with her dad for making an "unannounced storm cleanup" stop on the way to school.

Steven must have noticed it too. "Olivia, honey, aren't you going to speak to your grandmother?"

But Olivia kept her back turned to them both.

Steven persisted, *"Olivia?"*

When Olivia reluctantly turned around, her eyes were wet with tears. She threw the sticks down on the ground and ran up to where Julia was standing on the porch. Julia had to steady herself as Olivia all but threw herself onto her with a tight embrace. Her shoulders shook as she sobbed.

Julia didn't know what to think. She put her arms around Olivia while casting a questioning look to Steven. She had seen Olivia openly display her emotions before, as teenage girls will do from time to time, but this was different.

"Why don't we take this party inside?" Julia said while maintaining eye contact with Steven, who shrugged his shoulders as if to say he didn't know what could be wrong with Olivia. Julia smiled down at Olivia and gently swept her hair back out of her face. "Is that okay?"

Olivia nodded and sniffed.

Once inside the townhouse, Julia retrieved a tissue from a box on a lamp table and handed it to Olivia. Olive blew her nose as they stepped into the kitchen where, at least in Julia's world, all meaningful conversations took place. Three chairs scraped against the hardwood floor as each of them took a seat at the table. Julia reached across and took Olivia's hand.

After casting a side glance at Steven, she tried to lessen the seriousness of the moment. "I know you're not a fan of yard work, but my goodness, that was a bit much out there, don't you think?"

Olivia's face relaxed into a smile, and she laughed. Then her brow furrowed once more as she looked at Julia and said, "I'm just worried about you, Grandma."

At that moment, Julia witnessed something an adult sees when a youngster takes a small step from adolescence to adulthood. The Olivia now sitting at her kitchen table expressing concern for her grandmother barely resembled the Olivia who had stood in her kitchen arguing with her mother days earlier. That girl had faded into the background—at least for the moment—and a mature, selfless, young woman had taken her place. This more adult version of Olivia would likely make several guest appearances during Olivia's teen years before taking a permanent role at the helm of her life.

"Why on earth would you be worried about me?" Julia asked.

Olivia looked over at Steven as if to ask for permission. Steven displayed a blank expression indicating that he remained clueless about what could be wrong with his daughter. Then Olivia mouthed the words, *The phone call?*

Before Steven could respond, Olivia proceeded. "Grandma, I heard you talking on that old telephone the other night. You thought you were talking to your mom. At least, that's what it sounded like."

Julia's stomach knotted. She needed to brush up on her lying skills. Olivia hadn't bought her cover-up story about blowing a fuse. How was she going to explain this? She'd planned on keeping the details between her and Margaret—an option that no longer existed.

She looked at Olivia. "How many tardies do you have at school this semester?"

"I don't think I have any. Why?"

"Because you're going to have one today. Margaret will be here in a few minutes. We'll tell you the whole story."

Joseph looked down at the paperwork that Perry Thomas had just handed him. "So…what's this?"

"One of Dalton Larkins' clients, Hannah Vinmeyer, called me specifically to handle this for her."

"Yes, you mentioned that at church yesterday. I didn't recall her name, though."

"You wouldn't. But that doesn't mean you don't know her."

Joseph's eyebrows creased. "I don't understand."

Perry slid his chair closer and folded his hands on his desk. "I don't know how to tell you this…except simply to tell you."

Joseph's heart began to race. "Perry, is something wrong? Does this have anything to do with Margaret's past?"

Perry shook his head. "No. It doesn't have anything at all to do with Margaret."

"That's a relief. Margaret has been worried that—"

"Joseph, your mother is alive."

Joseph's breath caught in his throat. He cocked his head to one side. "I'm sorry, what did you say?"

"Your mother is alive."

Joseph shook his head. "That's impossible. I…I went to her funeral. I saw the car from the accident. There's no way she could have survived."

"Did you actually see your mom lying in state?"

Joseph's mind raced. He felt dizzy but tried to collect himself to make sense of all of this. He squinted as he attempted to focus. "Uh…no. Mom never wanted that. Besides, she was cremated."

"Look, I realize this is a lot to process. You undoubtedly have a million questions swirling in your head. I can answer most without violating attorney-client privilege. But there's more."

Joseph didn't know if he could take anymore. He took off his glasses and wiped the sweat from his forehead.

"She wants to see you."

Chapter Twenty-Three

1975

Esther balanced a teacup on a saucer while sliding aside a few magazines on the kitchen table. After making room, she gingerly set the teacup down. She shook her head and clicked her tongue. "Miss Frances, do you think you have enough catalogs here? I would think that big ol' fat Sears catalog would have everything you'd need for ordering Christmas gifts. Miss Frances?"

Frances stared out the kitchen window. It was a foggy, grey morning in November—an accurate depiction of her own mood and state of mind. The pencil she held in her hand had gone slack minutes earlier when she'd lost concentration. She was only vaguely aware that Esther had even walked into the room.

"Miss Frances?" Esther's voice was louder this time and Frances jumped.

She put the pencil down and slowly picked up the teacup. "Thank you, Esther. You have no idea how much I need this."

Esther sat down across the table. "Well, I reckon I do." She tilted her head to one side, her warm, brown eyes radiating a teddy-bear type of comfort and calm. "Miss Frances, are you okay?"

Still holding the teacup, Frances sighed and slumped back in her chair, her left hand resting on her belly. She looked over at Esther. Esther hailed from modest means, something Frances envied about her from time to time. She reasoned that it enabled Esther to see life more clearly.

Frances had found that wealth and affluence often muddied those waters. In her experience, maintaining a certain societal status resembled a boxing match. A contender who wanted to stay in the ring must be willing to absorb a few bloody blows and kidney punches. The prize, ironically enough, was being allowed to stay in and endure more. A few knockouts would cloud your thinking. Stay in the game long enough, though, and you stopped thinking—and feeling—altogether.

Frances detected genuine concern in Esther's eyes. She wondered what Esther saw in hers: Torment? Regret? Was her unhappiness evident, or had she successfully sold the lie that everything was okay?

Frances set her teacup down on the table. "Esther, what do you see when you look at me?"

Esther leaned back and shook her head. "Now, Miss Frances, you know that's not for me to say."

Frances' lips raised slightly into a dry smile. "If not you, then who?"

Esther hung her head and nodded. Most likely, Esther understood that Frances didn't have anybody else. When Esther looked back up, her eyes displayed sympathy. Esther then looked toward the ceiling as if she was asking God for help. She maintained her gaze for so long that Frances was tempted to look to see if God really was up there. Then Esther broke the silence. She looked directly at Frances and spoke plainly.

"Miss Frances, I see sadness when I look at you. I see a woman who drives through life on an empty gas tank. I see a woman in a one-sided marriage. Mr. Gates may have the high-paying job, but you do all the work around here to keep your family together. I don't think you feel appreciated in your own home, except by that sweet little Margaret." Esther leaned in as she lowered her voice to just above a whisper. "You have everything anybody could ever want—except for real happiness."

Tears began to trickle down Frances' cheeks as she raised her eyebrows. "So, I really don't have very much, do I?"

Esther stood up and pulled her chair around to sit beside Frances. Putting her arms around her, she pulled her into an embrace. Frances reveled in having someone demonstrate this kind of care for her, even for just a moment. She rested her head on Esther's shoulder. She could feel Esther shaking her head and her voice shook as she spoke. "I'm sorry, Miss Frances, but I just don't understand what you ever saw in Mr. Gates."

Frances didn't bother to wipe at the tears that continued to fall down her face. She answered weakly, "He wasn't always like this."

"Well, I don't know what he was like before, but I know what he's like now."

Frances pulled away and looked at Esther. "I wish you could have known him back then. He was kind, considerate, and— believe it or not—fun."

She picked up a Christmas catalog that displayed children playing in the snow on the cover. She chuckled as she said, "It was snowing the first time we met." She placed the magazine back on the table and picked up a napkin to wipe her eyes. Her heart grew heavy, and her smile faded. "But then something changed."

Esther pulled Frances back into an embrace. "Well, maybe that man is still in there somewhere and that little boy you're carrying will inherit his good traits."

Frances rested her head on Esther's shoulder once more and replied weakly, "That's not possible."

"Of course it is," Esther replied as she gently rocked Frances in her arms. "With God, all things are possible!"

"Not this time, Esther," Frances whispered. "Not this time."

Chapter Twenty-Four

"Hi!" Margaret said when Julia answered the door. Julia immediately stepped aside, which provided Margaret with a clear view of the kitchen table. She was surprised to see Steven and Olivia seated there. She whispered to Julia, "I'm sorry, did I get the date wrong?"

"No," Julia replied. "You're right on time. Would you like a cup of coffee?"

Margaret maintained a questioning look in Julia's direction as she walked inside. She took a seat at the table in a chair beside Olivia's. "Sure," she responded, her voice trailing off as she set her purse down on the floor beside her chair. She exchanged suspiciously subdued greetings with Steven and Olivia while Julia clanged cups and spoons in the kitchen.

A moment later, Julia set a hot cup coffee on the table in front of Margaret and eased herself down in the one seat left at the head of the table. "We don't have much time this morning. Olivia has school, and if Steven wants to keep his job, I'm certain he needs to get to work."

Margaret looked at Steven, expecting him to chuckle at Julia's remark. He didn't. He nervously shuffled in his seat while Olivia

128

kept her head down. Everyone—including Julia—appeared ill at ease.

Margaret leaned back in her chair and folded her arms, "Okay, people. We all know each other here. Did one of you run over somebody's cat or something? What is wrong?"

More silence.

"I thought we were on a tight schedule?" Margaret persisted, focusing on Julia.

Julia looked from Margaret to Steven and then to Olivia. "I guess we don't know who should go first: those with the questions or those expected to provide the answers, which explains the gridlock."

Margaret's patience was wearing thin. She leaned in toward the table. "Julia, could you be any vaguer? What's going on?"

To Margaret's surprise, it was Olivia who spoke next. What surprised Margaret even more was how she spoke—calm and articulate. It was as if she'd grown up overnight.

"This all started because I was—*am*—worried about Grandma. I kind of lost it outside earlier this morning, which explains why my eyes are probably red and swollen from crying. I was here the other night, and it sounded like Grandma was talking to her mom on that old telephone. Grandma said you knew about the incident and could help explain what happened. I just want to make sure—" Olivia's voice cracked. "I just want to make sure that Grandma is okay."

Margaret's pride over Olivia's heartfelt delivery temporarily overshadowed the gravity of her words. Margaret wished she had the time to focus on that aspect—to encourage Olivia for her mature, selfless behavior. In her line of work, she found that any opportunity to praise a teen for when they get it right can go a long way toward helping them to keep it right. But that would have to wait. For now, she could only hope to get it right herself and to help Julia smooth this whole thing over.

"Thank you, Oliva," Margaret responded as she offered her an affirming nod. "Now I understand now why no one wanted to go first. I don't know what your grandmother has told you, but I can assure you of one thing: Your grandmother is okay." Margaret looked at Julia as she spoke. "I don't know of anyone who could experience all that she has—including more than one time-warp phone call—and remain sane!"

Steven looked at Julia. "So, you really did hear your mom's voice on a phone call? On the same old telephone?"

Julia nodded. "I don't know how or why it happened. What I do know is that it *did* happen. It was scary and, yes, it made me question my *own* sanity at first. I took a chance and reached out to Margaret, who assured me I wasn't crazy. She had been having dreams lately that she wanted to talk to *me* about. We both needed answers. We've found a few in the book that I wrote. Oddly enough, the phone call, Margaret's dreams, and the events in my book all took place in the same time period."

"The time period when the first call took place?" Olivia asked.

"That's right, honey."

Margaret decided it might prove more helpful to focus on what *resulted* from that first phone call all those years ago instead of trying to provide answers that neither she nor Julia had yet.

"Just think about all that God did the first time. Because of that phone call and Julia reconnecting with the Morgans, God delivered me from committing suicide. And He didn't just allow me to survive. He gave me the opportunity to help others so they wouldn't have to suffer the way I did."

"Don't forget that you led Horace to Christ before he died," Julia added.

Steven raised his index finger. "Preston also found out he was Horace's son and came into a hefty inheritance."

"And Grandma wrote a best-seller!" Olivia glanced over at Julia and smiled.

A book that is increasing in value every day, Margaret thought.

"Well, I'm certainly glad that someone remembered that!" Julia said, winking at Olivia. "What Margaret is saying though is that if God didn't fail us the last time we walked through the valley-of-a-phone-call-from-the-past, He won't fail us this time. Olivia, I apologize for not being completely honest with you the other night. I hadn't wrapped my *own* head around it at the time. I didn't want to worry you, but it seems that I worried you anyway."

"It's okay, Grandma. Now that we know what's going on—well, sort of—we can pray about it."

Julia enthusiastically patted Olivia's hand. "I think that's the best thing we can do. In fact, why don't we pray right now? Would you mind leading us?"

Steven conspicuously cleared his throat and cast a stern look at Olivia.

Olivia smiled sheepishly. "It's okay, Dad. I wasn't going to put up a fight this time. In fact, why don't we all join hands?"

Margaret watched as Julia's face displayed a proud smile.

"I'm sorry we didn't get to finish cleaning up your yard," Steven said as he headed for Julia's front door.

"Don't worry about that yard. We had more important things to *clean up* this morning. Do you need to write Olivia a note to excuse her for being late? Speaking of Olivia, where did she go?"

"I'm right here, Grandma. I had to take a quick phone call. Dad, do you remember me telling you about Edward's dad's car? He finally let him drive it to school today. Edward is on a break between classes and wants to pick me up."

"Olivia, we don't know him all that well. And I'm not excited about you riding in some fast, tricked-out car."

"It's not like that, Dad."

Steven's nose wrinkled, and he shook his head. "I don't know, I'm not sure."

"The school is only three blocks away. How about we compromise? You can follow us to make sure I arrive safely."

"You would be willing to let me do that?"

Olivia nodded. "For a chance to ride in that car, I'd let you ride with us! Wait, I didn't mean that."

Steven chuckled. "I didn't think so. Well, where is this mystery kid with the cool car anyway? You need to get to school."

"I'm already late; what's five more minutes?"

"Speaking of late, Margaret and I need to get started with our prayer time," Julia said. "We've got a lot of ground to cover." She reached out to Olivia, "Give me a quick hug before you take off with this Edward character!"

Olivia was hugging Julia when the sound of a car pulling up to the house caused her to jerk her head around.

"That's Edward!" she exclaimed, as she pulled back and rushed around her grandmother to open the front door.

Margaret put her hand on Julia's shoulder to steady her. Julia chuckled. "That's the second time today she's almost knocked me down!"

Steven shook his head. "And that's my cue to follow them to school—before Olivia changes her mind!"

Julia locked arms with Margaret as they approached the doorway. Margaret expected to see Olivia's ride look like what Steven had described: tricked-out and fast. But Olivia had been right. It wasn't like that. When Margaret saw the car, she got a funny feeling in the pit of her stomach.

She watched as Edward stepped out of the car and shook hands with Steven. Olivia bounced into the passenger's side of the front seat.

"Julia, that car. It's a different color, but it looks like—"

"Wait, I've seen it before!" Julia said. "I spotted it when I stopped for gas on Sunday. The guy who owned it said his father bought it at an auction several years ago."

Margaret quickened her pace walking through the yard towards the car. Julia grabbed her hand, causing her to turn around.

"It used to belong to Horace Bennington," Julia said softly.

"I know," Margaret replied as she swallowed hard. "There's something I need to see before this kid drives away."

Margaret's heart raced as she approached the car. She walked over to look at the rear quarter panel. She reached out to touch what was left of a scratch that seemed out of place on this otherwise perfectly restored car.

With her other hand, she touched what was left of a scar over her right eye.

Chapter Twenty-Five

"It's a really nice car, Mr. Bennington," Margaret said, pretending to be impressed.

She looked toward her house where she should be warming up her flute for the band concert that night. She had just arrived home from school when Horace Bennington pulled into the driveway. Why would he think she would care about a car he had just bought? Wouldn't that be something that would interest teenage boys, like his two sons? Why was he showing it off to her?

"Would you like to take a ride in it?"

Margaret knew not to ride with strangers, but Horace Bennington wasn't a stranger. He was her father's business partner, and she'd known him for most of her life. Still, she felt uneasy about it.

"I think that's a grand idea!" Margaret heard her father loudly exclaim as he walked across the patio and joined her and Horace Bennington out in the driveway.

"But Daddy, I need to get ready for the concert," Margaret said, trying to be polite while making her point.

"Well, I don't think Mr. Bennington is suggesting a cross-country road trip," James Gates said with a boisterous chuckle.

"Just a drive around the block. You may never get another chance to ride in a car like this one, Margaret." James gingerly patted the hood like it was a new puppy and not a car.

"Well, okay, just let me take my flute and bookbag inside."

"Don't be silly. Just set all of that down on the patio. Mr. Bennington is a busy man. He doesn't have all afternoon!"

Margaret reluctantly released the bookbag from her shoulder, placing it and her flute case in a chair on the patio.

Horace opened the passenger side door for her. As they drove away, Margaret watched her dad wave goodbye.

James Gates stood in the driveway until Horace's car faded from his view. The decision to give Margaret to him was one in a growing list of sins and offenses. His partnership with Horace had long since derailed any train transporting morally sound cargo into—or out of—his life. To cope with the guilt, he'd learned to compartmentalize. Margaret's case in particular had to be approached as a business deal: nothing more, nothing less. In short, James owed a debt to Horace, and Horace had dictated the terms of repayment.

James knew Margaret would feel betrayed in the short term. One day she'd understand how difficult it was to maintain a certain standard of living. Sacrifices had to be made. At least, that's what he kept telling himself. But why would even *he* believe someone like James Gates? The self-loathing began to seep into his soul like black ink: the same black ink that would replace the red in the business ledgers. The corporation would, indeed, show a profit now. But deep down, James knew that more had been lost than gained. Much more.

He walked back into the house and poured himself a drink.

Margaret put up a brave fight that afternoon. She managed to momentarily escape out of the backseat of the car. Running into a wooded area nearby, she frantically looked for something—anything—she could defend herself with. She picked up a rock just before Horace caught up with her and dragged her back to the car. In the struggle, she aimed the rock at Horace, but it flew out of her hand and hit his car instead. She saw his eyes flash with rage as he picked the rock up and struck her across her forehead. Margaret had never seen so much blood.

Yet.

Later that same evening, Margaret sat on the side of her bed, watching through the window as a spring rain rinsed the pollen off the back patio. Tears silently slid down her face as she observed raindrops sliding down her bookbag and flute case; both remained in the chair where she'd left them earlier. Her hand trembled as she tentatively touched the gash just above her right eye.

She jumped when she heard a tap on her door.

"Margaret?"

Despite her not responding, her father walked in anyway.

Numerous questions skated across her mind. Could she approach her father for intervention, or was he party to what had happened that afternoon? Was it a coincidence that he'd walked out of the house when he did and encouraged her to leave with Horace? Could the two of them have planned the whole thing? The thought made her sick to her stomach.

Worse yet…what if it was all her fault? Did she do something wrong? She felt so ashamed and dirty. The emotional—and physical—pain was crushing her beyond what she thought she could bear. She discreetly checked where she was sitting to see if blood had leaked onto her nightgown. It had. She reached for the blanket at the foot of her bed and used it to cover her lap. Would her dad react in anger if he found out? Her thoughts had become a mangled heap of unanswered questions, fear, and guilt.

She quickly used both hands to smooth her hair down over the gash on her forehead. She remained expressionless as her dad sat down beside her. He, too, didn't make eye contact but instead stared out the window.

"Margaret, do you like your pretty bedroom?"

When Margaret didn't answer, he stood and began walking around her room, picking up a stuffed animal or a knick-knack and then setting it back down again.

Margaret kept silent but wanted to see what he was doing. She shifted to where she could look over her shoulder and watch his movements.

He turned his head and looked around her room. "We had it painted pink because your mother and I knew it was your favorite color." He straightened a framed band achievement certificate that had been hanging a little crooked on the wall next to her dresser. "I'm certain no other student in the band program has an instrument as expensive as yours." He lifted the sleeve of a sweater draped across her dresser. "...or designer clothes as nice as yours." He paused and looked in her direction. She quickly turned her head back to face the window.

He walked over to the bed and squatted down in front of her. She stared straight ahead but could see him in her peripheral vision. "These things all came at a cost, Margaret. Everything in life does. I've certainly paid it by working long hours and giving up things I wanted to do. Now it's your turn to do your part. Do you understand?"

Margaret nodded stoically.

"That's my girl." He kissed the top of her head and left her room, shutting the door behind him.

Margaret sat in silence as her heart shattered into a million pieces. The gash on her forehead paled in comparison to this stab wound to her soul. She wanted so badly to confront her dad for allowing this to happen. But this wasn't the dad she had grown up with: the one who took her shopping for a new porcelain doll each Christmas. The dad who helped her blow out the candles on her birthday cake. And—Margaret angrily wiped the tears off her cheeks—the dad who laughed as she caught snowflakes on her tongue and who had taught her how to make a snow angel. The man in her room tonight was someone who loved money, status, and prestige more than his own daughter. That man wasn't her dad. No, that man died this afternoon when he let her get into a car with Horace Bennington.

He even waved good-bye.

Chapter Twenty-Six

Julia and Margaret sat quietly on Julia's living room couch. The steady cadence of the wall clock provided the only background noise. For Julia, the rhythm offered a bit of comfort. The clock was doing what it had been designed to do—mark the passage of time. It stood in stark contrast to James Gates' actions all those years ago. His involvement in Margaret's abuse went against everything God designed fathers to do. Among the most important was to protect their children from wolf-like predators.

James Gates hadn't merely failed to defend his daughter. He'd thrown her to the wolf himself.

"Fathers aren't supposed to sacrifice their children; they're supposed to protect them," Julia said as she put her hand on Margaret's shoulder.

"Yeah, I know," Margaret responded weakly.

"Margaret, I'm so sorry. I knew you had missed the band concert because of Horace raping you, but I never knew the details."

Margaret briefly looked up at Julia. "That's because I never told you."

"Well, there's something *I* never told *you*." Julia turned in her seat to face her. "One of the main reasons Bill and I paid for you to receive those facial treatments years ago was to help get rid of that one scar. From the appearance, we concluded that it must have resulted from a deep cut. We didn't want to ask how you'd gotten it."

"Now you know that the cut from my dad went even deeper."

"Did you ever tell your mother what happened?"

Margaret shook her head. "No. I was too afraid."

"Why were you afraid? I don't think she would have blamed you."

Margaret paused before answering. Even with Margaret's years of work counseling troubled teens, Julia wondered if she still found it difficult to talk about her past. It's one thing to draw from a healing experience; it's another to revisit the pain.

Margaret hung her head. "I feared that she already knew. I couldn't bear the thought of having been betrayed by *both* of my parents."

"I can understand why you'd feel that way, but if your mother was in on it, then why would Horace later rape *her*? What would cause him to become so enraged? Let's face it; if he was going to sleep around, he preferred young girls."

"Like Gina Merino," Margaret appeared to say it to herself as much as to Julia. Her eyebrows snapped together. "You're right, Julia. It doesn't make any sense. Unfortunately, there's no one still living that can clear that up for us. Hang on—that's my phone buzzing."

Margaret took her phone out of her purse and looked at the screen. "It's Joseph. I need to take this. He told me he would call me after he met with Perry Thomas."

Julia didn't want to admit it, but the mention of Perry's name produced a flutter of butterflies in her stomach. "Of course," Julia responded as she stood and pointed toward the kitchen and whispered, "I'll tidy up while you talk to Joseph."

Julia busied herself rinsing off the cups and plates in the sink and transferring them to the dishwasher.

"I take it back," Margaret said a few minutes later.

"You take *what* back?"

"Someone may still be alive who could answer that question, especially if she and my mom had become business partners."

"What are you saying?"

"I can't believe it's true, but Joseph assured me that it is." Margaret swallowed hard. "Joseph's mother is alive."

Julia gasped. "Are you serious?"

"Needless to say, Joseph is in shock. He wants to share this development with that detective we met with yesterday. His mother wants to meet with him, so maybe—"

"You can get an answer to your question!"

Margaret smiled and nodded. "At least I hope I can. Joseph is on his way to the police precinct right now."

"Then what are you still doing *here*? Go!" Julia said as she hurried over and picked up Margaret's purse by the kitchen table.

She placed the strap on Margaret's shoulder for her. "Do you need me to drive you there?"

Margaret shook her head. "No, I'm fine. But you're right. I should be there when he talks to them—for moral support if nothing else."

Julia watched from the doorway as Margaret drove down the street. The remaining leaves and sticks littering her yard from the storm the day before caught her attention once more.

"You're the least of my concerns now," she said as she shut the door and went back inside.

"Okay, let me get this straight." Norman closed his eyes while reciting from memory what Monica had just told him. "Margaret confirmed it was Frances Gates and not Ellen Bennington at the locksmith's shop that day. We can base that on the ill-fitting rain-coat, the hair color and style that were not consistent with Ellen Bennington's, the signature that didn't match Ellen Bennington's, and the pregnancy—" Norman stumbled as he searched for the right words, "fishy-sick episode."

Monica nodded. "And the fact that the two ladies had become business partners."

"All of this is interesting, but we have to get back to what we're actually investigating: who owns that cocaine? When someone purchased it, they broke the law."

Monica's brow furrowed. "You can't purchase cocaine unless someone sells it to you. Norman, that was a lot of cocaine."

Norman leaned back in his chair. "So, we could be talking about it belonging to a dealer and not a user. We've visited that idea before. Why would a dealer leave that much cocaine just sitting there? Somebody missed out on a big payday."

Monica looked off into the distance. "Unless somebody else was looking for a different kind of payday."

Norman could hear a ringtone sounding from Monica's cell-phone holstered to her hip. "You gonna get that?"

Monica's hands moved to answer her phone, but her eyes remained focused as if she wasn't ready to mentally change gears just yet.

"Monica Berry." Her eyes grew wide. "Mr. Bennington?" She looked over to Norman and mouthed the words, *It's Joseph Bennington.* "We would be grateful for any help you can provide. Ten minutes from now? Yes, we will be here. See you then."

Monica hadn't put her cellphone back in the holster before it rang again.

"My, aren't you popular this morning?" Norman said with a half-grin.

Monica briefly looked down at her phone and then silenced the call.

"You don't have to reject the call so quickly; it's not like *I'm* calling you." Norman teased.

Norman expected Monica to laugh and jab back. Instead, her face displayed no emotion, and she said flatly, "It's nobody important."

"Meaning it *is* somebody you know. You really shouldn't describe your date for this Friday night as *nobody important,*" Norman joked, secretly hoping that the phone call wasn't from a romantic interest.

"Why are you being so nosey?" Monica asked.

"Why are you being so secretive?" Norman retorted.

"Fine," Monica said. "It was my brother, okay?"

Norman drew his head back in surprise. "I didn't know you had a brother. Younger or older?"

"You *really are* being nosey. He's younger—much younger. Now can we get back to the *important* phone call: Joseph Bennington's? He said he has new information that could help our case."

"At least that shows that he's not upset with us. And by us, I mean *you.*"

"Point taken. I'm just curious what Joseph wants to share with us that he didn't feel comfortable sharing over the phone. Do you think—"

Monica was interrupted mid-sentence by the sound of a knock at Norman's office door.

"Boy, that was fast. Did Joseph helicopter over here?" Monica got up from her seat and opened the door. Her breath caught in her throat.

"Hello, Monica."

"Calvin?"

Chapter Twenty-Seven

1975

A maid assigned to watch by the front door called back to the kitchen, "Miss Ellen? He just drove up."

Ellen glanced over at the butler, Bivens, who was putting the finishing touches on a floral centerpiece in the middle of the dining room table. Of all the staff at the estate, Bivens ranked as Ellen's favorite. He had worked there longer than any of the other employees. His calm, dignified display of decorum wasn't merely something he flipped on like a switch when he clocked in each day. Ellen had engaged in many after-hours' conversations with him over the years. He proved to be the same person enjoying an after-hours beer in jeans and a sweatshirt as when he wore his uniform and served champagne to dignitaries.

"Relax, Madam." Bivens looked up from placing a lily in the flower arrangement. "Everything will be ready on time. I only need to light the candles."

"Thank you, Bivens," Ellen responded, her eyes expressing gratitude while also nervously imploring him to be accurate in what he was saying.

Ellen had arranged for the staff to cook Horace's favorite lunch. Oddly enough, it wasn't anything fancy. Though he may raise his pinky while snacking on caviar and toast points at the country club, Horace's meal of choice had always been down-home, Southern cooking. To make sure this meal featured all his favorites, Ellen included fried chicken, mashed potatoes and gravy, green beans, and freshly baked biscuits.

Horace brushed past the maid at the front door. Ellen peeked around the corner and watched while he briefly stopped at a foyer table to pick up a stack of mail.

"Ellen, have you seen my post office box key?" Horace called out. "I'm expecting business documents to arrive any day now." He thumbed through the envelopes and then tossed them back down on the table. He loosened his tie as he walked toward the kitchen. "You said it was important that I come home for lunch today. I certainly hope so. I had to skip an important meeting with a new client. Ellen?"

"Come to the kitchen, dear!"

By the time Horace stepped into the kitchen, Bivens—true to what he had promised—was leaning over the dining room table lighting two white taper candles elegantly displayed in silver candlesticks.

Ellen stood at the dining room entrance that joined the kitchen by a swinging door. She observed that Horace was taken aback by the meal preparations. His eyes lit up as he stepped over to the stove. The lid on a pot with steam escaping through the sides clanked as he raised it to peek inside.

In addition to ensuring that the meal would impress Horace, Ellen invested extra time and effort preparing herself that morning. A string of pearls complimented a form-fitting, off-the-shoulder red sweater dress that fell just above her knee. She had flawlessly applied her makeup, and a pair of black pumps graced her feet.

Horace rarely gave Ellen compliments. There was the occasional, "Here comes my wife with those beautiful eyes," that he would spout out at a cocktail party to portray himself as the doting husband. In private, though, he barely gave her the time of day, much less words of affirmation. But when she walked into the kitchen, his jaw dropped.

"Wow! You look stunning. And do I smell all my favorite foods? What's the occasion?"

Ellen's voice was as smooth as velvet. "Do I need a special occasion to prepare a special lunch for my hard-working husband? You've earned this, Horace…and so much more."

She all but floated over to where he was standing and locked her arm inside his. She gracefully escorted him into the dining room, her free arm extended with her palm up, like a game show host showcasing a prize. "Look around, Horace. Our nice house, these priceless antiques, our cars? Your long hours at the office made all of it possible. I just wanted to make sure you knew, well, how I felt. Going forward, I want to really show you how I feel about all that you've done. This luncheon merely marks the beginning."

A clap of thunder sounded from outside.

Bivens had posted himself in the dining room doorway. A line of staff members stood in the kitchen waiting for him to give the nod to start serving the first course.

An hour later, Ellen walked Horace to the door where she gave him a kiss.

"Don't forget your umbrella, darling. It's pouring outside."

She watched as he raised the umbrella and sprinted to his car. She felt confident that the meal had sufficiently filled both his stomach…and his ego.

Bivens walked up behind her, drying his hands on a dish-towel. They both stood there until Horace drove out of sight.

"Madam, why do I have a feeling we just fattened up the sacrificial lamb?" Bivens asked in his usual regal manner.

Ellen turned to face him and smiled. "Because we just did."

The heels of her black pumps clicked against the hardwood floors as she made her way back into the kitchen.

Chapter Twenty-Eight

1975

James met Horace at his office door and handed him a cigar.

"How was lunch with Ellen today?"

"Lunch was quite satisfying." Horace held up the cigar. "I'm assuming this means your luncheon with Dominic Martin was, also?"

"Very. By the way, he wants us to start calling him by his street name."

"Which is?"

"Mr. White."

Horace shook his head and scoffed, "He doesn't score any points for originality, now does he?"

"No, but he makes up for it with his entrepreneurial savvy. But back to this all-so-important luncheon at the Bennington estate," James said as he lit a match and cupped it in his hand. "What was the occasion?"

"Actually," Horace said as he leaned his cigar into the flame and took a few puffs, "I think Ellen has finally seen the light. She arranged the luncheon to thank me for all that I've done for our family."

"She should be grateful. Speaking of gratitude, I appreciate your fronting the capital for this new venture. With a baby on the way, I've got to tighten the purse strings a little."

Horace rolled his eyes. "Which means you'll be forced to buy Margaret a *used* Porsche instead of a *new* one for her sixteenth birthday?"

James chuckled but then quickly became serious. "Speaking of Margaret," he looked down as he spoke. "I realize our arrangement was payment for—"

"The last venture that was your idea and that went south. I lost a lot of money on that one." Horace stepped over toward the window and looked outside as he spoke. "I have to say that your daughter has more than balanced those scales." He briefly looked back over his shoulder to James. "You know, she started out feisty, and I liked that." Turning to face the window once more, he continued, "Now she behaves in a much more compliant manner. It's almost as if she understands that it's—"

"Just business?" James asked.

"Yes!" Horace turned around and looked at James. Then he said matter-of-factly, "She is her father's daughter, you know."

"And as her father, I'm beginning to feel guilty. She had to get stitches for that gash you gave her as a souvenir the first time."

Horace poked out his lip and folded his arms. He even changed his voice to sound like a child. "That was self-defense. She hit me first."

James knew it was wrong, but he laughed at Horace's antics anyway. Still, he felt the need to help Margaret. The window of opportunity for him to emerge as her advocate and protector had long since slammed shut. Any current demonstration of decency on his part would do little to repair the past. Was he doing this for Margaret, or to ease his own conscience?

"Since this payday should more than offset those losses, can we call it even?" James asked, keenly aware of his cowardly word choice by not calling the situation for what it really was.

"For now. But if anything goes wrong with this deal, we'll have to renegotiate the terms."

"Speaking of which, Dominic, er, Mr. White said the package should have already arrived; he mailed it directly to you. It's high-quality stuff so, when we sell it, you'll get your investment back and then some."

"I think we call that a profit, Mr. Gates."

"I think we do," James said as he puffed on his own cigar. "And you've had quite a profitable day."

Horace sat down in his leather chair and propped his feet up on his desk. "I'd say so. I've got a fat wallet in one back pocket and Ellen in the other."

James took a seat in a chair facing Horace's desk. He used his cigar to emphasize his words, "If your wallet gets any fatter and Ellen keeps feeding you those lunches, you might have to use your profits to buy some bigger pants."

Horace leaned his head back and laughed, his front teeth showing with the cigar wedged in between.

"Ellen—you look lovely! Please come in." Frances held the back door open as Ellen made her way inside.

"I wish I could say the same for you. You look dreadful."

"Your coat is a little short on me. And I *am* pregnant, you know. These buttons are about to pop."

"It's not that. Green is not your color. Are you feeling ill?"

"The locksmith was eating fish for lunch. I thought I was going to get sick all over his shop."

"That would make me nauseous, and I'm not even pregnant."

Frances removed a small bag containing two keys from the raincoat pocket. "Here are the two keys." She held each one up in turn. "The original and the copy."

"That's perfect," Ellen said as she took them both. "I now

have my own key and can intercept any other packages that might arrive. I'll also emerge the hero when I suddenly discover where," Ellen used her fingers as quotations marks, "Horace left his post office key."

Frances pointed to a padded envelope on the counter. "That's the package."

Ellen picked it up and smiled. "Dalton Larkins is worth every penny. We would never have known what Horace and James were up to if he hadn't hired that private investigator. This is one way we can get back at them and do some good for society at the same time."

"But couldn't Dalton get disbarred?"

"He's a lot smarter than that. Remember, when he gave us the tip, he emphasized it was just hearsay. He left it up to us whether or not we wanted to look into it further. He doesn't want to know what we decided to do; that keeps him in the clear. Now back to, well, *what we decided to do*. First, we steam the envelope open. Then we switch the contents of the bag with—"

Frances rummaged through a paper grocery bag sitting at her feet and set a box on the counter. Her eyes lit up as she said, "Baking soda!"

"We re-seal the package and put it back in the post office box. If anybody asks why I'm bringing it back, I'll just say that I thought it was for me and that Horace prefers picking up business packages himself."

"When you say 'I', does that mean you'll go to the post office yourself? Because if you're going to be you, you need to wear what I was wearing earlier when I was pretending to be you."

"Believe it or not, I understand what you just said. Let's finish this, and then I'll relieve you of that raincoat and head for the post office."

Frances put her hand on Ellen's shoulder. "Have you thought through what's going to happen as a result of what we're doing?"

Ellen looked surprised. "Of course I have. James and Horace

will think they're selling cocaine when they're actually peddling a leavening agent. Nobody gets addicted to that evil powder, and James and Horace won't have any recourse whatsoever. The dealer won't believe them, and they certainly can't go to the police…this time."

"How do we know for certain that what's in that plastic bag isn't fake already?"

"We don't. What we *do* know is that what we're putting in the bag is."

"What do we do with the cocaine we assume is real? Do we just throw it away?"

Ellen smiled. "My dear, it's not ours to dispose of, now, is it? Think about it: Who owns this cocaine?"

"Horace and James, of course."

"Then that's who should end up with it. Eventually."

Chapter Twenty-Nine

"*Calvin, what are you doing here?*" Monica hissed as she nervously looked over her shoulder at Norman and then back at him.

Calvin towered over her, having grown a few inches taller and filled out handsomely since the last time she'd seen him. These changes most likely occurred during his college career—years Monica had missed out on. She felt a pang of guilt.

Calvin spoke in his signature quiet manner, which should have caused Monica to calm down but only served to stoke her anger.

"Monica, I'm sorry. I wrote you letters. I emailed you. I tried calling, FaceTiming—have I left out any form of communication? I drove from Mississippi to see you. That phone call a couple of minutes ago—which, by the way, I know you silenced—was my last attempt to reach you before I dropped by your workplace."

Monica avoided eye contact with him as he spoke, looking at wanted posters on the wall, framed pictures of former police commissioners—anything instead of his round, tawny eyes. They were the same shade as hers, but his displayed a peace she secretly coveted.

Calvin must have noticed her lack of engagement. He put his

hands on her shoulders, forcing her to look at him. "We have to talk."

"Well, this isn't the time or the place."

"Then what is?" Calvin said with an exasperated laugh. "Just give me five minutes."

Monica squinted her eyes shut to collect herself. She turned to look at Norman. "I need to take care of this. Do you think Joseph will feel comfortable speaking with you?"

"You can ask him yourself," Norman said as he pointed past Monica. "He just walked up."

Monica felt like she was crumbling on the inside. She needed to redeem herself with Norman for her rogue visit with the Benningtons. This meeting provided that opportunity. She'd rather miss it from having the flu than this.

"Joseph and Norman," Monica said as she attempted to portray a professional demeanor, "I'd like for you to meet my brother, Calvin Berry. Calvin drove here from Mississippi to surprise me."

"Hi Calvin," Norman called from his desk. Calvin smiled and waved in response.

Joseph smiled and shook Calvin's hand. "Wait—*the* Calvin Berry who played center for the Ole Miss Rebel basketball team? *The* Calvin Berry whose winning shot won the state championship two years ago?"

Monica felt a wave of humiliation as Calvin responded, "Yeah, I'm that Calvin. But, hey, we had a great team that year. It wasn't all me. I just got in a lucky shot at the buzzer."

Joseph shook his head. "That wasn't luck, son. You displayed amazing talent and timing!"

Ready to get the uncomfortable introductions out of the way, Monica nearly cut Joseph off as she said, "And Calvin, Joseph," she extended her right hand in Norman's direction, "this is my partner, Detective Norman Lasko." Glancing at Joseph and Norman in turn, she concluded, "I'll only be a few minutes, gentlemen, and then I'll join the meeting."

Monica was grateful Norman's office was on the second floor, where she and Calvin could talk privately. She shut the door and pulled him out into the hall.

"Your timing could not have been worse. You have no idea how important this meeting is!"

"More important than your family, Monica?"

This time the guilt arrived in a wave that pounded against the levy of Monica's heart. But the wall she had constructed over the years stood steady. Still, she felt it only right to own up to where her actions had wounded Calvin. He may be bearing the brunt of her anger, but deep down, she knew he wasn't the source.

"I'm sorry, Calvin." She swallowed hard. "I'm sorry that I missed your high school graduation, and your college basketball games. I just couldn't go back to Mississippi. It was too painful then, and it's too painful now."

To her surprise, Calvin smiled and brushed aside a strand of hair that had fallen onto her face. "Sis, I don't care about any of that. I just want you to make things right with Dad before he dies."

Monica recoiled. "He doesn't deserve it."

"Maybe not. But *you* deserve closure."

Monica was fighting a losing battle holding back her tears. They began trailing down her face. "I don't want closure, Calvin. I just want to be left alone to live my life. I've worked hard to put the past behind me. My only regret is that you got bundled with it." She paused and wiped her eyes with the back of her hand. "Look, you can visit me any time you want to. I'll even pay for your gas or your plane ticket. But I am not, and I repeat—*not*—going back to Mississippi to visit our father. I've got too many scars."

"But Monica, God can heal those scars. And forgiveness brings its own kind of healing. I don't understand—"

"No, you don't. You were too young."

"You need this."

Monica straightened her stance. "What I *need* is to get back to that meeting with Joseph Bennington. Are we finished here?"

Calvin paused for a moment. Monica felt as if he was searching her eyes for any sign of hope that she would change her mind. She made sure that none existed. Finally, he shook his head and shrugged his shoulders. "I guess we are."

Monica waited until he had turned the corner and walked down the staircase leading to the front door. She backed up to the cold, concrete wall and slid down until she was sitting on the floor. Her face contorted in anger and frustration as she silently sobbed.

But she only allowed her emotions a short time of expression before corralling them back inside her heart. It was time to get back to work. She briefly stepped into the hall bathroom. After splashing water on her face and tidying up her hair, she returned to Norman's office.

Margaret stepped out from the side hall she'd ducked into a few minutes earlier. She had wanted to give Calvin and Monica privacy for their emotionally charged exchange. Yet she couldn't help but overhear it. There was something she felt she needed to do before she joined the meeting.

A few moments later, she knocked on Norman's office door. Monica answered it—her still red and swollen eyes lighting up when she saw Margaret.

"Hi," Margaret said with a smile. "I'm sorry I'm late."

"Mrs. Bennington! I arrived a minute ago myself. We're just getting started."

Margaret pretended this was news to her. "Good! I'm glad neither of us missed anything."

Monica's eyes began to cloud over. She spoke just above a whisper, "Oh, Mrs. Bennington, you have no idea what I've missed."

Margaret put her hand on Monica's shoulder. "Would you like to join me for lunch when this meeting is over? We can talk about it then."

Monica nodded. "I'd like that."

"And Monica?"

"Yes?"

"It's *Margaret*."

Chapter Thirty

"What's this dish called again? It smells delicious, and I'm starving!" Steven waited for Holly to look up from measuring oil and vinegar for a homemade salad dressing. When she glanced over in his direction, he picked up a large spatula from the counter and held it over the dish.

"Don't you dare!" Holly said as she bounded across the kitchen and jerked it from his hand. "It has to look perfect for the judges."

Steven laughed and grabbed the spatula back from Holly. He pretended it was a microphone as he followed her back to the other side of the kitchen. "And now, ladies and gentlemen, the winner of this year's cookoff is not only a genius in the kitchen but is also the most gorgeous creature you've ever seen. That's right folks; we're talking about none other than the one, the only —Steven Sparrow!"

Holly laughed and then playfully gripped his chin in her hand. "Yes, you are the most gorgeous creature, at least in my kitchen! But if you don't stop distracting me, I'm never going to finish this salad dressing. Now, make yourself useful and take that cooler to the car."

As Steven lifted the cooler and headed out the back door,

Holly focused back on her recipe. "Let's see…half of a cup of salad oil, vinegar, two cloves of garlic—wait, where's my garlic?"

She stepped over to the refrigerator. Leaning over, she rummaged through the bottom bin. "Gotcha!" she said as she picked up a fresh head of garlic and stood back up.

When she did, the room started spinning. "Whoa," she said out loud. She grabbed the side of the counter for balance and took a couple of deep breaths. *Okay, Holly, this is not the time to get sick.*

"I put the cooler in the back of the SUV. What's next?" Steven called out as he came back into the kitchen. "Holly? Are you okay?" Steven walked over to where she was leaning over the counter and put his hand on her shoulder.

"I think so," she said as she briefly glanced up at him. "I started feeling dizzy all of a sudden."

"Do you need to sit down? Let me get you a glass of water."

"Good idea," Holly said, forcing a smile. "Maybe I'm just a little dehydrated."

The water from the refrigerator dispenser made a hissing noise as Steven filled a glass and handed it to Holly.

After a few sips, the dizziness passed. *Thank God*, she thought. She looked up at Steven and nodded. "I think that helped."

Steven stepped back and raised an eyebrow. "I know what this is, Madam Sparrow," he said in an exaggerated French accent. "*Les* competitors are trying to *sabotage!* They know your exquisite cuisine will win *le* blue ribbon." He picked up the garlic head from the counter and shook it at her as he spoke. "They poisoned *les* garlic cloves!"

Holly couldn't help but laugh. "You know you're crazy, right?" She wiped a bead of sweat from her forehead. "Okay, let's get back to this salad dressing. How about you mince two garlic cloves while I blend the other seasonings?"

"You got it."

Holly added a tablespoon of seasonings and used a whisk to blend it with the oil and vinegar. She looked over to where Steven had peeled the skin off the garlic cloves and was chopping each with a small paring knife. Even though the dizziness had passed, the episode rattled her. She found it difficult to concentrate.

Steven must have noticed. He set the knife down on the cutting board and stepped over to the other side of the counter. He cupped her face in his hands. "Hey, are you sure you feel up to this?"

"I'm sure," she responded and then scrunched up her nose. "Eww. Your hands smell like garlic."

Steven backed up, pretending to be offended. He picked up the cutting board containing the chopped garlic and leftover cloves and shoved it onto the counter in front of Holly. "Next time, *Madame* can chop her own garlic!"

Holly laughed and shook her head. "Not a chance. I can't do this without my sous-chef. But we need to hurry—the competition kicks off in a couple of hours."

"Holly, you need to remember something."

"What's that?" Holly asked as she stirred in the chopped garlic and poured the mixture into a plastic container.

"It's *gorgeous* sous-chef," Steven said and then dodged a garlic clove Holly threw at him.

Chapter Thirty-One

Joseph had only shared with Margaret over the phone that his mother was alive. In what turned out to be a bombshell of a meeting with the detectives, Margaret learned that Ellen had been in witness protection for taking down a dangerous drug dealer. The information Perry had provided Joseph with was limited; he wasn't privy to all the details. If they wanted to learn more, they would have to hear it from Ellen herself.

Something that concerned Margaret was how, when Joseph was sharing what he *did* know about Ellen's situation, he seemed disconnected from it. It was almost as if he was talking about someone else's mother. Margaret planned to check on him as soon as she finished lunch with Monica.

"I've lived in this area for years and I don't think I've ever eaten at this restaurant," Monica said as she glanced around before taking a seat across from Margaret.

"I chose it for the privacy, plus they serve a delicious Caprese salad!"

"Mrs. Bennington—"

Margaret raised her chin and cast a corrective glance at Monica.

Monica smiled. "*Margaret*. Thank you for meeting with me. I feel like such a mess right now. I'm sorry I fell apart on you back at the police station."

Margaret didn't want Monica to feel embarrassed about what had happened earlier. She needed to find a way to make her feel more comfortable. She prayed a silent prayer, *Lord, please help me to represent your love and tender heart for Monica. And please give me wisdom. The last thing I want to do is make a bad situation worse.*

"I'm a well-known counselor," Margaret said matter-of-factly as she reached for a roll from the small basket in the middle of the table. Placing it on her bread plate, she scooped up a pat of butter with her knife and began spreading it on the bread. "People come to me from all over the country to fall apart."

Monica laughed. "That makes me feel better."

Good—that broke the ice.

"Can I be honest with you?" Margaret asked.

Monica rolled her eyes and mumbled, "Why not? People are coming from *all over the country* today to be honest with me."

"Like Calvin?"

Monica's eyes widened in surprise, but only for a moment. "You didn't arrive late for that meeting, did you? You overheard our conversation."

"Nice work, Detective." Margaret smiled and then took a bite of her roll.

"You probably think I'm a terrible, selfish person not to visit my own father on his deathbed. I know that's what it sounded like. But you haven't heard my side of the story."

"I may not need to hear it," Margaret said, looking into Monica's eyes. "I may have seen it."

"What do you mean?"

Margaret reached across the table and put her hand on Monica's. "Those scars on your arms? They tell a story. Most of the ones I come across in my line of work result from a person cutting or shooting up. But you've never hurt yourself or done drugs, have you?" Margaret continued in a gentle voice, "I think yours happened when, as a little girl, you were forced to cook for your family, and you kept accidentally burning herself."

Monica's eyes filled with tears. She spoke just above a whisper, "Nice work, Detective."

Margaret leaned back in her chair. "You know, my job and yours aren't all that different. We both collect evidence, look for clues, and help provide answers. We want to help people live happy and safe lives."

"Serve and protect," Monica said as she used her napkin to wipe her eyes.

"The one person in our lives that should make us feel protected, especially when we're young, is our fathers. Mine didn't provide that for me, and I get the feeling that yours didn't provide it for you."

"No, he didn't. And you nailed it," Monica said as she rolled up her sleeves.

Margaret had to keep herself from gasping. "I'm so sorry, Monica."

"It all started when we lost my mother. She died on Calvin's third birthday."

"Do you want to talk about it? I'm here to listen and help in any way that I can. But if it's too painful—"

Monica shook her head. "No, it's okay. It's not like I don't think about it all the time. There are days when I can't believe it happened over twenty years ago. Other days it feels like a lifetime."

Margaret nodded in agreement. "Time can be tricky like that."

Monica's gaze became distant, as if she was traveling back to that day. "The sky was so clear that April morning. I can still smell the daffodils as Mama and I spread a white tablecloth on the picnic table in the backyard. After that, she let me help her blow up the balloons." Monica paused to look at Margaret. "I kept letting the air out of the ones I blew up because I thought it sounded funny. We laughed and laughed."

Margaret smiled but didn't respond. She didn't want to break Monica's concentration.

"The children showed up for Calvin's party around five that afternoon. Pop grilled hot dogs, and we ate cake and had a big old time. The sun was just setting when Calvin decided to play with a basketball Pop bought for him. It was Calvin's favorite gift. Pop always said that Calvin was going to be a basketball player, and he was right."

Monica looked away once again. "Pop told me to keep an eye on Calvin while he went inside to take a shower. Mama was busy cleaning up all the plates, cups, and wrapping paper the children had strewn across the yard. Monica's voice cracked. "I knew how hard Mama had worked to make Calvin's day special. I just wanted to give her a bouquet of flowers, that's all. I was picking daffodils when that basketball rolled down into the street. Calvin ran after it. Mama got to him before I did and brought him back into the yard."

"But the basketball—" Margaret had a feeling she knew where the story was going.

"Was still in the street. Calvin started crying. Mama acted on impulse. She didn't look before she ran out to get it. That truck didn't have time to stop."

"Monica." Margaret's voice was firm. "That wasn't your fault."

Monica looked at Margaret. Her face twisted as if she was confused. "Pop said it *was*. He yelled at me and said that if I'd been watching Calvin like I was supposed to, it never would have happened."

Monica placed her forearms on the table with her palms facing up. "This was my punishment. I had to do all the tasks that Mama had done—all except for taking care of Calvin, that is. Pop said he didn't trust me to do that anymore. But I had to cook breakfast for them every morning, pack lunches, cook dinner, and clean the house."

"Monica, did your father ever sexually abuse you?" Margaret said as she waved away a waiter who had walked up to take their order.

"No. He didn't take my innocence, just my childhood. That's why, as soon as I could leave home, I did. And I've never looked back."

"Until today?"

"Until today. I felt so guilty when I saw how much Calvin cared about me."

"Do you love Calvin?"

"Of course, I do! I've missed out on so much of his life."

Margaret thought for a moment and then said, "Maybe you don't need closure with your father. Maybe Calvin is the one who needs it."

"What do you mean?"

"*You* may be able to live with your decision not to visit your father. *Calvin* may not be able to. What if you not visiting him is something that bothers Calvin for the rest of his life."

"So, you're suggesting—"

"That you make it about Calvin and not your father. Do it because you love Calvin."

Monica nodded. "Maybe you're right."

"I know what you're going through. I forgave the man who abused me. Oddly enough, he was on his deathbed, too."

"Oh, God, this is going to be *so* hard," Monica said as she placed her elbows on the table and rested her head in her hands.

"You're right. It's not going to be easy. But you'll only have to talk with your father for a few minutes, and then it will be over. Compare that to the regret you could experience for the rest of your life. That would be harder…*much* harder."

"Calvin's already left for Mississippi. I guess I could ask Norman about catching a flight out next weekend."

Margaret scrunched up her nose and raised her shoulders. "I

may or may not have followed Calvin out of the police station earlier today and asked him to stay in town a little longer. I took a chance that you and I might get an opportunity to talk."

Monica's mouth fell open. "Calvin's still in town?"

Margaret pointed across the room. "Yep." She leaned in and spoke in low tones. "I told him about the Caprese salad they serve here."

Monica turned to see Calvin getting up from a table and walking toward her. She smiled back at Margaret before quickly standing and meeting him in the middle of the restaurant.

Margaret watched as Calvin swooped Monica up in his arms. He held her there for several minutes while she quietly wept.

The waiter came back and leaned in toward Margaret. "Ma'am, is everything okay?"

Margaret smiled as she maintained her gaze on Calvin and Monica. "You have no idea."

The waiter turned to walk away again.

"Wait," Margaret said.

"Yes, ma'am?"

Margaret looked up at the waiter. "I think we're ready to order now. We'll start with two Caprese salads." She looked back over at Monica and Calvin. "Make that three."

Chapter Thirty-Two

"The chef uses fresh basil, whole milk mozzarella, and ripe tomatoes. That's why the Caprese salad tastes so amazing here," Monica said as she and Margaret walked toward the front of the restaurant. "And thank you for paying for lunch. You shouldn't have. I'm the one who owes you."

"I tell you what," Margaret said. "Promise me you'll read Julia's book that I gave you, and we'll call it even."

Monica smiled. "Deal."

"So, when you stepped outside to call Norman earlier, did he agree to let you take a few days off?"

Monica nodded. "He said that none of our current cases are that urgent. I was the one pushing for us to complete the case involving your and Joseph's mothers. I haven't been able to stop thinking about it. Some cases are like that. They latch onto your mind and heart and won't let go. I guess it's part of the whole *serve and protect* thing."

Margaret turned to face Monica. "Have you considered that this case wasn't so much about you serving and protecting, but about someone doing that for you?"

Monica shoved her hands into her jacket pockets. "It might take a long time for me to wrap my mind around that concept."

Then she reluctantly nodded. "But it's a good one to wrap my mind around."

Margaret reached out and embraced her. Unlike a day earlier, Monica embraced her back.

Margaret glanced over toward Calvin. "If I can stand on my tiptoes, I'd like to give that brother of yours a hug, too!"

"Or I can bend over," Calvin said with a half shrug. "I'm used to it."

After a hearty embrace that convinced Margaret she'd need to schedule an appointment with her chiropractor, she watched as Calvin and Monica walked outside. Then she thought she lipread Calvin telling Monica that he would be right back.

He darted back inside the restaurant and approached Margaret. "Thank you so much for spending time with my sister today. It's nothing short of a miracle that she's going back to Mississippi with me."

Margaret put her hand on his arm. "Calvin, Monica isn't out of the woods yet, but it's a step in the right direction. She's going to need you to be there for her. In basketball terms, I'm passing the ball to you."

Calvin pointed in her direction. "And I will do my best for the team."

As he opened the restaurant door to leave, Margaret called after him. "Hey, Calvin?"

"Yes?"

"Who knows? You might just score another winning shot—right at the buzzer."

Calvin jerked his head back in surprise.

Margaret grinned. "My husband isn't the only one in our house who follows college basketball."

Margaret could feel her phone vibrating in her purse. She waved goodbye to Monica and Calvin with one hand and pulled her phone out with the other.

"Hello, Joseph? Yes, I just finished lunch with Monica and Calvin. Wait…what are you talking about? What check? Last

Sunday's donations? You can't be serious…Okay, I'm on my way home right now."

Margaret hurried out to her car. After getting in and clicking the seatbelt in place, she dialed Julia's number on her cellphone. She put the call on speaker. After a couple of rings, Julia answered.

"I was just thinking about you. How did the meeting go?"

"Which one?" Margaret said, looking over her shoulder as she backed her car out of the parking space. "I had a lunch meeting with Monica and her brother after the meeting at the police station. It's been an intense day, to say the least. That's not why I'm calling."

"What's going on?" Julia asked.

"Joseph was going through the donations from the church service yesterday. You won't believe who wrote a five-figure check."

"Please don't say Perry Thomas. I'm certain he's financially secure, but I'm not ready—"

"Get your mind off Perry. I know you like him, but this isn't about him."

"What? I do not. I mean, I don't *not* like him. Hey, you're the one dropping his name all the time. Moving on—that's got to be a huge donation!"

Margaret checked her mirrors before pulling out onto the highway. "Tell me about it. Joseph didn't give me the exact amount, but the fact that it's five figures means it's the biggest donation we've received since he gave that chunk of his inheritance money to renovate the Manor."

"So, who was the generous donor?"

"A lady named Hannah Vinmeyer."

"That's Perry's client, right?"

"Yep," Margaret said as she pulled into her subdivision. "Perry's client *and* Joseph's mother."

Chapter Thirty-Three

Julia couldn't imagine what Margaret and Joseph must be going through. Finding out that someone you'd assumed for years was dead, only to find out they're still alive? Julia wanted to help out somehow, perhaps by providing a meal for them. Then again, Joseph and Margaret probably needed time alone to process news of this magnitude. Plus, Julia had already committed her time to another cause tonight—the local Bake-N-Cook where Holly was competing.

And maybe that was a good thing. She felt grateful to have something to do that didn't involve voices from the past, relatives coming back from the dead, and other such heavy issues. Tonight, would be a time for her to support Holly, sample food from aspiring cooks and bakers, and relax a little. She went into her bedroom to pick out an outfit. Upon opening the top drawer of her dresser, she caught her reflection in the mirror.

She stopped for a moment. She reached around and loosened her hair out of the ponytail holder, allowing it to fall to her shoulders. She took note that her grey roots were showing. She'd have to rummage for it, but she remembered having a root-coverup product somewhere in the bathroom. She touched her hands to her face. Then she turned her head side to side.

When was the last time she'd put on make-up? She had cleaned up a little for Margaret's presentation at the church last week, but how long has it been since she felt like she looked *pretty?*

"Wrong drawer," she said out loud as she slid the drawer shut and made her way into her bathroom. She opened the bottom drawer of her sink vanity to reveal a sizeable collection of facial cleansers, serums, and moisturizers, along with a variety of makeup items. A few had never been opened.

"Right drawer," she said as she began pulling the items out one by one. She looked back towards her bedroom. "Where's that blue sweater and pair of cream-colored dress pants Holly bought me for my birthday?"

She stopped and, once again, stared at her reflection in the mirror.

"Okay, Julia. Just like that old cassette recorder, it's time for you to come out of storage."

Holly stood statuesque as one of the judges scooped out samples of her dishes and put them on a plate. She spotted a printed label titled *Holly Sparrow Entry #10* taped to the underside.

The judge looked up at her, "Do you have a copy of your recipes? All entries must be prepared from original recipes."

"Yes," Holly said, leaning down for a folder she had placed on a chair behind her table. "They're all right here. I made extras in case you need them."

As she looked at the judge, the room started spinning again. She leaned against the table and willed herself not to react.

The judge nodded as he flipped through the pages. "Thank you. We'll announce the winners soon."

"Thank *you,*" Holly responded as the judge walked over to the area of the room where the other judges had congregated.

Steven had stepped away when the judge approached her

table. As soon as he left, Steven returned. "How did it go? Did he comment on any of your dishes?"

Holly shook her head. "No, he's not allowed. I do think he was impressed that my recipes were so organized."

Holly sat down in the chair behind her table and unscrewed the top from a water bottle she'd stashed there. "I got a little dizzy…*again*."

Steven squatted down in front of her chair. "Maybe you should make an appointment with your doctor."

Holly set the water bottle back down on the floor and gave a half-smile. "I'm not all that worried. It's probably just from being nervous about tonight."

"Still, it wouldn't hurt to get checked out." He raised his eyebrows and shook his finger at Holly. "You know it's never smart—"

"To be your own doctor," Holly laughed as she finished the familiar adage. "One of my mom's many quotes. Which, by the way, where is Ms. Julia Burch? She said she would be attending tonight."

"Since I'm taller than you, let me look around," Steven said as he stood up and panned the civic center lobby where the event was being held. He craned his head toward the door. Holly watched as his jaw dropped and he covered his mouth with his hand.

"What is it?" she asked, looking over to where he was staring. Holly's eyes grew wide. "Oh. My. God. Is that my mother?"

They both maintained their gaze across the room as Steven answered, "I would say that Ms. Julia Burch has definitely arrived."

Holly slowly nodded. "Indeed, she has."

Margaret rushed into the house to find Joseph sitting alone at the kitchen table. She could see where he had separated the cash donations into one stack and the checks into another, both to be deposited into the Gates Manor Foundation account. She was familiar with his routine. Each time they conducted a fundraiser, whatever funds the donors didn't submit electronically, Joseph—being old school—made sure to separate the cash from the checks before taking it all to the bank.

Margaret slowed her pace and quietly slipped her purse from her shoulder, allowing it to ease onto the floor. She set her keys on the counter. She pulled out a chair next to Joseph's and sat down.

Without making eye contact, Joseph took the one check he'd separated from the others and slid it over to Margaret.

Margaret picked up the check. "Fifty thousand dollars?" She said it louder than she'd intended. "When you mentioned five figures, my mind landed on ten or fifteen. But *fifty?*"

Then she noticed the calligraphy handwriting. It was shaky, consistent with an older woman's, but elegant, nonetheless.

"Hannah Vinmeyer's name, but your mother's handwriting."

"You know, federal agents assign each Witness Protection member a name that doesn't resemble their real one. I'd have to say that Hannah Vinmeyer is *very different* from Ellen Bennington, except for the syllable count. And, yes, it's a large donation. I don't know how I missed seeing her last Sunday. Then again, would I have even recognized her? It's been so long, and she's in her early nineties now."

Joseph's thoughts were bouncing around, and understandably so. Margaret decided the best thing to do was let him talk, regardless of whether or not he was making sense.

For the first time since Margaret sat down, Joseph turned to look at her. "Can you believe my mother helped take down a dangerous drug dealer?"

Margaret didn't hesitate. "Yes, I can. Living with your father was a warmup lap for what she did." She smiled. "I think she could have taken down all organized crime if she'd put her mind to it."

Joseph smiled weakly and then stared down at the floor. When he looked back up, he had tears in his eyes. He whispered, "Margaret, my mother is alive."

Margaret spoke soothingly as she rubbed his back. "I know, Joseph. It's a lot to take in."

He put his head on her shoulder, and she wrapped her arms around him. His shoulders shook as he sobbed.

"*A lot* to take in."

Chapter Thirty-Four

Julia tentatively walked through the door in her blue sweater, cream-colored dress pants, and nude pumps. After giving herself a facial, applying makeup, putting a few hot rollers in her hair—and touching up her grey roots—she almost didn't feel like herself. As soon as she spotted Holly and Steven, she snaked her way through the crowd to where they stood.

"Please tell me they haven't announced the winners yet. I'm running late. It took me a little longer to get ready than I thought it would."

Holly took a couple of steps back. "I'd say the extra time paid off. Mom, you look amazing!"

Steven nodded. "I'm going to have to beat the men off of both you ladies tonight!"

Julia smiled and shook her head. "You just haven't seen me wearing makeup in a long time…or dressed in anything other than a sweatshirt and a pair of jeans! It felt good to do a little 'self-care'—is that what they call it these days? I can't take credit for the outfit, though."

"I can! I remember buying it for you," Holly responded as she reached around to the back of Julia's sweater and tugged at it. "What I *forgot* was to remove the price tag." She chuckled as she held the small piece of cardboard in front of Julia. "And so did you!"

Julia laughed. "I told you I'm out of practice!"

Julia jumped as the public address system squealed to life. Guests across the room covered their ears. "Sorry about that, folks. May I have your attention, please? I'm Councilman Jim Warner, and I'm honored to announce the winners of tonight's competition. Will all participants please report to the front of the room?"

"This is it!" Holly said nervously.

Julia and Steven both wished her good luck as Holly joined the other contestants up front, where a table covered in a black cloth displayed a row of awards arranged from the smallest to the largest.

Jim continued, "As a reminder, all proceeds from the registration fees, ticket sales, and sponsorships go toward restocking the shelves at the local soup kitchen and providing meals for needy school children over the summer. Before I announce the winners, please give a round of applause for our judges, who volunteered their time for this event."

Julia clapped along with everyone else as she looked around to see if she recognized anyone in the crowd.

"Now, for the winners!"

Julia watched as Jim stepped back to pick up the first trophy. Reading from a list he was holding, he announced, "The award for Best Presentation goes to...Hilda Belmore for her patriotic-themed cake decorating."

The guests applauded as an older woman stepped forward to receive her plaque.

"The next award, Best Pasta, goes to the contestant with... would anybody like to guess?" The crowd laughed, and a few people yelled out, "The best pasta!"

Jim chuckled and then spoke into the microphone. "I can't pull anything over you people. This award goes to...Joann Bravino!"

Julia watched as Jim distributed the awards. She kept hoping to hear Holly's name. With each presentation, the contestant's spouse, or any other family members in attendance, joined them for a photo that would appear in the "Community Events" section of Sunday's newspaper.

"Okay, folks," Jim said as he turned around to look behind him. "As you can see, we have only one award left: the Judges Choice Award. This award applies to those contestants who entered a complete meal into the competition—which I think was everyone except for Miss Hilda, who has the market cornered with her desserts." Jim paused to point out into the audience. A few people standing around Hilda patted her on the back. She just waved them off and laughed.

"The Judge's Choice Award," Jim continued, "is based on the ingenuity of the recipes and how the flavors of each dish complement the others as a complete meal. This year's Judges Choice Award goes to a newcomer—Holly Sparrow!"

Julia's heart all but exploded. She bounced up and down with excitement, and she and Steven hugged each other. Holly turned around and looked back at them, her face glowing. She walked up to accept the award and shook Jim's hand.

Julia and Steven made their way through the crowd to stand beside Holly for the picture. Holly smiled big for the camera, but something about her seemed off to Julia. She dismissed it as exhaustion. After all, Holly had worked tirelessly to create those recipes and prepare all that food.

As the photographer stepped aside, Julia did a doubletake as she saw Perry Thomas walking toward her. She glanced over at Holly and Steven. They had immediately been swarmed with guests coming forward to congratulate Holly.

It frustrated Julia that Perry's smile made her knees weak. She didn't want to feel this way. More importantly, she didn't want Margaret to be right. There would be no living with her if somehow she and Perry ended up becoming more than friends.

Perry extended his hand. "Congratulations to the, uh, mother of the competition winner?"

Julia laughed and shook his hand. "Thank you! I'm proud of her."

"I've got to admit; she proved to be a fierce competitor."

"Wait…were you a contestant tonight?"

Perry chuckled. "Yes, but I didn't enter to take home a trophy. It was just fun to participate in a community event and support a worthy cause. Plus, it showed me how badly I need to brush up on my cooking skills."

Julia laughed and gave a half-shrug. "I was grateful to have a nice event to attend that got me out of the house." For some reason, she felt like she needed to explain. She didn't want Perry to draw any wrong conclusions. "My husband passed away five years ago. Getting back in circulation has been a slow process for me."

"I understand. I lost my wife three years ago."

"Then you really do understand," Julia said to herself as much as to Perry.

"Well, tonight certainly was the perfect night to have your picture taken. You look lovely, and I'm certain your picture will look lovely as well."

Julia could feel her cheeks turning red, but she maintained her cool. "Not unless the photographer is skilled at using Photoshop!"

They both laughed, and then Perry looked down at his shoes. "Even though I've been a fan of your writing for years, I know we just officially met. But would you like to, maybe, go to dinner with me sometime?"

Julia smiled. "I'd love—"

Julia heard voices behind her shouting, "Can someone help her? Call 9-1-1! Ma'am, are you okay?"

Julia watched as Perry's eyebrows snapped together. He pushed past her and rushed over to where Holly was lying on the floor. Julia whirled around to see Steven leaning over Holly and dialing a number on his cellphone.

Her legs felt like lead. She couldn't move fast enough. She could hear Steven yelling to someone on his phone—she assumed it was the 911 operator. "Please hurry! Yes, she experienced a couple of dizzy spells today but insisted she was fine. Get here, quick!"

Julia's breath quickened as she knelt beside Holly. "Holly, are you okay? Can you hear me?"

With the hospital located near the civic center, the ambulance arrived within a couple of minutes. The crowd parted as four paramedics rushed in with a stretcher. After asking Steven a few questions, they helped Holly sit up.

One paramedic squatted down at Holly's side and unwound a stethoscope looped around his neck. Another clicked on a penlight and held Holly's eyelids open to check her pupil dilation. As they attempted to help Holly stand up, she collapsed into their arms. Julia could see the panic in Steven's eyes.

One of the paramedics had been taking Holly's blood pressure. The Velcro cuff crackled as she quickly removed it and looked at one of the other paramedics. "Her BP is low. Start an IV. She needs to go to the E.R."

"Can I ride with her?" Steven asked.

The paramedics looked at each other. "Okay, just stay out of the way."

Steven nodded. "Understood." He turned to Julia. "I'll see you at the hospital."

Perry put his hand on Julia's shoulder. "Do you need me to drive you?"

Julia didn't know what she needed right now. Everything had happened so fast. She just wanted Holly to be okay. "I don't want to put you out. I'll be fine."

Perry's voice was kind but firm. "I really think I need to drive you."

Julia pointed toward the door, trying her best not to cry. "My car's out front."

Chapter Thirty-Five

Julia felt grateful that the hospital was only a short drive away. After circling the parking lot for what felt like hours, Perry finally located an empty spot. He had barely put the car in park when Julia jumped out of the passenger's side and sprinted across the parking lot—a feat which proved especially challenging in high heels. She made her way through the revolving door leading to the emergency room lobby. Perry managed to keep up and followed her inside.

She approached the receptionist at the front desk. Her hands shook as she fumbled with her wallet to produce her driver's license for identification. "My name is Julia Burch," she said, trying to catch her breath. "My daughter, Holly Burch Sparrow, was just brought in."

The receptionist clicked several keys on her computer. "She's in triage. A doctor is with her now. Have a seat, and I'll let you know when you can go back."

Julia turned to Perry. "You don't have to stay. There's no telling how long this will take. Just drive my car back to the civic center. Joseph can give me a ride over there later to pick it up. I have a spare key."

"Why don't I stay until you get to see Holly? Once the doctor examines her, you'll have a better idea of what's going and what you need to do next."

Perry's calm response struck a stark contrast to the anxiety that had hijacked Julia's emotions.

She nodded. "That makes sense."

"Why don't you sit down? There's a vending machine across the hall. Can I get you anything?"

"You're probably going to think it's the last thing I need, but I could really use—"

"A cup of coffee?"

"Yeah. Make it dark roast."

A few minutes later, Julia had a cup in hand. She took a sip of the coffee and set the cup on a lamp table beside her seat. While she was grateful for Perry's company, she regretted that he was stuck sitting with her in a hospital waiting room. She felt certain this was not the kind of 'community event' he had planned on participating in this evening.

He took a seat across from her in one of the dark blue vinyl and chrome chairs soldered together four in a row. His act of kindness tonight knocked Julia off the fence regarding how she felt about him. She liked Perry. But then her mind would zigzag through the maze of memories she had made with Bill. A steady stream of guilt dripped into her heart as if she was betraying her late husband.

"Julia Burch?" the hospital receptionist called out.

Julia and Perry exchanged glances and Julia jumped to her feet.

"You can go back now," the receptionist said as she pointed over her shoulder.

"I'll wait here," Perry said. "Somebody's got to guard your coffee," he added with a friendly wink.

Julia managed a smile as she headed towards the triage unit. She looked back at him. "I shouldn't be long."

Perry held up a hand. "Take all the time you need."

As Julia entered the triage unit, the double doors closing

behind her made a whirring noise. She quickly made her way past a row of curtains providing the only privacy for the patients on the other side. She carefully read each name scribbled on a dry erase board until she found Holly's. She pulled back the curtain and was shocked to see Holly sitting up and drinking from a paper cup.

After closing the curtain behind her, her voice trembled as she said, "Holly, sweetheart, how are you? You gave us a scare tonight!"

Holly passed the cup off to Steven and extended her arms. Julia dropped her purse to the floor and rushed over to embrace her. "So, what's going on? What did the doctor say?"

Steven handed the cup back to Holly and she took a sip. "This is orange juice, by the way," Holly said, holding it up as if raising a toast. "Evidently something is going on with my blood sugar. They drew a vial of blood when I first arrived. The doctor said she'd be back within the hour with the results."

Julia shook her head. "I'm just glad you're sitting up and coherent!"

Holly nodded. "I've never passed out before. It's not something I want to repeat."

Steven took Holly's free hand and grinned. "I told Holly that we were all shocked that she won, but none of us passed out over it."

They all laughed. Julia appreciated Steven's humor. But underneath his smile she could see that he was concerned…and tired.

"Holly Sparrow?" a female hospital staff member issued a greeting simultaneous with pulling back the curtain. "I'm Dr. Deering." She pressed the button on a wall-mounted hand sanitizer dispenser and rubbed the liquid onto her hands.

Dr. Deering was tall with salt-and-pepper hair pulled back into a ponytail. Like Steven, she appeared tired. She had circles under her eyes and her ponytail looked like it had seen better days. With the Covid staff shortages, Julia wondered how many shifts this doctor had been covering.

"Doctor, this is my mother, Julia Burch."

The doctor leaned over to shake Julia's hand. "Nice to meet you."

Dr. Deering focused on a small iPad she had placed on the tray table at the foot of Holly's bed. She momentarily took off her glasses to rub her eyes and then put them back on again.

"Okay, Holly, your bloodwork came back, and we now know what's causing your dizzy spells."

"It's not diabetes, is it?" Steven asked.

The doctor shook her head. "No, but Holly *will* need to make some dietary adjustments, specifically regarding staying hydrated."

"The paramedics said her blood pressure was low—"

"And she will need to keep an eye on that. I recommend buying a cuff that she can use at home. That way, she can check it anytime she feels the need."

Julia almost felt sorry for Dr. Deering. She couldn't say what she'd come to say for having to answer all of Steven's anxiety-filled questions. As he presented the next one, it was as if this weary physician decided to just roll with it.

"So, what she has, it is treatable?"

Dr. Deering leaned on the tray table, resting her chin on her fist. "I guess you could say it's treatable."

"But if it goes away, will it come back?"

The doctor looked at Steven and then at Holly. With a vacant expression and a voice devoid of emotion, she replied, "Usually freshman year of college…to drop off its laundry."

Steven looked confused. "I'm sorry, what?"

The doctor looked at Holly. "You're pregnant."

Chapter Thirty-Six

1975

A loud boom jarred Ellen Bennington awake. A second one sounded that made her think it had originated downstairs. She looked at the clock on her nightstand. *One thirty? What's going on?*

Turning to ask Horace if he had also heard the noise, she discovered he wasn't in bed with her. She immediately sat up. She ran her hand through her hair and swung her feet over the side of the bed. Grabbing a bathrobe draped over a chair by the door, she slipped it on and cautiously tiptoed downstairs.

She noticed that Horace had left his office door cracked open. The light from a single lamp cast a narrow, rectangular shadow in the hall. She tentatively tapped on the door. "Horace, is everything alright?"

When he didn't respond, she opened the door and saw where two chairs had been thrown against the wall. Horace was leaning over his desk, his eyes wild with anger.

"Horace? What on earth?" Ellen asked as she stood in the doorway.

Horace didn't look at her but stared down at the floor. "Ellen, go back to bed," he growled.

Ellen crossed her arms. "I will not. Not until you tell me what has caused this," she paused and looked around the room, "this *tirade!*"

Horace's head remained low. He only looked up with his eyes. "I'll tell you what's wrong. That double-crossing business partner of mine has done it again."

Ellen flippantly rolled her eyes. "Oh, please. Did you and James have another lover's quarrel?" She waved her hand dismissively. "Just kiss and make up so I can get some sleep!"

This time, Horace growled so loudly that it caused Ellen to jump. He angrily swept the folders and paperwork on his desk to one side, causing them to scatter onto the floor.

Fear gripped Ellen's heart. She'd never seen Horace like this. Yet she knew to remain calm.

"I'm sorry, darling, you *really are* upset. What did James do?"

"I trusted him, Ellen. I invested my hard-earned money toward a new venture that he convinced me was a sure thing. It could have been if we'd worked with the right distributor. But James picked a crook who gave us a fake product."

Ellen began to feel weak. Her stomach knotted.

"James knows how I'll get back at him for this. It didn't seem to bother him last time, but it will this time. I'll make sure of it." Horace stormed out of his office and headed down the hall toward the front door.

Ellen panicked. She knew he was talking about Margaret. He would abuse her worse than before. What could she do? Then she thought about Frances being pregnant—with Horace's child—but pregnant, nonetheless. She couldn't be responsible for anything happening to Frances or the baby. She had to think fast.

She followed Horace down the hall. She blurted out, "James didn't do anything. It was…it was *me.*"

Horace slowly turned around. "What are you talking about?"

"I feel terrible. I should have come to you sooner." She sighed. "I ordered you a gift. I went to the locksmith's shop and made a copy of your post office key. I wanted to intercept the package before you saw it and ruined the surprise. I mistook the package containing the cocaine for the gift."

When Ellen said the word *cocaine*, Horace's eyes grew intense.

"When I opened it and saw what it was, well, I couldn't *unsee* it. I made a few connections, and I sold it for you. I replaced yours with a harmless powder so that no one could accuse you of any wrongdoing. I thought I was doing a good thing. I've really been trying lately, Horace. The luncheon, the gift—"

Horace appeared only to be concerned about one thing. He tilted his head. "How much money did you make?"

Ellen could feel her heart pounding, but she couldn't stop now. She could only hope that Horace would buy her story.

"Well, it's not so much the money I made; it's what I did with it. I hope you'll be proud of me. I made an investment, darling. One that will go into your name once it's up and running and, most importantly, profitable. Right now, it's just an apartment building on the outskirts of town. Once they put in that new highway, the property value will skyrocket."

"I haven't heard of any new highway. You know this for a fact?"

"Well, it's several years in the future, but yes, I do. I don't expect you to have time to research such details."

She walked up closer to him and put her hands on his chest. "I meant what I said the other day. I want to show you how I feel about all you've done for us, Horace. Maybe my technique needs a little work, but my heart is in the right place."

She could see Horace's expression softening. "James knew nothing about this then?" He seemed to be asking the question to himself.

"Nothing," Ellen said with the most soothing voice she could muster. "So there's no need to lash out at him."

"And you'll get the deed to that property to me? I want to see all the documentation. I want to know where my money is going."

"Of course." She paused and kissed him on the cheek. "Now, why don't you go upstairs to bed while I turn off the lamp in your office. I'll have Bivens tidy up in there first thing in the morning."

"Good idea," Horace said as he turned and ascended the stairs. Ellen smiled and watched until he had reached the top and closed the bedroom door.

She walked into his office, careful not to trip over the overturned chairs. She turned off the lamp and then, in the darkness, fell to her knees and wept.

Chapter Thirty-Seven

No one spoke. The doctor looked at each of them. "Did you hear what I said?"

Holly's mouth had dropped open. Steven's face had turned the shade of Holly's bed sheets. Julia looked at them and then at the doctor. It wasn't her place to be the first to react to this news, but in her heart, she was dancing with joy. This wasn't even close to the diagnosis she had feared the doctor would deliver.

"Are you sure?" Holly asked.

"From your bloodwork, I'd say you're around eight weeks. So, yes, I'm sure."

Holly looked at Steven and laughed. "We're gonna have a baby!"

Steven beamed and squeezed her hand. Then his eyes grew wide. "And a teenager getting her driver's permit!" He looked at the doctor and then at Julia. "At the same time!"

Dr. Deering chuckled and then directed her attention back to Holly. "I've arranged for a nutritionist to meet with you before you're discharged tonight. If you already have a fifteen-year-old, you're that much older with this pregnancy. You'll need to take extra care of yourself. Be sure to follow up with your obstetrician as soon as possible."

Holly shook her head in disbelief. "Okay! I'll do that. Thank you, Dr. Deering."

As soon as the doctor left and swooshed the curtain closed once again, Julia squealed, "You're pregnant!"

Holly wept as she laughed. "I can't believe this! I was bracing myself for bad news, like a brain tumor or some other terminal illness." She looked up at Steven. "Two wins in one night?"

Steven smiled. "I think we need to stop and give thanks."

"I agree," Julia said. They all held hands and bowed their heads.

Steven cleared his throat and then prayed, "Lord, thank you for this miracle. We were expecting a very different outcome tonight. We feared the worst, but you have blessed us with the very best: the gift of life. We ask that you keep Holly and the baby healthy for the duration of this pregnancy. We pray these things in Christ's name. Amen."

"Amen," Julia chimed in. She paused and then said, "I have a question."

"What is it?" Holly asked.

"Who's going to stop by the store to purchase the zip-ties we'll need to restrain Olivia? We all know she's going to lose her mind when she finds out!"

"Yes, she is!" Holly laughed. "Steven, should we call her tonight at Kelly's or wait until tomorrow."

Steven scratched his chin. "I say we make a stop on the way home."

"For zip ties?"

"No, silly. I think we should stop by Kelly's house and tell Olivia tonight. It's not that late. I'll call Kelly's parents to let them know. Julia, you're welcome to come along."

"As much as I'd like to see her reaction, I need to get Perry back to the civic center to pick up his car. He drove me over here. Make this about your family tonight—your *growing* family!"

Holly sat up straight in the bed. "Who's Perry?"

Julia couldn't believe she'd just let Perry's name slip. She wasn't prepared to tell her family about him yet. After all, what was there to tell? It was way too early to put a label on their relationship. They were barely even friends.

She stuttered, "Actually, he's...he's an old friend of Joseph's. Yes, that's it. I only met him recently." Her eyes lit up as she remembered another detail. "He participated in the competition tonight and said you proved to be a fierce competitor."

"*That* Perry!" Holly said as she threw her hands up, "Perry Thomas. I've met him. He's such a nice guy—a widower. A *handsome* widower who's a retired attorney. Did I mention he's handsome and a nice guy? He's also a widower."

Julia laughed. "Enough! We're just acquaintances. He and I just happened to be chatting when you fainted. He offered to drive me over here."

"Where is he now?" Steven asked.

"He's in the waiting room," Julia said, pointing in that direction.

"I'd love to meet him sometime and, you know, rub Holly's win in his face a little."

"Steven!" Holly said, shaking her head.

"You're right. I'm sorry. His *handsome, widower, attorney* face. Did I mention he's a widower?"

"Ignore him," Holly said. "Please tell Perry that Steven and I said hello. And if he ever wants to drop by and drool over my award, I'll let him. For a fee, of course."

Julia laughed as she picked up her purse. "How about I tell him you said hello?" She stepped over and pulled the curtain back. Looking over her shoulder, she called, "Take care, you two!"

She closed the curtain and then took a few steps toward the double doors. She stopped and backed up. Pulling the curtain back open once more, she whispered, "You three!"

As Julia walked back into the waiting room, she stepped over to where she and Perry had been sitting earlier. Perry's head was resting on his shoulder, and he was softly snoring. Someone had rolled up a sweater and put it between his head and the metal top of the chair. Julia looked around. A lovely African American woman was sitting in the row of chairs across from Perry. She looked to be in her early seventies. She smiled at Julia and then pointed to Perry. "He looked so uncomfortable," she said.

"Thank you," Julia said quietly, not wanting to awaken Perry. She looked at this woman. She had twinkle—a light about her eyes—that, while Julia couldn't put her finger on it, looked strangely familiar.

"You look like you've had a long day, dear," the woman said as she patted the seat next to her. "Come, sit down."

Julia hesitated but then decided to take her up on her offer. After all, they were in a public waiting room, and this lady had a kind face.

"Is that your husband over there?" she asked.

Julia immediately put up a hand. "Oh no, he's just a friend. We hardly know each other. My husband passed away."

Julia didn't know why she volunteered that last piece of information, but the woman's response wasn't what Julia expected. In a strange way, she acted as if she already knew.

"Hmm." The woman said. "Hardly know each other, and yet he's been sitting over there waiting…and praying for the past hour." She leaned in closer and whispered, "He didn't know I was watching."

"Praying? "Julia asked, her curiosity piqued.

"Umm-hmm," the woman responded. "Talking to God. And God was listening."

Julia looked back over at Perry, who was still asleep.

"So, this handsome, praying gentleman over there who's not your husband. Do you like him?"

Julia turned back to face the woman, "I do. But I haven't known him all that long. It's not like we're dating."

The woman tilted her head to one side. "Why do you feel like you have to apologize for wanting to be happy?"

Julia studied the woman's face. Even though she was a total stranger, Julia couldn't shake the feeling that they had met before. She shrugged her shoulders. "I don't know."

"Honey," she said, taking Julia's hand into hers. "You're not dishonoring your late husband by moving on. Just because he finished living his life doesn't mean you have to stop living yours. Do you think he'd want that for you?"

Julia shook her head. "No, he wouldn't."

The lady smiled. "I can tell you for certain that he wouldn't. Live your life. Keep Jesus in the center of it, and everything's gonna work out fine."

"Thank you," Julia said and, without thinking, hugged the woman.

The woman touched Julia's face with her hand. "Living a full, happy life devoted to Jesus is the best way you can honor your husband's memory." She paused and smiled, her eyes twinkling. "That and naming your grandson after him."

"What?" Julia asked.

"I said what time did you get back?" Julia turned around to see Perry rubbing his eyes. "I guess I fell asleep." He picked up the sweater on his shoulder and held it up. "Where did this come from?"

Julia turned and stepped over to where he was sitting and took the sweater from him. "The nicest lady! Ma'am, what's your name?"

Julia turned back around, but the woman was gone.

Without looking at Perry, she tossed the sweater back to him and quickly searched through the waiting room, but there was no sign of the woman anywhere. Julia circled back to where the woman had been sitting. In the chair was a single gardenia bloom. Julia slowly picked it up and held it in her palm.

"Impossible," she whispered.

Perry stood behind her. "Are you alright? How's Holly?"

Julia turned to face him. "The doctor said Holly is fine. I'll elaborate on that in a minute. Just to be clear: This didn't count as our first date. I'd still like to go to dinner with you. Especially now that we have something to celebrate."

Perry took a couple of steps back. "Wow! Okay, I agree. A hospital waiting room makes for a lousy first date. What are we celebrating? Holly's win tonight? A good report from the doctor?"

Julia raised her shoulders and squealed, "A *pregnancy*! I'm going to be a grandmother again!"

Perry's jaw dropped, and he laughed. "That's wonderful news! Congratulations!" He hesitated but then pulled Julia into a hug. As she momentarily nestled her head on his chest, she clutched the gardenia bloom in her hand.

Thank you, Minnie Morgan.

Chapter Thirty-Eight

Steven and Holly pulled into the driveway at Kelly's house. Steven put the car in Park and looked at his watch. "It's ten o'clock. Even though Kelly's parents said it would be okay to stop by, do you think the girls are in bed already?"

"They're high school freshmen. Even if they are in bed, I guarantee you they're not asleep. They'll be yacking until the wee hours of the morning. I can't believe Olivia talked you into letting her stay over at Kelly's on a school night."

"You asked me to make arrangements for her since she didn't want to be the only fifteen-year-old at the Bake-N-Cook. Besides, she assured me that they were going to study," Steven said as he unbuckled his seatbelt.

Holly rolled her eyes. "They *always* say they're going to study. That's code for ditching their homework, eating all of the cheese puffs in the pantry, and watching movies."

Steven got out of the car and walked around to open Holly's door. As she stepped out, he continued, "I didn't want her to stay at home by herself. We didn't know how late the competition would run. And, since we took that little two-hour tour of Community Hospital's triage unit on our way home, it's even better that she was at Kelly's."

They had walked a few steps up the sidewalk when Holly took Steven's arm, causing him to stop.

"Thank you for being there for me tonight. Your quick action to call 911 probably saved my life...and our baby's life."

Steven touched his hand to her cheek. "I've never been so scared in my life." His voice cracked. "I thought I was going to lose you."

Holly smiled. "God had other plans. Tonight definitely wasn't about losing!" She took a deep breath. "Steven?"

"Yes?"

"Take your hand off my face—it still smells like garlic."

After a brief but friendly greeting at the front door, Kelly's parents excused themselves so that Holly, Steven, and Olivia could talk privately. Holly made herself comfortable on the living room couch and Steven settled in beside her. Olivia plopped down in a chair across the room.

She shrugged her shoulders. "So...what's so important that it couldn't wait until tomorrow? Kelly and I were already on the second Twilight movie."

"What happened to studying?" Steven asked with a raised eyebrow.

Olivia grinned. "Oh, right, we were *studying* the second Twilight movie."

"I was right," Holly mumbled under her breath.

"First of all," Steven began, "Your mom won the big prize at the competition tonight!"

Olivia's eyes lit up and her hand flew to her chest. "That's great! Congratulations! Where is the trophy? I want to see it!"

Holly smiled. "It's in the car. I can show it to you later."

"Okay," Olivia said, settling back in her chair once more.

Holly looked over at Steven. She wasn't sure how to proceed from here. But Olivia steered the conversation.

"That's great news, but you could have told me that over the phone. I'm proud of you, Mom, but it's not like you won *Miss Universe*."

Steven nodded slowly. "You're right. What we *didn't* want to tell you over the phone is that Mom got sick at the competition tonight."

"What do you mean?"

Holly sighed. "I fainted. Your dad had to call 911."

"What?" Olivia said, jumping to her feet. "Are you okay?"

"The paramedics decided that I needed to be evaluated at the hospital. Both my blood pressure and my blood sugar were dangerously low. The emergency room doctor ran a blood test."

Olivia's lip trembled. "Mom, are you okay? You don't have cancer or a brain tumor, do you? Oh my gosh, that's why you came over tonight!"

Holly shook her head. "No, it was nothing like that. But the bloodwork did show what was causing the change in my blood sugar and my blood pressure, which caused me to pass out."

"Which was...?" Olivia stretched out the word "was" as she looked from Holly to Steven and back to Holly again.

"Olivia," Steven said. "You're going to have a sibling. Your mom's pregnant."

Olivia's eyes widened. "Shut up! Shut up! No way! Are you serious?"

Holly beamed. "We're serious!"

Olivia squealed and started bouncing up and down. "That's so awesome," she said and then laughed, "and the *last* thing I thought you were going to tell me! I'm so excited! I'm going to have a little brother or sister!"

She bounded across the room and all but jumped on both Holly and Steven to embrace them both. Then she stopped and backed up.

"Ewwww! That means that you—" she pointed to each of them in turn.

"Where do you think *you* came from?" Steven asked as he dramatically extended his arms.

"That's different. I don't know how. It just is."

Steven and Holly both laughed.

"Come here, you little pollywog," Steven said as the three of them embraced once more.

"Do you have any names picked out yet?"

Holly laughed as she swept Olivia's hair back off her face. "No, we haven't gotten that far yet."

Oliva tapped her finger to her lip as if she was deep in thought.

"I think that, if it's a boy, you should name him after Dad and Grandpa Bill. You know, combine the two names."

Holly and Steven looked at each other. "That's actually a very sweet thought," Holly said, a little taken aback that Olivia would come up with that.

Something about the idea tugged at her heart.

William Steven Sparrow. What a beautiful name!

Chapter Thirty-Nine

onica winced as she took a sip of the hotel coffee. *It tastes like something Norman would have perked.*

She'd hoped for a good night's sleep but didn't count on it happening. Her emotions were still churning over being back in Mississippi. She just kept focusing on Margaret's words. *Make it about Calvin. Do it because you love Calvin.*

"Good morning, sunshine!" a cheerful male voice called out, walking up from behind and ruffling Monica on the top of her head.

She jumped. After turning around and seeing it was Calvin, she lovingly pushed him away, "Don't sneak up on me like that! I don't like to be surprised. I carry a weapon, remember?"

Calvin laughed and leaned over to speak in her ear, "Which one? Your mouth or that Glock stuffed in the back of your pants?"

Monica laughed. "Touché!" Then she turned to look at him as he sat beside her at the counter in the hotel restaurant. "Your coffee must have been better than mine this morning. You're all bright-eyed and bushy-tailed—not to mention on point with your sarcasm."

"I was just messing with you. Have you eaten yet?"

"Unfortunately, yes. After we see Pop, maybe we can hit up a restaurant for some real food." She raised her coffee cup to take a sip.

"I've got a better idea," Calvin said, leaning back in his seat. "How about I cook for you?"

Monica sputtered into her coffee. "*You* cook?"

"What?" Calvin said, jerking his head back in surprise. "You don't think I can play basketball, be *incredibly* handsome, and cook, too?"

Monica laughed and then shook her head, staring down at her coffee cup. "It's just that I was always the one—"

Calvin put his hand on her back. "I know you were. That's why, today, I want to do that for you."

Monica looked up at him and offered a half-smile. "You're on."

Calvin pulled out his cellphone and studied the screen. "Visiting hours start soon. Are you ready?"

Monica shook her head. "As ready as I'll ever be."

As the hospital elevator whirred upward, so did Monica's anxiety.

To distract herself, she turned to Calvin and said, "When we visit Pop, do we have to go in one at a time?"

Suddenly Calvin pressed a button on the elevator. The elevator jerked and came to a stop.

Monica panicked. "What are you doing, fool? This thing could get stuck! Why did you do that?"

"There's something I haven't told you. I was afraid that, if I did, you wouldn't come back to see Pop."

"You pick *right now* to tell me? Are you crazy? Take your hand off that button!"

"No," Calvin said firmly. "I need to tell you something."

"So, tell me already!"

"Dad remarried a few years ago."

Monica looked down at the elevator floor. She couldn't believe what she was hearing. Attempting to control her anger, she took a deep breath before looking up at Calvin again. "As I mentioned at the hotel when you snuck up me, I don't like surprises, especially one like this. How could you have left out a detail like that?"

"Monica—"

"You're telling me that not only do I have to visit my abusive father who robbed me of a normal childhood, but I also have to suck up to some heifer he hitched his wagon to?"

"She's a wonderful person…she's been like a mother to me."

"A WHAT? No," Monica said as she started pacing in the elevator like a caged animal. "No, no, *hell* no! Ain't no way I'm gonna call that woman—" Monica stopped pacing and leaned against one of the elevator walls. She covered her face with her hands. "I knew this was a mistake. I should have never come."

Calvin didn't say anything. After a few seconds, Monica looked over at him. He just stared back.

"Well?" she asked. "Aren't you going to answer for this?"

"I don't know, Monica. Are you going to let me?"

Monica didn't respond, but with her back against the elevator wall, she slid down until she was sitting on the floor.

"I'll take that as a yes," Calvin said as he eased down to sit across from her. "Did anyone ever tell you that you jump to conclusions?"

"No, they tell me I'm good at arriving at them, hence the detective title."

"You might want to brush up on waiting until you have more evidence before you rush to judgment, at least when it comes to family matters."

"Evelyn isn't like Pop—the Pop you remember, that is. I believe God sent her to him. Among other things, she's the one that got him going to church again. As a result, a few months ago, he gave his life to Christ. That's when I started trying to get in touch with you. Then he got the cancer diagnosis. I knew we were running out of time, so I drove to North Carolina to see you. All I'm asking is that you spend a few minutes with him and then meet Evelyn. Give her a chance. I think you'll be pleasantly surprised."

"If I say yes, will you get the elevator started again?"

"Do you promise not to yell at me again?"

"Again, if I say yes, will you get the elevator started again?"

Calvin laughed. "Okay, you win. And Monica?"

"Yes?"

"That gun isn't loaded, is it?"

"Don't make me show you." Monica laughed as she stood up. "Now, quit pushing *my* buttons and push the damn elevator button."

Calvin laughed, pushed the button, and pulled Monica into a playful hug.

As the elevator doors creaked open, a full-figured, African American woman dressed in a light blue skirt suit stood in front of the nurse's station. She was wiping her eyes with a tissue.

"Evelyn?" Calvin rushed over to where she was standing and put his hands on her shoulders.

"Calvin!" the woman said with more volume than Monica was comfortable with, "Calvin, he's gone...he's gone...your daddy's gone!"

Chapter Forty

Monica's stomach twisted. She was too late. What if she hadn't lost her temper in the elevator? What if she had arrived a week—or even a day—earlier? Was Evelyn going to reprimand her? Even though they'd never met, she could only imagine the contempt Evelyn felt for her as the wayward daughter who never came to visit.

Monica slowly walked over to where Calvin himself was weeping while attempting to comfort Evelyn.

When he saw Monica, Calvin wiped his eyes and said, "Evelyn, I want you to meet my sister, Monica."

Monica's heart raced. *Here it comes.*

"Monica?" Evelyn said.

She looked down. "Yes, ma'am."

"Baby girl, come here and let me give you a hug. I've been waiting to meet you. I don't mince words, so just let me go on and say how sorry I am for the way your father treated you. I loved your father, but you better believe I gave him what-for when I found out how he made you a servant in your own home. That wasn't right, and none of the stuff that happened back then was your fault, you hear me? Come here, child."

Evelyn's unexpected—not to mention lengthy and unfiltered

—greeting didn't leave Monica any time to calculate her response. She burst into tears and said, "Thank you, Evelyn."

Evelyn wrapped her arms around Monica and let her cry. She patted her back and kept repeating, "It wasn't your fault. You were just a child. Jesus is gonna heal that heart of yours. It's gonna be alright."

This wasn't at all what Monica had expected. She had forgotten what it felt like to have a mother's arms wrapped around her. Who knew that such mercy and compassion could be delivered through a perfect stranger?

And her dad's wife at that.

Evelyn insisted that Calvin find a vending machine and purchase a bottle of Gatorade for Monica. She handed him a few dollars from her purse. "This baby's been crying a lot. She needs to replace her electrolytes."

Monica secretly reveled in the attention. Calvin must have noticed. He looked over at her and mouthed, "See?"

After Calvin had stepped away, Evelyn took Monica's hand. "Come with me. I want to show you something."

She walked down the hall past the nurse's station and opened the door to a patient's room. She switched on the light and led Monica inside to where a sheet had been pulled over a body stretched out on a bed.

"Since you're a detective, I know this isn't the first time you've seen a dead body. But it's the first time you've seen your daddy's. I know this isn't going to be easy, but it's important."

Monica held her breath as Evelyn slowly pulled back the sheet to reveal her dad's face and neck. She first looked at Evelyn, who now had tears streaming down her cheeks. Then she slowly let her eyes fall downward. There he was. Her Pop.

He looked different from what she last remembered, and not merely because he had aged.

Evelyn was right. As a detective, Monica was no stranger to viewing dead bodies. One was a drug dealer lying in the street bleeding out from a gunshot wound to the chest. Another was a missing person she and Norman had discovered in a dumpster. She knew from experience that just because a person had died doesn't mean they're going to look peaceful. And that's what was different about her dad.

"He looks peaceful," Monica whispered.

"He didn't always. For a long time, peace stayed just out of reach for John," Evelyn said as she maintained her gaze down at Monica's dad. "Until he encountered the love and forgiveness of Jesus, that is."

Evelyn reached over, took Monica's hand, and looked into her eyes. "Your daddy's biggest regrets were your mother's death and how he made you feel responsible for it. Deep down, he knew that blaming you was just a cover for how he blamed himself. It was easier to take it out on a defenseless nine-year-old. He knew you'd believe it was your fault." She looked down. "Maybe, over time, he started believing it himself." She looked back up at Monica. "I told him that Calvin had been his and your mother's responsibility that day, not yours. You were just a child yourself at the time. Nine years old." She shook her head. "Accidents happen, Monica." Evelyn continued in a voice so tender that Monica began to weep. "It doesn't do any good to start dishing out blame, but it was your mother's decision to run out in the street and get that basketball. Our choices have consequences."

Monica sniffed and wiped her tears with the back of her hand. "You have no idea how much I needed to hear that. You're the only one—"

"No child, I'm not the only one who saw it that way. Jesus saw it. He worked a long, long time to soften up your daddy's heart. Do you know what your daddy needed more than anything?"

Monica shook her head.

"To know that Jesus *understood*. Jesus knew the pain in your daddy's heart, just like He knows the pain in yours. You see, Jesus doesn't wait until we've got the floors swept and the kitchen all cleaned up before He knocks on the door of our hearts. He comes to us when we're at our worst: bleeding, broken, and don't know which way to turn. If we let Him, He'll squat down, pick us up, and help us clean up the mess we've made of our lives. He'll forgive us and give us a fresh start."

Evelyn turned back to look at Monica's dad. "The week after John gave his life to Christ, he told me he wanted to get a tattoo." She wiped her tears with the tissue in her hand and then chuckled. "Most folks just buy a cross necklace, but not your dad. He wanted something that represented the one thing he wanted forgiveness for more than anything else. I didn't know what to expect until he came home and showed me. Then it made sense."

Evelyn pulled back the sheet further to reveal Monica's father's arms.

Monica leaned in closer. She immediately put her hand to her mouth. The tattoo on his left arm read *His scars*. The one on the right arm read, *My Forgiveness*.

Evelyn put her arm around Monica. "You're not the only one with scars on your arms—Jesus has them, too. His were from being nailed to a cross where He took the punishment for your sins and mine. But He didn't stay in that tomb. He's alive, and He's knocking on the door of your heart. Jesus understands, Monica. He understands."

Evelyn turned Monica's arms to where her hands were facing up. She slid up Monica's sleeves. Monica could see her swallow hard. She looked up and then cupped Monica's face in her hands. "The ones on the inside look even worse, don't they?"

Inside Monica's heart, the levy began to crumble, row by row, brick by brick, until it completely collapsed. Years of pinned-up emotion and pain coursed through her soul. Her shoulders began to shake, and she sobbed.

Evelyn firmly embraced her. "I know, baby girl," she said as she patted Monica's back. "You just let it out. It's okay. Jesus is healing all that pain."

Monica wasn't sure how long she cried or when Calvin entered the room. All she knew was that, along with Evelyn's embrace, she could feel the warmth of his hand resting on her shoulder.

"Would you like to pray, Monica?" he asked softly.

Monica shook her head and buried it in Evelyn's chest. "Why would God listen to me? All I've done is yell at Him most of my life."

"If Jesus can forgive the Roman soldiers for driving those nails into his wrists, I think He can forgive Monica Berry for giving Him a little lip."

His response made her laugh. After wiping her eyes with a tissue Evelyn had provided, she stepped over to a small sink on the other side of the room. She splashed a little water on her face and then patted it dry with a paper towel from the wall dispenser. She paused and looked in the mirror.

Something had changed.

"I look different," she said to herself. She turned toward Evelyn and Calvin and repeated, "I look different."

Evelyn nodded and smiled. "I think that's called *peace.*"

For the first time, the peace she'd admired in Calvin's eyes and even witnessed today on her father's face, she now saw in the mirror.

"You ain't seen nothing yet, baby girl," Evelyn said. She lovingly pushed Calvin in Monica's direction. "Get on over there and pray for your sister to receive Christ, Mr. College Basketball Star. Go win one for the Lord's team today."

Calvin glanced over at Monica. "I don't know. Do you think she can be quiet long enough for me to pray for her?"

Monica laughed and then extended both arms toward Calvin and Evelyn. They all joined hands. "Little brother, the only words I can come up with are," she looked heavenward and said, "thank you."

Calvin smiled. "That's the best thing I've heard come out of your mouth this whole trip. Now, let's pray."

Monica couldn't believe the joy and peace that had overtaken her heart. It was like the arrival of springtime after an endless, brutal winter. Still, there was something she needed to do before she left her father's room—and the state of Mississippi.

Evelyn had walked back over to her father's bed and was about to pull the sheet back up when Monica put her hand on her arm.

"Can I have a few minutes alone with him?"

Evelyn nodded. "Of course, you can. Take your time. Calvin and I will be downstairs in the lobby."

Monica waited until she heard the door close behind them. She looked down at her father.

"Hey, Pop. I know we haven't seen each other in a long time. That's mostly my fault, even though for years I blamed you. I guess we have that in common, you and me: blaming others for our mistakes. In fact, I'm discovering that you and I are a lot more alike than I realized. Now Calvin? He took after Mama." Monica looked off into the distance. "Tenderhearted, softspoken...*rational*." She chuckled and shook her head. "Always seeing the best in people."

She looked back down at her father. "I'm not like that, and neither were you. Maybe the right way is somewhere in the middle...where we acknowledge that a person needs to change...and then we give them the chance."

"I mainly wanted to say that I forgive you for what you did to me, and I hope you'll forgive me for not giving you that second chance." She began to cry. "I'm so sorry, Pop." She shook her head. "That's the *last thing* I thought I'd be saying at this moment, but it's the truth. I was wrong for blaming you for my bitterness and sour outlook on life. That was my choice. I needed to change, but I couldn't do it on my own." She looked down at his tattoos once more. "Neither could you." She smiled and touched his face. "I'm just glad that Jesus didn't give up on either one of us."

Monica checked her watch and took a deep breath. "I've got a lunch date with Calvin and then a plane to catch, so I'd better get going. I won't be able to travel back for your funeral, but I think this visit was more important. You know, I thought I was coming here today to say goodbye." She smiled. "Evidently, today wasn't about goodbyes. I'm going to see you again in heaven."

She reached down and kissed his forehead. "I love you, Pop."

Taking the sheet in her hands, she gently pulled it back over him. She picked up the bottle of Gatorade Calvin had set on the bedside table. After looking back over her shoulder a final time, she flipped off the light switch and quietly closed the door behind her.

Chapter Forty-One

"I don't know, Joseph," Norman said as he cradled the phone between his neck and his shoulder. He used a spoon to scoop coffee from a bag with a large *M* scribbled on the front. "Today should be a mother and son reunion, not a police interrogation."

"I'm convinced that Perry Thomas discovering that my mother is still alive wasn't just for our family's benefit," Joseph replied. "You need to be able to close this case. I wouldn't know which questions to ask—that's your department. Besides, Perry already cleared it with my mother."

"As long as you're sure," Norman said as he poured water into the coffeemaker and flipped on the switch.

"Are *you* sure you can work your schedule around going to Virginia today? Perry urged us to make the trip sooner rather than later—my mother isn't well."

"Of course. And while I appreciate the offer to ride with you and Margaret, I'll just follow you in my car. I never know when I might get called back to the office."

"I understand. I wish Monica could have ridden shotgun with you today. I hear she's out of town visiting her family."

"Monica is where she needs to be. I'll fill her in on everything when she gets back from Mississippi later today."

"Thank you, Norman. Margaret and I will see you shortly."

Norman removed the carafe and put his cup under the steaming brown stream gurgling from the coffeemaker. When enough had dripped into his cup for him to take a few sips, he replaced the carafe.

"Monica," he said out loud, "if only you could be here for this meeting. I'm certain it will be one for the records. You've been right about everything regarding this case—so far." He breathed in the aroma rising from his cup and took a sip. He tilted his head to one side. "You're also right about the coffee. I hate to admit it, but yours does taste better."

Norman took note that the police radio was unusually quiet as he drove to Virginia. He even checked the dials to make sure he still had a signal, but everything seemed to be in working order. No chatter from the radio—combined with the absence of Monica's—made for a deafeningly quiet ride. He found himself alone with his thoughts, something he typically avoided whenever possible.

Monica visiting her father and Joseph reuniting with his mother prompted Norman to think about his own family. The Virginia countryside itself would have brought up the topic as it represented where Norman spent his childhood. He hadn't been back to the house where he'd grown up since his high school graduation: an event that took place more years ago than he cared to calculate. However, the scenic backdrop mother nature displayed today did little to offset the bleak memories it surfaced.

Norman's parents had divorced when he was ten. As an only child, his companions back then were the characters on the cops and robbers shows he watched on television. They'd provided him with solace, both in how they'd transported him to a different place and time and how he could turn up the volume to drown out the sound of his parents fighting. He'd adopted the mindset at an early age that if you can just put the bad guys away, everybody else will have a happy ending.

Both of Norman's parents were well-educated and held high-profile jobs. This had only served to make the details of their divorce more complicated, not to mention more public. They dodged television cameras for several years as they darted in and out of courtrooms, haggling over who got what.

Norman lived for the occasions when his aunt and uncle would rescue him from the fray, allowing him to stay at their house for a few days to experience a taste of normalcy. Norman smiled as he pictured a seven-year-old version of himself running through the wooded area behind his aunt and uncle's house, ducking in and out of bushes and trees as he played cops and robbers with his cousins. The fun would end all too soon, however, and he'd find himself being driven back home to where his parents slept in separate bedrooms and parked their only child in front of the television like it was a live-in babysitter.

As a little boy, all he had wanted was for his parents to be happy. He was too young to remember all of it, but he'd seen pictures of how they had started that way. First, there was the framed photo of a glowing bride and groom on a sunset river-boat cruise in Italy. Another—his favorite—captured a trip to Disney World. True to the spirit of Disneyworld, it was a magical moment. His parents were all smiles as they stood behind a three-year-old Norman donning Mickey Mouse ears and waving at the camera. He never knew who took the first bite of the poison apple that killed their marriage. But if they could no longer make each other happy, then perhaps, he'd thought at the time, he could do it for them.

He'd attempted to do so by making the A Honor Roll in grade school and excelling at sports in middle school. He'd worked hard to graduate first in his high school class, beating out students headed for ivy league colleges. But even his best efforts fell short of making a dent in the misery that seemed to encase his parents. Neither ever remarried. Norman reasoned his mom was married to her career, and his dad preferred bedding down each night with a cigarette and a bottle of Scotch.

Norman tried to put a positive spin on his dysfunctional childhood. He reasoned that it had helped him with his police work; he just stuck with the facts and what made sense. He never gave in to false hope or relied on hunches. All in all, his early experiences had made him solid in his career choice but hollow when it came to personal relationships.

His thoughts were interrupted by his Apple watch alerting him to a call. It was Joseph. After issuing a couple of voice commands, Norman could hear Joseph on the speaker.

"Norman, the house is located just a mile up the road. I'm not sure what the parking accommodations will be, but we'll figure all that out when we arrive."

"Sounds good," Norman replied.

After seeing Joseph turn on his left turn signal, Norman did the same. The driveway was narrow, having been crowded out by thick overgrowth. Some of the limbs were so close that Norman could hear them brush against his car. He hoped they wouldn't leave scratches, something he'd check for when he reached the clearing. The gravel crunched under his tires as he drove slowly towards the house, which was visible now. He blinked hard. He couldn't believe his eyes.

"No way," he said as he pulled to a stop and put the car in park.

The paint color was different. Someone had torn down the side porch and added a handicap ramp to the front. Other than that, it was undeniable: Ellen Bennington was living in the house where Norman had grown up.

What are the chances? He hadn't returned here since he'd packed up his SUV and headed off to college. In the decades that had passed, new construction and road reroutes left him clueless that he was turning into the driveway of his parents' old homeplace.

Stepping inside this house would put him back where he spent a lonely and sad childhood. It would make him uncomfortable, to say the least. But today couldn't be about him. He would force himself to set all of that aside and focus on what this was all about: Joseph seeing his mother alive and him seeing this case *closed*.

He waited until Joseph and Margaret got out of their car. He put his hand on Joseph's shoulder. He could see the trepidation in his eyes. It was what he felt, but for different reasons. Joseph was returning to a place where a parent he thought dead was actually alive. Norman was returning to a place where a marriage started out alive but ended up dead.

Norman took his place at the back of the procession, walking up the front porch steps. Joseph rang the doorbell, and a nurse wearing pink scrubs opened the main door. She unlocked the screen door and stepped out onto the porch.

She smiled at Joseph and extended her hand. "I'm Flora. You must be Joseph."

"Yes, and this is my wife, Margaret, and our friend, Norman Lasko. It's nice to meet you."

"I just wanted to remind you that Hannah—that's who I've known her as—is on oxygen. No open flames of any sort. She's been looking forward to this visit. You can follow me inside."

Norman watched as Joseph looked over at Margaret, squeezed her hand, and stepped inside the house.

Chapter Forty-Two

Julia crunched on a piece of toast as she watched a bird in her backyard build a nest in a tree. The sun had to fight for atmospheric territory this morning, defeating a dense streak of purple clouds before victoriously illuminating the eastern sky.

Last night had left her with mixed emotions. She felt over-joyed at how the evening had ended but getting there hadn't been a smooth ride. She couldn't wait to fill Margaret in on all that had taken place. Margaret had texted her earlier to let her know that she and Joseph would be meeting with Ellen today. Julia promised herself that she wouldn't steal the headline of that reunion but would wait to talk with Margaret later.

Even though Julia's body had been exhausted last night, she hadn't been able to locate the off switch for her mind. So, she'd picked up her book again, intending only to read a few chapters. She'd hoped that, in addition to helping her fall asleep, she'd pick up a few more clues along the way.

By the time she'd gotten to the point where she was too tired to read another chapter, there were no more chapters to read. It was one-thirty and she'd read the book in its entirety. While it had helped her to relax, it hadn't provided any new insight. The latter disappointed her. Then again, perhaps she and Margaret had already gleaned all they needed from it.

She turned around to pick up her breakfast plate from where she'd set it on the kitchen table. She glanced down at the old telephone. *No more answers there either*, she thought. She popped the tape out of the compartment and held it in her hand. Her mind went back to her book. The cassette tape she'd found in the closet at her parents' house—the one she'd taken to the school where she'd hoped to speak with Mr. Morgan. Where was it? And where was her dad's old cassette player? She'd already unpacked all the boxes from the garage.

Wait. What if I stored the old tape recorder in the same box as the telephone when I boxed them up years ago? It makes sense that I would have.

Julia slid the box out from where she had left it in the corner near the kitchen table. She could feel the weight of something in it, but that didn't necessarily mean it was the tape recorder. She leaned over and removed a layer of newspaper and bubble wrap. Sure enough, underneath was the old cassette tape player with the cord wrapped around it.

Lifting it out, she placed it on the table. She unwrapped the cord and put it aside. Pushing the button that released the tape compartment, she could see that a tape was still in there. She reached for her reading glasses and hurriedly put them on. She leaned in closer to read the label.

Julia's Spring Band Concert, May 1975.

She smiled. It was the right cassette tape—one she'd played over and over. When she had listened to it before, she'd only been interested in hearing the music and Mr. Morgan winning the award from the State Band Committee. What if there was something in the background that she'd never paid attention to…or hadn't previously had a reason to?

She plugged one end of the cord into the machine and the other into the wall receptacle. She held her breath as she pushed play.

The machine made a clicking noise as the tape's reel began to turn. Julia turned up the volume and took a seat at the table.

Walking into his parents' old house was like a trip back in time for Norman—an unplanned trip at that. He understood why the federal marshal had selected it for Ellen. While it paled in size to the Bennington estate, it held its own when it came to quality construction and tasteful décor.

Back in the day, it was quite an impressive purchase for a young couple just starting out. Of course, each of his parents purchased larger and more elaborate homes for themselves after the divorce. He never understood why they waited so long to sell this one. He often wondered if it represented something to them that they couldn't reduce to monetary terms. He remembered riding by it one last time before heading to college. He hadn't been back since—until today, that is.

The house had sat unoccupied for years before his parents had finally put it up for sale. Now it provided refuge for a woman who could have had any house she wanted at one time in her life. She lived in this one for the security and peace of mind it could provide. Norman shook his head as he looked around. *I hope you have better luck with that than I did.*

"Right this way," Flora said as she led them into a knotty-pine paneled den which was to the left of a bright and open kitchen. Norman ignored the emotional triggers that were like invisible hands reaching out to grab him as he took in the all-too-familiar surroundings. As they approached the den entrance, he could hear the hum of an oxygen machine.

The next sound he heard was from Joseph.

"Mother!" Joseph called out. Norman looked past Joseph to see an older woman in a wheelchair dressed in black pants and a red sweater. Her snow-white hair was neatly brushed back and fell just at her neck. She was lovely at ninety; Norman could only imagine how beautiful she'd been as a young woman. Of all her features, her eyes sported the most beautiful shade of blue Norman had ever seen.

"Joseph!" she said softly. "Come here, son."

Joseph collapsed to his knees in front of her wheelchair. Weeping, he took her hands into his and kissed them. She spoke tenderly to him when she said, "It's not everyday you find out your mother is still alive."

Joseph continued to weep as he reached up to his mother, cupping her face in his hands. "I've missed you so much!"

He buried his head in her embrace and wept. Norman wiped his own eyes, as did Margaret and Flora. Norman had experienced numerous emotional scenes, having worked in law enforcement for as long as he had. Nothing compared to this.

After a few moments, Joseph took off his glasses and wiped his eyes on his shirt sleeve. "Mother, this is—"

"Margaret," Ellen said, cutting him off. Norman watched as Margaret leaned over to hug Ellen and kiss her cheek.

Joseph put his glasses back on. "Mother, does Wyatt know?"

Ellen shook her head. "No, and he doesn't need to. He went through enough when he found out that Gina Merino was his birth mother. My sources tell me that he and Gina—and her husband, George Ortiz—have a wonderful relationship. I didn't want to do anything to disrupt that."

Joseph nodded. "Wyatt is doing well. He travels all over the country with his prison ministry."

Ellen smiled. "My sources tell me that, too. Trust me—it's not that I don't want to see him. It was a difficult decision, but I think it's the right one."

"Mother…" Joseph paused as if trying to compose himself. "I know it wasn't your choice, but how could you just leave us? We were devastated by your death, especially such a tragic one."

Ellen took his hand. "It was the hardest thing I've ever done, Joseph. Sometimes the price tag for a good deed is higher than you expect it to be. I know you have so many questions. I plan to address as many of them today as I can, both yours and that young man's standing behind you."

As if he had forgotten an item on his checklist, Joseph turned around and motioned for Norman to step forward. "I apologize, Norman. This is the detective I told you about, Mother. His name is Norman Lasko."

Norman extended his hand to shake Ellen's. "It's an honor to meet you, ma'am."

"Well, thank you. Likewise, I'm sure. What did you say your last name was?"

Perhaps she didn't hear him, so he spoke loudly.

"Lasko."

Ellen laughed. "It's my lungs that are shot, not my ears. I just wanted to make sure I heard you correctly. The prior owner of this house—that was their last name." She paused. "In fact, I was told they had a son that graduated Valedictorian of his high school class. That wouldn't be you now, would it?"

Norman could feel everyone's eyes bore in on him. He would answer the question but attempt to downplay the topic of his family.

"Believe it or not," Norman said with a smile, "that was me."

Margaret's mouth dropped open. "That's great, Norman! Wait, this was the house you grew up in?"

Norman displayed a sheepish smile and gave a half shrug. "Guilty again."

"No way!" Joseph exclaimed. "You must have so many memories here."

"That would be true," Norman said. He felt a twinge of panic as he caught Margaret looking at him as if she'd transitioned into counselor mode.

Time to steer this car back onto the highway.

"So, Mrs. Bennington, you may know that we made an interesting discovery at the old Durledge Apartments that they're tearing down: an apartment complex you and Frances Gates put in your husbands' names."

To Norman's astonishment, Ellen replied, "You must be talking about that bag of cocaine. They finally found it." She rolled her eyes. "Took them long enough. Horace and James have long since passed. Worse, so have the statute of limitations on drug possession. Am I right, detective?"

Norman couldn't help but chuckle. "You're right. But you helped to put the dealer away years ago."

"Yes, that wretched excuse for a man destroyed so many lives. Why don't you all sit down, and I'll tell you the story."

Flora squatted down beside Ellen's chair. "Miss Hannah, don't overdo it, okay? I'll be in the kitchen if you need me."

Ellen patted her hand. "I'll be fine. Would you mind heating some water? I think I'd like a cup of tea. Would anyone else like tea, or is this a coffee-drinking crowd?"

Norman looked around as no one said anything.

Ellen smiled. "How about we prepare both?"

Chapter Forty-Three

After everyone had poured themselves either a cup of coffee or tea, they filtered back into the den. Flora set a cup of tea on the table beside Ellen's wheelchair and then stepped out of the room, closing the door behind her. Norman watched as Ellen took a sip and then waited until everyone had taken their seats before she began.

"I want to start by saying that no matter how well we plan our futures, none of us can *see* the future. If I had known that Horace would turn into such a monster, I don't know that I would have married him." She looked up and shook her head. "God knows there were plenty of times I wished I hadn't.

"As powerful as Horace was, I didn't think I had any recourse. Back in the 1970s, there weren't many options for women in abusive situations. Men traditionally held the purse strings. Until the Equal Credit Opportunity Act in 1974, a woman couldn't even secure a bank loan without a man's signature. After a while, I just resigned myself to make the best of it." Ellen looked over at Margaret. "Your mother did the same regarding her marriage to your father.

"That all changed one morning in the fall of 1975 when Frances asked me to meet her at a park. That's when she told me she was pregnant with Horace's child." Ellen looked over at Margaret once again. "Your baby brother, Preston.

"We both decided we'd had enough. We hired an attorney who didn't have connections to Horace and James. We decided to hit them in the areas where they'd feel it the most, which of course, were their wallets and their reputations. That's when we bought the Durledge Apartments with an agreement that owner-ship would eventually be gifted to Horace and James. When the agreement took over, Horace and James would become the proud proprietors of run-down, government-subsidized hous-ing. Not only would they own property they couldn't give away, but it would also serve as a blemish on their flawless reputations as savvy businessmen."

"That's smart thinking," Norman admitted.

Ellen smiled. "We had a smart attorney."

"Since you and Dad were still married, wouldn't that have taken money away from you as well? And eventually from the estate? Granted, it would have upset Wyatt more than me. I'll never forget how enraged he was when we learned that Preston was our half-brother and entitled to a third of the inheritance." Joseph said.

"Joseph," Norman began. "I'm just curious. How did you find that out?"

"I took a hair sample from Dad just moments before the funeral director closed his casket. With so much on the line, I'll never forget how nervous I was to be the one carrying a piece of evidence that could impact so many lives."

Norman nodded and said, "That makes sense. I'm sure you dropped it off at the hospital lab as quickly as possible."

"That's one of the reasons I was so nervous. The lab was closed, and I had to wait until the following morning to drop it off along with a mouth swab I'd taken from Preston. I wasn't as worried about Preston's DNA evidence; I could always take another one. But Dad's hair sample? That was one and done."

Norman briefly looked up from taking notes. "Evidently, everything worked out though."

"I'd put it in a Ziploc bag for safe keeping until I could drop it off at the lab the next day. I remember Gina, our housekeeper, saying that I'd feel better if it was in a more secure container, like a small plastic one with a lid. A small detail, but I remember it made me feel better. The results came back conclusive: Horace was Preston's biological father."

Ellen smiled. "Gina was always there when we needed her. There was no task too big or too small. No one could ever say that about your father. He didn't have time for the little things, the things that most of us would consider as holding real value. Instead, he thought of everything in terms of profits and losses. The love of money took over his life. Money isn't necessarily a bad thing. We need it to survive. It's the *love of money* that corrupts us.

"To answer your question, Joseph, even if our plan backfired, Frances and I knew that our children would still receive a sizeable inheritance. We decided to hand down something of even greater worth. We wanted our children to know that their mothers weren't doormats and weren't going to turn a blind eye to their fathers' wrongdoing. Plus, Frances and I made a profit from our little business venture. Those years of rent payments? We each pocketed fifty thousand dollars."

Joseph's eyes lit up. "That's the check you wrote for the Manor! You donated the money?"

"I donated the *principle*, yes. The rest is in a savings account for your son's college education."

Joseph's hand went to his chest. "Mother, this is amazing."

"But what about the cocaine?" Norman asked.

"Frances and I intercepted the first shipment and replaced it with baking soda. Horace thought James had double-crossed him and was going to take it out on Margaret like he did the last time they had a failed business venture. Even though Frances and I had been in on it together, I told Horace I'd acted alone. I convinced him that I'd sold the cocaine and invested the proceeds in a real estate venture, one that would benefit him in the future. Horace insisted I provide him with financial updates on this venture; but, over time, he lost interest as bigger and more lucrative opportunities presented themselves.

"My telling Horace that I knew about the cocaine blew the lid off his secret venture. He never dabbled in it again. Of course, the dealer wasn't there for mine and Horace's exchange and assumed he had a bright future with James and Horace as clients. So, he moved his family to the area. In his mind, it was a matter of convenience; he could conduct the transactions in person."

Norman took a sip of his coffee. "But you still had the problem of the bag of cocaine."

"Yes, I'm getting to that. We decided to hide it in one of the apartments. Since the government had classified Durledge Apartments as subsidized housing, the buildings had been cheaply constructed. It didn't take much for Frances and me to pick an unoccupied unit, tinker with the wall behind the cabinets, and use it as a hiding place. Funny enough, we ourselves would go to this apartment from time to time—to hide, that is." She looked off in the distance. "Nobody knew us in that part of town. It was liberating to be a 'normal person' for a few hours. We'd order takeout, read, or I'd write in my diary."

Norman's eyes lit up. "So that was *your* diary key and your keepsake box? Why did you leave it all behind?"

"A few years into mine and Frances' venture, I found out that Dominic Martin—that was his name—didn't need Horace and James as clients after all. He had found a lucrative market among those less fortunate. I heard he had stooped so low as to have his son sell drugs to students at the high school. Anyway, I provided—"

Margaret held her hand up. "I'm sorry to interrupt, but what was his name again?"

"Dominic Martin," Ellen replied. "Why do you ask?"

"It's just that I haven't heard that name in years. His son and I were in band class together. And you're right; Dominic Jr. did sell drugs at the high school." Margaret paused as if she was composing herself. Her voice cracked as she said, "He sold them to me."

Ellen's eyes filled with compassion. "I'm so sorry, Margaret. That makes me even prouder of the fact that I helped put his father away, although it proved much riskier than I ever imagined. Not long after I'd provided the police with a tip on Dominic, someone leaked *my* name to *him*. The police had information that he was coming after me."

"That's when they staged the car accident and put you in Witness Protection?" Joseph asked, leaning forward in his chair.

"That's right," Ellen said. "To answer *your* question, Norman, I had to leave immediately. I didn't have time to return for my keepsake box, diary, or anything. I couldn't see the future to know that Margaret would rent the apartment years down the road."

Norman's eyes narrowed. "Wouldn't Dominic also come after Horace and James? I wouldn't think they'd be safe either."

"Evidently, neither did Horace and James. I don't have proof, but I think they arranged for Dominic to be killed in prison. Even with him dead, the federal marshal kept me in Witness Protection. Dominic was part of a much larger organization. They didn't think I'd ever be safe again."

"Wow," Norman said. "Unbelievable."

"So, Detective Lasko, I don't know if you'll be able to make any arrests, but at least now you have your answers."

"Ellen, I still have a question," Margaret said, shuffling in her seat. "It's wrong that Horace would be unfaithful under any circumstances; but when he was, he typically sought out teenage girls. With that in mind, why would he assault my mother?"

Ellen's countenance fell. "Because your mother found out that Horace was abusing you. She stood up to him. That's why he did it. Sexual assault is almost always about power, and power was Horace's drug, if you will. He was addicted to it."

Margaret slowly nodded. "I remember that day. I heard Horace let himself into our house and barge into my parents' bedroom. As soon as I knew it was him, all I wanted to do was hide. I was terrified of him." Joseph reached over and took her hand. She continued, "I heard a muffled argument, but I never knew what they were arguing about...nor did I really want to know. I literally put my hands over my ears."

"She was trying to protect you, Margaret. She only wished she had done it sooner. I don't think she ever completely forgave herself. In fact, the fifty thousand dollars that she earned from our joint venture? She put it into a private trust fund for you and Preston. Your father never knew about it. That money was what Preston used to pay for your rehab over the years. Even though your mother couldn't prevent your abuse, in some way she helped facilitate your healing."

Norman watched as Joseph squeezed Margaret's hand.

"Now, Detective Lasko—"

"Please, call me Norman."

"Okay, Norman. Can I ask you a few personal questions... since you just asked me a few?"

"Fair enough." Norman chuckled, but he began to feel uncomfortable. He loosened his tie.

Okay, Norman, he said to himself. *Just stay calm. How personal can this really get?*

<h1 style="text-align:center">Chapter Forty-Four</h1>

"So, I'm living in the house you grew up in?" Ellen asked with a twinkle in her eye.

She knows how much I'm already hating this conversation.

Norman looked around. "Yes, ma'am. I was an only child."

"After I moved in, I looked into the prior owners, never knowing that I'd one day be hosting their son. I didn't have to look far to learn that your parents divorced, and that it was an ugly and public divorce. I'm sorry you had to go through that."

"Well, thank you. But it's all in the past."

"Is it?" Ellen asked, her robin-egg blue eyes looking right through him. "Because either you have an aversion to jewelry, or you're not married. I don't see a ring. Do you have a girlfriend or someone special in your life? I told you these questions were going to be personal," she said with a wink.

Norman immediately thought of Monica. No, she's my business partner. This is just a business meeting to close a case, one I'll discuss with Monica later today. She's just someone I work with—nothing more.

But what came out of his mouth was, "It's complicated."

Ellen's expression went blank, and then she laughed. She had to stop for a moment to catch her breath and adjust the oxygen tube in her nose.

"You do know that Joseph's father abused Margaret, right? And that his older brother tried to kill her?" She shook her head. "I don't think it gets more complicated than that!

"Norman, when God wants two people to be together to fulfill His purposes, nothing can stop it. Maybe that's one of the reasons you're here today. I can look in your eyes and see sadness." Ellen stopped for a minute as if she was trying to reel in her emotions. Her voice cracked. "I know what sadness looks like; I lived with it for many, many years." She reached out her hand to him. "Come here, son."

Norman got up from his seat and squatted in front of her wheelchair. She took his hand, and, once again, her eyes seemed to look right into his soul.

"Don't let what someone did—or didn't do—in your past dictate your future. Don't be afraid to open up your heart to people, and whatever you do, don't be afraid to open it up to God. I don't know what your earthly father was like, but your Heavenly Father won't disappoint you. He loves you like no one else can. You think about that on your drive back to North Carolina."

"Yes, ma'am, I will."

"Good. Now, Margaret, Joseph, and I have a lot of catching up to do that's *not* police business." She smiled. "If you don't mind, I'll have Flora show you out."

He stood back up, leaned over, and kissed her cheek. He shook Joseph's hand and gave Margaret a quick hug. He had made his way to the den entrance when he heard Ellen call his name. He turned around. This time he saw gratitude in her eyes.

"Thank you for making the trip today. I feel much better now that I've come clean with this whole ordeal."

"No, ma'am." Norman stared down at the floor. "Thank you. You've given me a lot to think about."

Back outside, he paused to look at the house once more. Then he unlocked his car and put on his seatbelt. He issued a voice command to his cellphone.

"Call Monica."

Chapter Forty-Five

For as many times as she, her parents, and Mr. Morgan had played the old band concert tape, Julia was surprised it still worked. This time she was listening for a conversation, a strange noise, anything she might not have noticed before. So far, all she had heard was Mr. Morgan announcing the title of the songs, the band students playing the music, and the audience applauding.

By the time Mr. Morgan dismissed the audience for a ten-minute intermission, Julia was about to give up. Then she heard her parents talking with someone. She turned up the volume, but with an auditorium full of conversations, she couldn't make out who they were talking to or what they were saying. Her dad then switched off the machine, most likely to save the battery for the second half of the concert.

"Maybe I'm wasting my time," Julia said out loud. After the intermission, the band played a few more songs, and then the State Band Committee presented Mr. Morgan with his award. Julia's heart warmed. She rewound the tape to hear that part again. Afterward, the concert concluded.

Out of habit, she reached to turn the machine off. Then she heard something. Instead of leaving the tape recorder in his chair, her dad had picked it up to take it back home with him—

with the machine still running. She could hear a woman chatting with her mom.

"They played so well tonight! What's your student's name?"

"Julia. She plays the clarinet."

"My son is Dom—Dom Martin. He plays the trumpet. We just moved here. My name is Carrie."

She heard a few other words, but they sounded muffled as if her dad had the microphone close to his body. Then the tape went silent.

Dom Martin. Julia didn't recall the name as a fellow band student, but she couldn't be expected to remember everyone. It had been fifty years, after all. She powered up her laptop. After typing in a few prompts, she searched the name. Nothing came up.

Another dead end.

What if Dom was short for something?

She thought for a moment and then typed, *Dominic Martin.*

Her screen populated with several articles.

She read that Dominic was a Jr. His father, Dominic Sr., was a convicted drug dealer—among other crimes—who served only served five years of a ten-year sentence before being killed in prison.

I wonder how young Dominic turned out. According to his mother, they had just moved to the area. Margaret started experimenting with drugs that summer. That's when we lost touch. Julia looked at her watch. *I don't like breaking promises, even the ones I make to myself. But I've got to call Margaret!*

Monica thanked the taxi driver and rolled her suitcase up to her front door. So much had taken place since she had thrown a few items together and headed off to Mississippi with Calvin. It had only been a day and a half, but it felt like a lifetime ago. She planned to take a long, hot bath and hit the sack early, but not before reading a few chapters in the Bible Evelyn had bought for her at the hospital gift shop.

She'd just thrown her keys on the entry table when she heard her phone ringing. She checked the caller ID. It was Norman.

Norman, please don't ask me to come to work. I'm exhausted.

"Hey, Norman. I just got back home. What's going on?

"How was your trip? How's your dad?"

Okay, you're usually all business. You're behaving like a normal human being right now.

"I didn't get there before my father passed, but I still got to tell him goodbye. It's a long story. All in all, it was a life-changing trip."

"I'm sorry to hear about your father."

"Thank you."

"I'm driving back from Virginia. I just finished a meeting with Joseph, Margaret, and Ellen Bennington. Ellen's attorney, Perry Thomas, scheduled it for today. Since Ellen's health is failing, Perry didn't think we should put it off."

"You met with the Benningtons without me, or at least without checking with me first? One of the most powerful families in the area and—" Monica started laughing. "Sound familiar?"

"I guess I had that one coming." Norman chuckled. "I need to update you on all that I learned from that meeting. I was wondering if, especially with your dad's passing, I could treat you to dinner tonight. I'd offer to cook, but I haven't been to the store, and I'm fresh out of frozen pizza."

Monica laughed. "I've got a better idea. How about you come over to my place and I will cook for you? Not tonight, because I'm really tired. Would tomorrow night work?"

"I'll make it work. See you in the morning at the precinct?"

"Yeah. Have a safe drive back home."

Monica ended the call and made her way into her kitchen. She took a wine bottle from the rack on the wall and popped the cork. She poured herself a glass and made her way into her bedroom.

This hot bath is going to feel so good, she said to herself. Then she stopped.

Wait a minute. Did Norman just ask me out on a date?

~

Margaret heard her phone buzzing in her purse. She checked the caller ID.

"It's Julia," she said, looking at Joseph and then at Ellen. "I'll only be a minute."

"I thought you said it was Julia," Joseph said with a wink.

Margaret stepped into the kitchen and answered the call. "Julia?"

"I'm so sorry to interrupt your time with Joseph's mother, but I need to talk with you. A lot has happened in the last twelve hours."

"Such as?"

"First of all, we had a scare. Holly passed out at the cooking competition."

"What? Is she okay?"

"She's better than okay. She's pregnant."

"Thank God…and congratulations!"

"There's more to that story, but I'll save it for a later conversation. The main reason I called is that I finished reading the book. Unfortunately, no new clues surfaced. Then, for some reason, the spring concert tape that I referenced in the book came to mind. So, I dug out the old recorder and listened to the tape. I heard something that I hadn't heard before, only because I wasn't listening for it. Dominic Martin's mom and my mom were talking. Do you remember him? He may have gone by Dom. I can't seem to place him."

"Who did you just say?"

"Dom Martin. His dad was Dominic Sr. and did time for

dealing drugs but didn't complete his sentence because he was killed in prison."

"No, I know who he is. I just can't believe you made that discovery from the tape. Dominic's dad was the one Horace and James got mixed up with. We just learned his name. Ellen exposed him, which is why she went into Witness Protection."

"Horace knew this guy?"

"Yes, and I knew his son. He was in band class with us. You wouldn't remember him because he hung out with a different friend group. He was the one who introduced me to drugs."

"I realize it's been decades, but do you recall the first time? Did you go to Dom, or did he approach you?"

"If I remember correctly, he showed a romantic interest in me. After he'd earned my trust, he introduced me to a pill that was supposed to help relieve my anxiety. The rest is history. I became an addict. After high school, I don't think I ever saw him again. He was only a part of my life for a short period of time."

"That's all the time a snake needs in order to bite. I don't think it was a coincidence that Dom made such a brief appearance on the stage of your life. He played a minor character by design, which is why you never made the connection."

"What connection?"

"What if Horace targeted you through Dominic Jr.? Horace knew you were hurting and vulnerable. If you started using drugs, it would destroy your credibility. It was an insurance policy if you ever decided to expose him. All of the guilt and shame you've felt all these years. What if it wasn't your fault? What if you were intentionally baited?"

"But isn't that what drug dealers do anyway?"

"Yes, but this was personal if Horace was behind it. It makes so much sense. Ellen may be able to provide you with an answer."

Margaret sighed. "I don't know if I want to uncover yet another plot to destroy me, courtesy of Horace Bennington. I'm tired of kicking up the dust from my old life. Can't we just let it settle?"

"That's the whole idea! Margaret, this could be the key to you finally closing the door to your past. All that God has shown you recently has brought you healing and freedom that you didn't even know you needed. Why stop now when you're almost at the finish line?"

Julia could hear Margaret sigh once more. "Maybe you're right. I'll let you know what Ellen says."

Chapter Forty-Six

E *ven work feels different,* Monica thought the next day after Norman debriefed her on the Bennington meeting. *I didn't realize how angry I felt all the time.*

"I guess we'll just box up all the evidence and indicate on the box that the case is closed?" she asked.

"Maybe not *all* of the evidence," Norman said as he pursed his lips. "Since we didn't connect the diary and the keepsake box to any crime, I think we should send those items back to their original owner, Ellen Bennington."

"I think that's a great idea," Monica said. *Did Norman just grow a heart? Or has he this been this way all along and I never noticed?* "Well, if it's okay with my partner, I think I'll leave a little early this afternoon. I need to pick up a few last-minute items at the grocery store for dinner."

"I suppose that since you're cooking dinner for your partner, he shouldn't object!"

Monica chuckled as she slung her purse over her shoulder. "I'll see you at seven?"

"I'll be there. Is there anything I can bring?"

"You can bring a bottle of wine if you'd like. Besides not

bringing coffee—I don't trust you to pick out anything decent—there's one thing you absolutely cannot bring to my house."

Norman leaned back in his chair. "What's that?"

Monica's eyes widened. "Frozen pizza."

"Roger that. I'll make sure I thaw it out first," Norman said with a grin.

"Don't push it, Lasko," Monica said as she headed out his office door. She was already in the hall when she called out, "Seven o'clock sharp, and don't be late."

Norman waited until Monica was out of earshot when he dialed a number on his cellphone.

"Kevin, it's Norman Lasko."

"Hi Norman, what can I do for you?"

"Do you remember when I got you out of that speeding ticket a few months ago and you said you owed me? Can I cash in on that?"

"Of course! When were you thinking?"

"How about now? How busy are you?"

"We're open until six. Come on by and ask for me."

"I'll see you soon. Thank you, Kevin."

Okay, Norman. Just bite the bullet. People do this all the time. It will be worth it. Plus, you're long overdue.

Norman grabbed his jacket and headed out of his office.

Turning off the timer, Monica slid her hands into two oven mitts and carefully placed a bubbling eggplant parmesan on the top of her stove. She checked the table, straightening the silverware and holding the wine glasses up to the light to check for spots. The doorbell rang. She glanced down at her watch.

Seven o'clock on the nose.

On her way to open the door, she checked her reflection in the mirror over the foyer table. She stood on her tiptoes and looked through the peephole in her front door, just to be sure it was Norman.

But she wasn't sure.

She tentatively opened the door. "Norman? Is that you?"

 ⌘

With Steven and Olivia's yard clean-up project getting cut short the other day, Julia decided she'd finish the job herself. By the time she'd finished picking up all the debris, she'd almost filled an entire compost container.

Back inside her townhouse, she stopped at the kitchen sink to wash her hands. She shook her head as she looked down at her nails. "Julia, I see a manicure in your future," she said out loud. "Especially if there's a date with Perry in your future. Let's find the number of the girl who used to do your nails…if she's even in business anymore."

Julia picked up her phone and saw a missed call from Perry. Her heart did a little summersault.

Should I call him back? Would that look too forward? Or should I let him call me?

That problem was solved when her phone rang and she saw Perry's number displayed. She took a deep breath and calmly answered.

"Hello?"

"Hi, Julia! It's Perry. How are you?"

"I'm doing well. How about you?" Julia moved the phone away from her face and took another deep breath, willing her heart rate to slow down.

"I'm great. I just wanted to see if we could schedule a time to get together later this week. I'd love to take you to dinner at that new restaurant by Oakwood Lake. I was thinking maybe…Friday?"

Julia pretended to look at a calendar. "Let's see…yes, I'm free Friday night."

"Great! I'll pick you up around seven o'clock."

"Seven works for me. I'll see you then."

"I'm looking forward to it."

"Me, too, Perry."

Julia ended the call. Her heart was bursting with joy. In addition to getting a manicure, maybe she would ask Holly to help her pick out a new outfit for the occasion. However, before she did anything else, she needed to take care of a little unfinished business.

She stepped into her bedroom and picked up her wedding picture. She sat down on the side of the bed.

She took a deep breath. "Bill, I have something to tell you. I can't believe I'm saying this...but I'm going on a date later this week." She smiled. "I really like this man, and I think you'd like him, too."

She looked off into the distance for a moment. "I think it was F. Scott Fitzgerald who said, 'There are all kinds of love in this world, but never the same love twice.'" Tears filled her eyes as she looked back down at the photo. "No one could ever be you, and no relationship could ever replace what we had. But this could be an opportunity for me to experience love again. If God has brought this man into my life, that's all the more reason for me to give it a chance." She paused and wiped the tears from her eyes. "Just know that I still love you...and I always will."

Julia kissed the photo and gently set it back on her nightstand.

Chapter Forty-Seven

"Are you alright, dear? That must have been some phone conversation," Ellen said as she blew at the steam from the cup of tea Flora handed her.

"I'm just ready to move past painful topics," Margaret said with a heavy sigh as she slumped into the wing-back chair next to Joseph's. "Today should be for you and Joseph to revisit happy memories."

"There's still time for that. Today is also for answers."

"What did you and Julia discuss that has you looking so crestfallen?" Joseph asked, shifting in his seat to face her.

"It wasn't *all* bad. She did tell me that Holly is pregnant."

"That's great news!" Joseph said, and then cleared his throat. "What's the not-so-great news?"

"It seems that Dominic's son's name came up on an old band concert tape Julia was listening to. It's a little uncanny that it would surface yet again considering I haven't thought of him since high school. Whether I want to admit it or not, there could be a reason for that. Do you know if Horace could have used him to target me? As Julia said, if Horace could get me using drugs, it would discredit me and any attempt I made to expose him."

Ellen set her teacup down on the table beside her wheelchair. "You know, I never put two and two together, but that could have been the case. I'm certain that Dominic was none too happy when Horace and James decided that one deal gone sideways satisfied their appetite for the drug market. I seem to remember overhearing Dominic threatening to expose James and Horace's misadventure to their stockholders. Horace would have been desperate to find Dominic a stop-gap source of income, especially since he thought I acted alone in getting rid of the cocaine. He knew you were vulnerable. You were only fifteen years old— just a child. You don't need to feel guilty about any of that."

"I know it may sound irrational, but for years I felt guilty for Horace *abusing me*. Over time I accepted that it wasn't my fault. But the substance abuse? I took full responsibility for that. At least something good came from it, and I was able to help other victims. I often wonder what path I would have chosen if none of it had ever happened."

"You're looking at it all wrong, Margaret," Ellen said. "Your work at the Manor wasn't Plan B. You've ministered to others with a depth of compassion that could only have come through what you suffered. God placed a powerful calling on your life. Satan tried everything he could to destroy you, but he couldn't. The painful things you experienced only served to better equip you for the work God had called you to do.

"Since I've been in Witness Protection, I've read my Bible cover to cover—more than once. One thing I've learned is that God rarely chooses people with a spotless record. You may have made a few bad choices along the way, but so did Moses, King David…and let's not forget Peter, who went so far as to deny the Lord. Despite their mistakes, we hail them as heroes of the faith. And they weren't without their share of enemies, either. Those with callings on their lives almost always face opposition. You weren't targeted because you had a *defect*, Margaret. You were targeted because you had a *destiny*."

Margaret sat in silence as Ellen's words washed over her. The guilt she had carried all these years began to lift. She didn't realize just how heavy it had weighed on her until she felt it subside. She marveled at how she had to visit the past to discover that these suppressed emotions even existed. For years, she had focused so intently on helping the students at the Manor that she didn't realize that she herself still needed healing.

It took a moment for Margaret to collect her thoughts. Then she looked at Joseph and Ellen. "When all of this started with my dreams and Julia experiencing another phone call from the past, I wanted to know *why*. Now I understand, at least in regard to how it pertained to me. I had gunk in my engine that was slowing me down. Not that I wasn't effective in my work; God definitely was using me to help others. But I can only imagine how much *more* effective I'll be now that I've had a thorough tune up!

"The next question was, *why now*? At my age, I'd considered retiring. Now I'm thinking that God may still have work for me to do."

"Look at me," Ellen said. "I'm ninety years old, and I'm on oxygen. My days on this earthly journey are numbered. I've been waiting a long, long time to see why God still had me here. Now that I know, I have to say it's been worth the wait. Margaret, there are troubled teens out there who need the help you can provide. It's not time to turn in your keys to the Manor just yet."

"Thank you, Ellen. Thank you so much!" Margaret jumped to her feet and embraced her.

Ellen looked up at her and said, "And don't ever forget that your mother loved you very much. She'd be so proud of you, just like I am." She peered around Margaret to look at Joseph. "Thank you for bringing this one into the family!"

Joseph stood and squatted down in front of Ellen's wheelchair. "Mother, I've never said this to anyone before. So you'll be the first—"

"You're glad I'm not dead?" Ellen asked with a chuckle.

Joseph smiled and squeezed her hand. "More than you'll ever know."

Margaret chuckled and then glanced at her watch. "Oh my goodness! It's already three o'clock? Joseph and I should get going." She looked over at Ellen. "I'm sure you need your rest."

"The time has flown today," Joseph responded. "I'm glad we got all of the heavy topics out of the way early on. Some of those stories you shared from when I was a little boy? I had no idea. I haven't laughed that hard in years."

"I'd have to say the same," Ellen said with a smile.

"And, Flora, that chicken dish you whipped up for lunch was amazing!" Joseph continued. "Are you sure you don't want to come back to North Carolina with us?"

Flora laughed. "No, my place is here. I enjoy my work with home health. It's gratifying, especially when I meet nice people like Miss Hannah and her family. But I agree with Margaret. Miss Hannah does need to take her medicine and rest for a little while. I hope you'll visit again soon."

"As long as you'll have us, we'd love to," Margaret said.

"Can you put up with us again for a visit, Mother?" Joseph asked, kneeling in front of his mother's wheelchair once more. "Next time, I promise we won't bring any law enforcement with us."

"How about my grandson?" Ellen grinned. "Bring him, and we'll call it even."

The late afternoon sun shone on Joseph's side of the car as he and Margaret wound their way through the Virginia countryside and back across the North Carolina state line. Margaret could tell that Joseph was at peace. He laughed and talked like his old self. Margaret had something on her mind but had decided to wait until they were further down the road before she brought it up.

She eventually put her hand on Joseph's arm. "Can we make a stop in Enoburg?" she asked softly. "There's someone I need to talk to."

Chapter Forty-Eight

"Who are you, and what have you done with Norman?" Monica asked as she did a doubletake before opening the door to a well-dressed man with a stylish haircut and a bottle of wine tucked under his arm.

Norman extended his free hand. "I'm Norman Lasko." He lowered his voice. "The *man,* not the detective. And you are?"

Monica threw her head back and laughed. She couldn't help but be impressed. She took a couple of steps back. "Let me look at you! Nice haircut, stylish pants, cool V-neck sweater. Did you get your teeth whitened? Well, *Mr.* Lasko—not to be confused with *Detective* Lasko—I'm Monica Berry. Welcome to my home!"

"This has to be the best eggplant parmesan I've ever had. You are a superb cook."

Monica took a sip of her wine. "Let's just say I've had plenty of experience."

"Do I detect a back story to that response?" Norman asked as he took another bite.

"As a matter of fact, yes. I had quite the dysfunctional childhood. My mother died when Calvin was three years old. My father blamed me for her death—long story—and forced me to take over her duties in the home. I had to cook, clean, pack lunches, everything my mom had done for us. The only problem was that I was nine years old at the time, which is why I have," Monica said as she rolled up her shirt sleeves, "these."

Monica expected Norman to display the same response as everyone else who had seen her scars: controlled repulsion. Norman reacted differently. She watched as his eyes welled with tears. He quickly brushed them away.

"Monica." His voice cracked. "I'm so sorry."

She smiled reassuringly. "I'm okay with it now. When I went to see my dad, I found out that he wasn't that person anymore. He even had tattoos on his arms in the same place as my scars. His tattoos read, 'His Scars, My Forgiveness,' indicating how Jesus had forgiven him for how he treated me. I realized that he wasn't the only one who needed forgiveness; I needed it for blaming him for my anger and negative outlook on life. In other words, I needed Jesus, too. I asked Christ into my heart. I feel like a new person, Norman. It wasn't easy going back home, but I'm so glad I did."

"I'm glad you did, too. I'm proud of you."

"So, what about your childhood?" Monica asked as she used a pair of tongs to place another helping of salad on her plate and then Norman's.

"Funny you should ask. While you were in Mississippi, I took an unplanned trip to where *I* grew up. My family's house was where the Feds had placed Ellen Bennington for Witness Protection. I thought I was traveling to Virginia to tie up loose ends for the case. As it turns out, I had loose ends to tie up that had nothing to do with the case."

"Such as?"

"First of all, I didn't realize how many similarities you and I share regarding our upbringing."

"Wait...I was under the impression that your family was like the Kennedys of Virginia."

Norman chuckled. "My parents were well-off, but that didn't make us immune to dysfunction; ours just played out with a different narrative. My parents fell out of love with each other and became so wrapped up in their own pain that they forgot I was hurting, too. I had a sad and lonely childhood. As I got older, I tried to fix them by becoming an overachiever. I thought if they could be proud of me, it would help heal their pain. It didn't. So, like you, I left home after high school graduation and never looked back."

"How old were you when your parents divorced?" Monica asked, taking a bite of her salad.

"The divorce took a few years to finalize. When all was said and done, I was ten years old."

"Wow, around the same age as me."

"Correct me if I'm wrong, but, like you, I threw myself into my work to keep the pain at bay. Yesterday, I didn't have a choice but to come face to face with it."

"Besides working all the time, how else has it affected you?"

"I limited myself to what I considered to be safe relationships, like the professional ones I developed with my coworkers."

Monica nodded. "To quote the famous locksmith Tom Kimball, *the hardest thing to unlock is a human heart, especially one that's been hurt.*" She grinned at Norman and winked. "You probably thought I wasn't listening that day."

Norman smiled. "You're probably right. I'm impressed!"

"So, we've both kept our hearts closed off."

"I know I have. Otherwise I would have asked you out a long time ago," Norman said as he looked down at his food.

"Norman, I—"

He cautiously looked up at her. "I'm not saying it has to go anywhere, although I'd like for it to. Just giving it a chance is something I would never have considered until I spoke with Ellen Bennington. Besides—"

Monica reached over and put her hand on Norman's mouth. "Let me talk, Lasko. You don't have to justify anything. We already have a solid friendship. It may take me a while to get used to the idea, but who knows? When I think about how it all came about, I have to agree."

"Agree with what?" Norman leaned forward, his hazel eyes intent. The way he looked at her made her heart flutter. *I didn't see that coming,* she thought.

"That it's worth a shot. You know, just to see where it goes. One thing I'd like for us to do is to pray and commit it to God. Are you okay with that?"

"I wouldn't have it any other way. There's only one thing that concerns me. It should be pretty obvious. Your family may have a problem with it."

"That our skin colors are different?"

Norman shook his head and suddenly looked serious. "No, not that." He sighed. "You perk gourmet coffee, and I drink fossil fuel. That could be a real dealbreaker."

Once again, Monica threw her head back and laughed. Afterward she took his hand into hers. "I think there's hope for you yet."

He looked into her eyes. "I think so, too."

Monica smiled. "Now, how about we pray?"

Flora had just opened the front door, causing a draft that Ellen Bennington felt back in the den where she was sitting. She set aside the book she was reading and adjusted her cardigan sweater to where it overlapped in the front. Ellen was much weaker these days, having decided to come off of any respiratory assisting devices. She knew she had little time left and wanted to be able to enjoy a fire in the fireplace and the smell of a scented candle—small pleasures she'd been denied with an oxygen tank constantly in use.

She could hear footsteps as Flora entered the room carrying a medium-sized box wrapped in brown paper.

"Miss Hannah? The mailman just dropped off this package addressed to you. Do you want me to open it?"

"That's odd," Ellen said as she tilted her head to one side. "I wasn't expecting a delivery. Who's it from?"

Flora set the package down on the coffee table. She put on reading glasses that hung from a long silver chain around her neck. "It says here that it's from Detective Norman Lasko in North Carolina."

Ellen drew her head back in surprise. "What on earth would Norman be sending to me in the mail?"

"Only one way to find out," Flora said as she peeled off the packing tape and opened the box. After removing a layer of bubble wrap, she pulled out a silver-plated box that looked as if it had been recently polished.

Ellen's eyes lit up as Flora handed it to her. "Well, what do you know? It's my old keepsake box!" She fought a lump in her throat as she gingerly opened it and looked inside. She shook her head."Norman even returned my diary." She paused and then looked up at Flora. "Can you give me a few minutes alone?"

"Of course. Take all the time you need."

"Oh, and Flora? Would you mind putting another log on the fire? It's a little chilly in here."

After Flora had stoked the fire in the fireplace, Ellen picked up the diary. Her hands, gnarled from arthritis, struggled as she attempted to thumb through the contents. She stopped when she arrived at the section towards the back where a lock of hair lay pressed between two pages. She silently read:

> *Dear Diary,*
>
> *I guess the adage proves true that no good deed goes unpun-*
> *ished. My efforts to put a drug dealer in prison have put my own*

life at risk. As I write this last entry, I'm awaiting the Federal Marshal's phone call marking the beginning of my transition into Witness Protection.

Ironically, this preservation of my life has, thus far, caused me to die a thousand deaths. My world as I know it will cease to be. I will miss out on milestone moments in my sons' lives. And, whether by my feigned death—or my real one—I'll be absent when the Bennington estate is settled.

This grieves me, as issues still need to be settled that extend beyond bank accounts, properties, and other assets. Items of infinitely greater value must be reconciled: the greatest being the debt Horace owes Frances and Margaret Gates for the pain and suffering he caused them.

The locks of hair pressed between these final pages are remnants of those entrusted to Gina Merino for testing to prove that Horace is Preston Gates' father. As such, Preston is heir to one-third of all assets. I have instructed Gina to use whatever measures necessary to make sure these locks of hair are the ones tested. Gina was more than willing to assist since she, like Margaret, bears the scars of Horace's cruel thievery of her innocence.

Let the record show that I cut these locks from Horace's hair while he was sleeping. That is my account, Dear Diary; one I shall take to my grave.

While Horace has often credited success to big-picture and global thinking, I've discovered that, more often than not, it's the details that determine it. All it takes is one small detail to decide an outcome. The most significant can be the detail that gets over-looked, such as an expectant mother's miscalculation of her due date (Frances excelled as a literature major but was never proficient with numbers).

It shall cost me dearly, but I don't regret my decision to take a criminal off the streets. I have enabled justice to triumph. I can lay my head down at night, close my eyes, and sleep soundly. Perhaps those who are adversaries of what is right and good should sleep with one eye open. If nothing else, it could help them avoid things that go snip in the night.

In particular, it could have kept one barber from losing a key customer. Then again, James Gates always was particular about his appearance…especially his hair.

With warmest regards,
Ellen

Ellen's lips curled up into a smile as she read the last sentence.

She paused, gazed out the window, and said aloud, "Margaret and Joseph, I'm sorry that I didn't disclose everything. But there are certain keepsakes should forever remain under lock and key."

Ellen reached over and carefully set the box on a nearby table. Maneuvering her wheelchair closer to the fireplace, she tossed the diary into the flames.

Chapter Forty-Nine

Joseph and Margaret stopped at a florist shop in Enoburg where she purchased a bouquet of lilies. Afterward, they drove to the town cemetery. It took a few minutes for them to locate the gravesite. Margaret squatted down and placed the flowers on the marker.

Joseph put his hand on her shoulder. "I'm going to give you two a few minutes alone."

As Joseph stepped away, Margaret gingerly touched the inscription.

Francine Anne Heurnes Gales

"Mom, it's me. I brought you a bouquet of lilies—your favorite." Margaret stood back up and spotted a robin perched on one of the monuments. She smiled. "You won't believe who we just spent the day with—Ellen Bennington."

She thought for a moment. "It must have been so hard for you to stay married to Dad all those years. I understand now that you didn't feel like you had a choice." She shook her head. "You weren't strong like Ellen, but you were stronger than I gave you credit for, because somehow you did it. On top of that, you stood up for me when you knew you'd lose the fight. That takes real strength and courage. I don't know if anyone ever told you that or not. I would have told you sooner, but I didn't know just how brave you really were…until today.

"Mom, I feel more empowered than ever to keep doing what I'm doing. I still wrestle with my past, but I'm winning more battles than I used to." Her lip quivered. "You embodied the truth that just because we feel weak doesn't mean we have to quit. God gave you the strength to keep going, not just for Preston and me, but for all the people our lives would touch. You did a good job, Mom. I'm proud of you."

She looked over her shoulder to where Joseph was standing by the car. "I guess that does it for this visit. Joseph doesn't like driving after dark." She squatted down once more and touched the marker. "I love you, and I'll be back soon."

TWENTY YEARS LATER

J.J. Bennington opened the car door and extended his arm to an older woman with short white hair and blue eyes. Carrying a floral arrangement in one hand, she locked arms with him as he escorted her to a gravesite.

"Mom, I'm going to give you two a few minutes alone."

Margaret nodded and said, "Thank you." She leaned over and placed the bouquet on the base of the tombstone. She lovingly touched the inscription.

Julia Elizabeth Burch Thomas

"These are a few stems and blossoms from the gardenia bush in your front yard. Perry said that pruning it will help it produce even more blooms. He sure does miss you."

Margaret stood quietly for a moment as a cool spring breeze prompted her to pull her coat collar up around her neck.

"I'm sure Holly told you that Olivia is pregnant," Margaret

said with a smile. "She's due next January. William is finishing his junior year of college. Time sure does fly, doesn't it?"

She took a deep breath. "It breaks my heart to say this, but this will be my last visit. I just don't have the strength that I once had. Joseph swears I'm going to outlive him, but I'm not so sure about that. Although, I do have a birthday coming up; I'll be eighty-six." She shook her head. "I can remember when I didn't think I'd make it to *twenty-six*. Now I'm on the homestretch to ninety.

"You know, the older I get, the more life reminds me of a book." She smiled and looked down at the tombstone. "As a writer, I knew you'd appreciate that. It's like we're all characters in God's story of our lives. Our book contains a certain number of pages, just like we're assigned a certain number of years to live. It takes a long time to *write* a book, as you well know. But it only takes a little while to *read* one."

Margaret stopped and looked over toward the west where the sun was making its descent. She chuckled and said, "I must be a fast reader, because my eighty-six years went by so quickly." Margaret's eyes brimmed over with tears. "Julia…because you allowed God to work through you, my story has a happy ending. The best part is that it's not really an ending at all. I'll get to spend all of eternity in heaven with Jesus, the one who redeemed me and gave me a second chance at this life." She smiled. "And you'll be there, too."

She pulled a tissue from her jacket pocket and wiped her eyes. "I guess it's time for me to leave now. Before I do, I should let you know that Olivia has the old telephone now. Safe to say it's going to stay in the family. Who knew that God could use it to do so many seemingly impossible things?

Then again, that's what our God does best."

Acknowledgments

To Sherry, Amanda, Stephanie, Christa, and Liz for their editing genius. Their input and critiques help shape every book into a quality piece of literature—and make me a better writer in the process!

About the Author

Jan is an award-winning, North Carolina author who has enjoyed penning stories since elementary school. With two devotionals and three fiction novels to her credit, she continues to write fresh and relevant material that bring the truth of God's love to everyday life.

Also by Jan Hemby

The Gates Manor Band

Secrets and Surrender

Burnt Toast: Devotions for Imperfect People

Spilt Milk: Devotions for Imperfect People

Available everywhere books are sold.